IMPORTAN̄   ̣ ̣ ̣ ̣ IUN

A Moment in Time is an entirely fictional work and although names have been used from real people in the 1500's to make the plot more realistic, I obviously do not know what their real characters were like . The created characters, therefore are entirely fictional and bear no resemblance to the real people. I am grateful to the Throckmorton Family for allowing me to use their ancestors' names in my book.

A
Moment
In
Time

By Margot Bish

Chapter 1

"It couldn't have happened at a worse time," the voice on the end of the telephone exclaimed. "He says he's too old to carry on and we are putting the house on the market at the end of the week."

It didn't sound like the kind of conversation that would nearly cost me my life. Always a soft touch for someone in distress, I sighed internally. "Well, I'm not really taking on any new customers because my Mum is moving up to Redditch soon and I'm keeping Saturdays free to be with her but if you are also moving soon perhaps I can help you on Saturdays until she or you move. Where exactly are you?"
"Oh, that would be wonderful." The voice said. "We are on the edge of Feckenham, at Shurnock Court." She gave me careful directions and we agreed to meet on the next Saturday afternoon. I looked on the map to check where I was going and was impressed to find my destination actually marked on the map in that curly writing reserved for historic monuments. It looked a big place.

The weather was perfect for gardening, I reflected as I cycled up the steep side of the ridge and then freewheeled for miles down the other side almost into Feckenham. The sun was shining in a pure blue sky but there was a cooling light breeze to compensate for the heat. I arrived fifteen minutes early, cycling slowly along The Saltway, checking house names and playing the" If I was rich would I buy that house?" Game. When I reached Shurnock, I couldn't help an indrawn breath and a long slow whistle. This one I would definitely buy, but I would need to be seriously rich.

The gravel drive led to security gates with an intercom and then the gravel swept onwards into a vast parking area. It then crossed a moat before crunching up to a vast Tudor mansion. I felt an inner tremble and stifled it with a firm instruction. "OK, just pretend you do this kind of garden every day of the week. It's only like a load of small gardens all joined up." I pressed the intercom button and waited. "Who is it?" crackled the intercom. "Its Margot. I've come to help with your garden." "Come in," the voice invited and the gates swung slowly open. As I traversed the wide gravel expanse, the oak arched front door opened and a diminutive but agile lady emerged and walked purposefully to meet me. She held out a hand to shake as I dismounted and propped my bicycle against the house wall. "Pleased to meet you," she said with a relaxed smile. I grinned back, shook and said I was also pleased to be meeting her. "Where do you want me to start?" I asked. She grimaced. "I'll show you the worst bed," and led me past the house and then an outdoor swimming pool before swinging right around a small detached cottage with one room acting as pool changing room. The flowerbed was small but smothered in bindweed, nettles and the odd bramble or two. "Mind my lovely poppies. I adore them," she instructed. "Are you OK to do this?" I nodded. "Where do I put the rubbish, and do you have a fork and spade I can borrow?" We got that sorted and I set to. She nodded approvingly. "I'll leave you to it. How long can you stay?" I considered briefly. "Three hours?" She nodded, "Good." she said, turning away to return to the main house.

I worked methodically along the bed, enjoying turning the chaos of shrubs struggling to see daylight into something beautiful, There was an amazing sense of peace here. I wanted to keep coming to this place with its sense of great history and pondered how I could fit it in. If I could come early, I could do three hours a fortnight and still have time for my normal Saturday chores and hobbies. Carole, my new customer, returned after two hours carrying a tray with orange juice and biscuits and clutching some money. "I have to go out, so I brought you some orange juice and your money, Goodness you have done a lot. Will you be coming back?" "Yes please" I replied. "Every Saturday morning, if you like," I should mention that sometimes my subconscious over-rules my conscious mind. What happened to once a fortnight? "Agreed," Carole confirmed. I looked over the bed. "I've almost finished this, What do you want me to do next?" She gestured vaguely,"Just carry on round," She checked her watch and hurried off towards her car. I heard the engine start as I headed towards a flower bed nearer the house. The car started towards the gate but stopped and then reversed to stop next to me. A head popped out of the window. "Thanks for being so great," Carole called with a big smile. My smile was equally huge in response, and then she was gone.

With my three hours up, I hoped the gate was still open or automatically opened when approached from the inside, but first I thought I would have a quick look around to see what I needed to do next time. The whole place was beautiful. The moat became a lake on the far side of the house, beyond a vast lawn where Canada geese grazed under ancient apple and pear trees. The house was L-shaped with complicated additions at various levels. It wasn't actually enormous but it exuded an aura of greatness. Its history seeped into the present, periods of tranquillity interspersed with periods of turmoil and unrest. The next flowerbed was a struggling mass of nettles with what was probably a forsythia peeping through the stinging leaves and yet more brambles. I would work on that next visit and try to release that imprisoned forsythia. I was relieved to find the gate open.

My cycle home was euphoric, I was excited about the challenge ahead and hardly noticed the steepness of the two mile hill. My thoughts were mixed between the restoration of the garden and the history of the house. What a fantastic place. All week, Shurnock hopped in and out of my mind while I worked automatically on my regular contracts and then we were round to Saturday again. I woke early to another sunny day, my tabby cat purring in my ear and trampling my legs. It was only 5 o' clock but why waste the day? We breakfasted and I was on the road by 5.30. I had the world to myself and cycled almost recklessly down the steep hill from Astwood Bank accompanied only by the chirrup of sparrows in the hawthorn hedges and a recently arrived swooping swallow. I pedalled hard across the flat land which must once have been an ice age river valley or even the sea. Shurnock was still asleep when I arrived but I had noticed a public footpath went through the back fields with no barrier between it and the property except a stream with a bridge. I wheeled my bicycle over the bridge and left it propped outside the front door to show I was there if anyone looked. I briefly checked the flowerbed I had started with to make sure no weeds still showed and then headed for the strangled forsythia. I worked alone for an hour, enjoying the blanket of peace and then Carole appeared with a tray holding biscuits and two glasses of orange juice. "Good morning," my employer greeted me, cheerfully. "Isn't it a beautiful day? I brought you a drink and some biscuits. What time did you get here? How did you get in?" I explained about the footpath and said I'd arrived at 6.15. "It seemed too beautiful a morning to waste," I explained. Carole nodded. I had drained the juice and scoffed the biscuits and quickly returned to work. I was already on my third barrow of weeds which had to be wheeled a ten minute route to the bonfire pile. It took so much time , I was filling the barrow high. Carole watched with interest. "When is your birthday?" she suddenly asked. "Er, 31st March," I said. "Hmm" she said doubtfully. I gave her an enquiring glance. "That's Aries. Aries don't normally have your feel for the land." I paused. "My Mum says the signs have changed and I should be a Pisces," I suggested. "I love nature. I love being outside. I love the shape and feel of plants and helping them look beautiful. This is the best ever job. I feel stifled indoors." I added. She smiled enthusiastically. "So do I," she said. She nodded her head at the geese. "Those birds know that. They know they are safe here. I used to live in Wales where there was no electricity or mains water. I brought my sons up there. Now the National Trust own it." I tried to imagine having no mains water or electricity but failed. Everything would be extremely hard work, but on the other hand, it would be great living so closely with the natural world. "The next place I am going to live is going to be miles from anywhere." I felt just a touch of jealousy tinged with awe. The things you could do if you had money. I worked on and after a while Carole sighed and said she had best go and do some work on her computer, which she hated. "It'll be great when I've sold the business and can do away with all that," she said. I was packing up when she reappeared. "I may not be here next time you come," she said. "but my partner, Simon should be here so just carry on." I stood back to check my work. The forsythia could breathe but there was more work to do. "OK. I'll be back on this bed, I should think." "It already looks much better," Carole said. "Thank you," She handed me my wages and I went to fetch my bicycle. On the way home I spent more time imagining living where water came from a well. Did they have gas lights or candles? Did she have wood fires for heating the house or oil? My brain then skipped to the former occupiers of Shurnock. How many people had lived there? What were they like? My thoughts had been so absorbing, I had managed the hill unnoticed again. Maybe I was fitter than I thought. My subconscious was keen to return the next Saturday and woke me even before the cat at 4.45. The sun still shone. The land was slowly turning from fresh green to burnt brown, which was worrying for a gardener, but the sky blurring from pink and orange to brilliant blue lightened my heart. A buzzard mewed overhead. The faraway mountains and hills edged the scene in hazy purple and my spirit soared with the wings above me. Shurnock greeted me as a familiar figure. I fetched the barrow and fork but as I passed the cottage bed, I spotted a bramble I had missed in the dogwood. I took my secateurs and trowel, but as I bent to the prickles, I felt someone watching me. I glanced around and saw a man holding a wooden spade studying me. I realised he had come through a door in the wall beside the cottage. I gave him a nod, not sure if he was the retiring gardener. "Why be you removing they bla'berries?" he asked. "Er, they don't go with the shrubs," I stammered, surprised. He shook his head disapprovingly, but half turned away and strode forward, not around the bed, but across it and I saw a path open up through the rose and the man walked along it and faded away. I blinked and the path had gone. Did I just imagine that? The door was still there, shut. I opened it and found myself looking at the swimming pool. I turned and tried to find a way to explain where the old gardener had gone but from all angles, the rose existed and the path did not. " Well, wow, I've just spoken to a ghost." I told myself. It hadn't been frightening, just a bit disorientating and as I guiltily removed the bramble, I found the experience fading and an acceptance that here in this place, many periods of time might meet and mingle like waves on a beach. I retrieved my barrow and went to finish the forsythia bed wondering if I would meet any other people from the past. Half an hour later, I stood back and admired the freed forsythia, looking a little straggly in places but no longer encased in dead wood and weeds. I walked past the cottage bed to the bonfire pile nervously but all was still, all was normal. I walked round to the front bed and found bindweed suffocating the roses and other shrubs. I waded in. The sun shone down and made me thirsty. Where was this Simon with the drinks? There were no cars. I had the place to myself, apart from that other gardener. I wondered what century he worked in and what he grew. More food than flowers, I thought. I reached the end of my three hours and shrugged to myself. No money and no drink – it happened. I did have a couple of apples in my bag which were juicy enough to get me home. I would probably get paid next time. The lack of drink however made the hill more difficult. As I pushed my bicycle up the steep sloped tarmac, I entertained myself, looking at the houses and assessing which would have existed when Shurnock was built. There would have been more trees, I thought, and less fields, but hardly any houses. Maybe only Astwood Court, and even that would have been smaller. Did its moat used to go right round the property instead of its existing long pool? I gazed out over the fields and felt free and exhilarated. The steepest part of the hill was behind me and as I remounted my thoughts returned to the gardener. He wasn't the retiring gardener. His clothes were of a different era – the boots heavier but less well shaped.

In fact, I was now surprised I could have thought he was from our time because he'd been wearing a long cloak made from hemp and tights and breeches rather than trousers. My brain had been refusing to accept the facts to protect me from shock. A group of cars whizzed past me. The world had woken up. I envied that gardener in his car free world, but then, it had been a world of fear with real wars and battling soldiers, religious persecution ending in death, starvation and plague. I was better off here despite the odd bad driver nearly pushing me off the road.

I didn't tell anyone about the gardener. Even my best friends would wonder about my sanity, but I went back the next Saturday with a nervous eagerness. I wanted to ask that gardener about his life. I paused longer than necessary by the cottage bed but he didn't come. Eventually, I took the barrow along the side of the big house to the front bed. Today, I would get that bindweed cleared. On the way, I glanced down the other side of the house to admire the forsythia. I noticed that there were small doors like old fashioned front doors in that side of the house. Perhaps the original house had faced the other way. As I worked, happiness flooded through me. Once again, no one was about, but there was a car on the gravel. It was still early. The house seemed to approve of my work. The atmosphere was benign. The barrow soon filled and I wobbled off to the bonfire heap. Still no gardener. Oh well. I upended the barrow and retraced my steps. As I approached the cottage bed, the door in the wall opened and a lady stepped out. She carried a trug basket and had her skirts covered with an apron. It wasn't Carole. She didn't look my way but stepped forward across the flower bed and faded away as she passed in front of me. I found my mouth dry and swallowed convulsively. My insides trembled with a sort of excitement. It had happened again, but this time, I was looking into her time and she had been unaware of me. What made it happen? I walked on, wondering if I was going crazy. Could wishful thinking be making my imaginings appear real? At the path to the rear of the house I felt a pushing at my mind wanting me to edge the lawn, of all things. I ignored it. The bindweed was way more important. Every now and again, I found myself glancing at the front door, wondering if anyone was home and would bring me a drink. I had brought a bottle of water this time, but I wanted to check I was going to be paid, and I quite fancied a fresh orange juice. No one came. I finished my three hours and decided to try knocking on the door. No reply. I would just try if it was unlocked and shout if it was. I turned the iron ring latch and pushed and the heavy door swung open. I was in a small lobby with a spiral staircase ahead of me and a long room with a fireplace filling a third of the far wall to my right. The room was open to the roof and was daylight lit with large windows down both sides. I felt certain this was the original house, just a one room hall, maybe once divided in half to house animals as well as people. To my left, a door opened into a kitchen of vast proportions. No people. I called hopefully up the stairs but there was no reply. Was I stupid to keep coming back if I wasn't being paid? I pondered this on the way home. I would go one more time, and if I didn't get paid, I would give up. My thoughts went to the lady. Well, not really a lady, but maybe a dairy maid or a kitchen maid, as I had no sense of them owning a whole herd of cows. That pushing in my mind was odd, too, almost like an order, almost like a voice without sound telling me to smarten that lawn edge. The bindweed was almost done but there was a fair amount of deadwood to clear in those shrubs. I would do that first and then edge the lawn. When

I had time, I was going to research the history of Shurnock. Its ghosts were not demonic but the turmoil of tumbling time surely reflected a disruptive history. There was a message on my phone from Carole. "Hi Margot. I think we must have missed each other. Did you come this morning? We haven't paid you. Should I drop off a cheque for you?" She gave a phone number to ring. That was a relief. I rang her back. "Where were you working?" she asked. "In the front bed, on the bindweed," I explained. She clicked her tongue. "How silly," she said. "I had a feeling I should look there, but I didn't do it. Well, shall I drive over with your cheque?" I hate people wasting fuel so I replied, "No, it's fine. Just leave the cheque in the barn, maybe on the barrow if you won't be there next time." "Are you sure?" she said. "Yes, positive," I said. "I'll be out of the country for a while,"she said, "But Simon should be around." We disconnected. I reflected on the feeling she had mentioned. Were the people of the past communicating through feelings? I spoke to Mum on the phone the next morning. "I've found a buyer," she told me excitedly. "It's a lovely family with a small girl who loves the garden and there's no chain." "Oh great," I responded. My heart sank a little. The lawyers normally took about eight weeks to sort things. I had wanted more time than that at Shurnock. Carole hadn't mentioned a buyer. I was getting addicted, I chuckled to myself as I wondered if I could somehow find another slot to fit them into. Anyway, it was good that Mum would be nearer to me instead of a six hour train ride away. "Do you need help sorting the house?" I asked Mum. "Have you given your buyers your solicitor's name, and have you got theirs?" "I'm doing fine with the house," Mum said, "And, yes, we have swapped solicitors' details." "Well done," I said. We swapped our other news. I hesitated. Should I tell Mum about my experiences? She had told me about odd things she had experienced. I decided I would. She listened quietly and said, "How interesting. Let me know what you find out." I felt relieved she hadn't queried my state of my mind. "That gardener sounds like a sensible man, wanting to keep his blackberries. Local food is important," she commented. I laughed. "I felt really guilty, cutting them off at the base, but they will come back unless I keep cutting. How is your fruit bed?" "There are strawberry flowers and blossom on the cherry tree and on the raspberry canes. The peach tree still has curly leaves." "Poor old peach," I said. We made plans to talk the next week and rang off to carry on with our separate lives.

There was no cheque on the barrow. I cursed myself for not getting Carole to bring the cheque to me, and now she was out of the country for weeks. Should I give up? Well, I had promised myself I would do this week, and I was here now. I wheeled the barrow past the cottage without a thought of ghosts, but as I reached the back of the big house, I felt that tug in my mind again, but stronger. Someone wanted that edge smartened up. I stubbornly resisted. I was going to get that front bed tidy first. The voice in my mind gave up or lost its strength as I walked determinedly on. I weeded and cut out that dead wood and took my full barrow to the rubbish area and met no ghosts but the voice still insisted that I do that edge. I gave in to it. I enjoy edging. It has a rhythm that lulls the mind. Insert blade, push down, step, insert blade, push down, step. It hadn't been done for a while and the mat of grass was thick, but glancing back, I could see the precise edge appearing. I reached the end and rubbed the sweat from my face. Just got to pick up the unwanted turf and then remove the weeds in the revealed gravel. It already looked better.

Half way along I encountered a water mains inspection lid which had been completely concealed. I was just weeding around it when the hairs on the back of my neck started to rise. Out of the corner of my eye, I saw long skirts and, as I raised my head found an elegant lady watching me work. I scrambled to my feet. She stepped forward and tapped the inspection lid with her toe. "What is this?" she enquired. "Its an inspection cover to check the mains water," I replied. She tipped her head sideways, considering. "Explain, please." The clothes looked like those of a rich Tudor lady. Of course, I thought. There was no mains water in her time. "Um. The pipes carry water from the rivers into the house to taps and things for washing and to drink, and then take any dirty water away but in case it blocks or freezes they have lids you can lift to check the pipe." She nodded, still thoughtful. One question deserves another, I thought. "What is your name?" I asked. "Lady Jane," she said as if I should know the name. I nodded. I wanted to pinpoint the time. "Who is the king?" She was hesitant. "Henry." I tried to remember who was around then that she might know of. "Do you know William Shakespeare?" I asked curiously. She raised her chin arrogantly. "I know of the Shakespeares," she said, but obviously she didn't hold them in much regard. "What about Francis Drake?" She looked bewildered. "Do you mean the sailor?" "Yes," I said, thinking, he can't be famous yet and nor is William Shakespeare. I glanced down, wondering if I had just changed history by explaining mains water and when I looked up, she had gone and it occurred to me that the shape of the house behind where she had stood had changed. There had been plants of some sort where now there were paving slabs in the walled enclosure. Once, this area was a front garden, I turned and saw there would have been a sweeping slightly curved drive once leading from the Roman Saltway Road to this frontage. I heard a footstep behind me and turned to find Carole with her tray of juice, biscuits and a cheque trapped under a glass. "Hello!" she said. "|I saw you out of the window." "Oh," What had she seen? I felt sheepish about doing the lawn edge with overgrown shrubs and weeds still in the beds. "I think I've just met a lady from the past. She er wanted me to edge the lawn." Carole stifled an emotion. "Oh you've met her have you?" she said, and then, changing the subject, continued, " I moved my flight to tomorrow. Here's your cheque. I was thinking, could I pay straight into your bank account while I'm away? Simon is awfully absent-minded." I agreed, hesitantly, always a little nervous about giving people my bank details. "How's the house sale going?" I enquired. Carole grimaced. "Not a single viewer. The agent says its due to the threat of Brexit causing uncertainty." "Mm," I sympathised. "I haven't seen it in the paper. Where are they advertising?" She snorted. "I'll chase that up." "What about those magazines like Country Life?" I suggested. "I wanted those," she agreed " But they said I would have to pay extra for them." She was obviously not impressed with their efforts so far but she was a successful businesswoman so I reckoned she would sort them out. "I have found a buyer for the business, anyway." "Oh, good," I said. She handed me the tray. "I must go and pack for my business trip," she said and strode away purposefully. I felt surprisingly lonely when she had gone, but put some effort into finishing my edge. Lady Jane was right. It had really needed doing. With the path widened and the lawn edge sharp and straight the whole area looked balanced. Travelling up to that old front door would now look impressive. Would Lady Jane be able to see what I had done? She hadn't been worried about talking to someone across the centuries. Did she do it often? It had been a meeting of times, Not ghosts but each of us standing on the boundary of our era and looking into the time of that other person. We had each felt curiosity. Above all other emotions. I felt that I liked her. She had a quiet confidence and a thirst for knowledge, a sharpness of mind. I felt she had in her past conquered disasters and come through it stronger than before. There was quite a similarity to Carole, I thought with a spurt of surprise, and wondered about Carole's past life before her isolation in Wales. My mind was filled with the two ladies over the next week. Part of me wanted to look Lady Jane up online and find out everything I could about her. Part thought this would colour my future encounters if there were any and I wanted to learn directly from Lady Jane. I settled for looking up the company name on Carole's cheque. Phew! She was worth millions, owning both hotels and an organic and natural medicines business that went worldwide. She had none of the arrogance I associated with money. How had she avoided that attitude? I admired her more. Mum was keen to know about my visit. "Did you see the gardener?" she asked. "No, but I met someone who might be the lady of the house." I recounted our conversation. "I realised after that Drake and Shakespeare were Elizabeth I so it fits she might know them but they wouldn't be famous." I said. "Oh. How exciting," Mum said, "I hope you get to talk to her again." I giggled. "I wondered if I looked in a science or history book if mains water would now appear earlier in history, Mind you, perhaps piped water appeared earlier at Shurnock and its just the historians didn't know about it. It makes my brain boggle a bit thinking about it." We moved on to discussing removal vans and the logistics involved. I promised I would make a day free of gardening to meet the removals van and sort the furniture while Mum travelled up by coach and train.

 I took a drink and some crisps and apples with me for the next visit, expecting the place to be empty. There were no vibes by the lawn edge. Lady Jane must be happy with her edge and there was no sign of the people by the cottage. Accompanied by a bright eyed and inquisitive robin who sang cheerfully in between darts to the ground to remove unearthed grubs, I worked my way along the smaller beds, cutting back grasses and overgrown climbers and, in the hot weather, thinking I would love to jump into the most inviting swimming pool. I was deterred by the lack of a towel. With those beds tidy, I walked around the kitchen side of the house and across the grass to see what was growing near the moat lake. Thinking about the different ages of the different wings of the house, I turned under the apple tree to study the roof line, and the world shimmered and changed, The kitchen wing had gone, and gazing up above me, the apple tree was tiny stretching only a metre above my head. I felt nauseous and breathless. My brain refused to accept the message from my eyes. I squeezed them shut, counted to five and opened them. I was looking at the end of the hall. There was no porch, no staircase to a second storey. My neck felt stiff and unwilling to turn. I shuffled my feet round and found the gardener walking away from me pushing a wooden wheeled barrow towards a large vegetable garden. My clothes were the same. My tools were the same but everything around me was different, except that the moat and its lake were still there. I had somehow slipped back in time. How had it happened and how did I get back, or rather forward to my time? It had happened when I turned. If I turned the other way in the same spot? Nothing changed. I swallowed an uncomfortable lump in my throat. What else? I walked hopefully backwards and forwards over the spot and spun round both ways. Nothing. I was determined not to panic. Think. I knew of other time slip spots didn't I? I would try those. I half ran, half walked, worried that the gardener would see me and think me a suspicious character. What could I say if someone came out of the house? If it was Lady Jane, would she know me? Could she help me? The front doors were, as expected now on the other side of the house, and earth paths meandered through a herb garden buzzing with bees and alive with colourful fluttering butterflies. There was no inspection cover but I could work out where it would be, If I walked from the front door I should be following Lady Jane's footsteps. It didn't work. I felt clammy, shivery, even though the sun still shone. Deep breaths. Do not faint. I would feel safer away from the main building. I would try the cottage bed. I was disorientated by the moat which continued around the property in this time, and there was no cottage and no swimming pool, just a walled courtyard with chickens and a cow and a couple of pigs in a sty. Next to the sty was a door in the wall. I hurried to it, paused, taking a deep breath. Why should this work when the other places didn't. I tried not to hope too much. It might not work. It HAD to work. I opened the door, stepped through, saw the kitchen maid's path ahead of me but the land to the sides were hazy with the shape of a rose in a flower bed. Stay there. I willed the haze to become firmer. How did I change times?If I stepped into the haze would it disappear or become more real? I eased another step forward to clear the doorway and then, holding my breath, stepped sideways. My time materialised around me and there was a yelp. "Golly. Where did you come from?" a male voice exclaimed. A young man was standing almost right next to me, looking backwards over his shoulder at me. "You gave me a heart attack." My heart was thumping too. "Sorry," It came out as a croak. "I came through that door." I said, clearing my throat and wiping the clammy sweat from my face. Looking at the face in front of me, I reckoned I was looking at Carole's son. "I'm Glynn," he announced. "Mum said to keep an eye out for you and bring you a drink if I saw you. I made the drink when I saw you out the front and then I couldn't find you." I nodded. I went to look at the lake and the fruit trees and then thought I'd check here for the next most important job." "There's quite a lot to do," Glynn gave me his Mum's shy smile. "Yes, but I'll get there," I said and mentally added, If I don't keep falling through time. Glynn held out a glass and a bottle of ginger beer. "Thanks," I said gratefully. "See you," he said and left with his mother's lack of fuss. I felt wobbly and unnerved and leant against the cottage wall, sliding my spine down the bricks and sitting with my knees close to my chin so I could rest my trembling arms on them. My heart beat was slowing to strong powerful thuds and my breathing eased back to a normal pace, but my brain still fluttered like those butterflies, dancing from one unlikely scenario to another. I looked at my watch. Another hour's gardening to do. I pushed back to my feet and taking another steadying breath, set off back to the front bed where I had left my bag. In the courtyard beyond the swimming pool was an overgrown pyracanthus. I would work there. I found myself moving slowly, almost shuffling to avoid stepping through time. "Pull yourself together," I muttered and lengthened my stride. It was lucky it was hot, disguising the terror generated sweat as the sweat of hard work. I clipped away at the thorny network, getting about halfway before running out of time. With relief I pushed my bicycle out of the gate, mounted and headed for home. I felt exhausted, almost ill. As the road steepened, I stopped, drank my drink and ate the crisps. I'd walk the hill. There was no rush. I needed to think what had happened and try to make some sense of it. I couldn't really have gone back in time. It must have been a dream or wishful thinking or something. By the time I reached the ridgeway, high above the Feckenham plain, I was convinced my overactive imagination had got the better of me and caused some sort of hallucination. I wouldn't mention it to Mum. Bubble met me at the door. "LA-A-A-T-E" she mewed at me. "Yes I am" I agreed. "Lunch?" she suggested. I should mention, Bubble is a cat of few words, but they are always straight to the point. It was a good idea. We shared a cheese sandwich and finished each with our favourite biscuits. I spent the afternoon reading a good book in a semi shaded part of the garden, with Bubble lazing alongside me on the blanket, her relaxed sprawl emanating an atmosphere of calm. Feeling sleepy, I closed the book on its bookmark, put my forearm over my closed eyes and allowed myself to think about Lady Jane and how it would be to live with her in the 1500's. If I had gone back in time and got stuck there, how would I manage? I slid into dreamless sleep before any plan formed.

Mum was frustrated. The man she was buying off had died. Now she would have to wait for the estate to be sorted. "Is your buyer OK with that?" I asked. "Apparently, he hasn't got a buyer for his house so he doesn't mind waiting," Mum said. "Well that's OK, then. We'll just have to be patient." Quietly, I was grateful for the delay. I wanted to meet Lady Jane again on the borders of time and I wanted to make those gardens tidy before Carole sold the house. If I could ask Lady Jane about the time slips, maybe I wouldn't stumble into any more. This week, I would visit the library and look up ghosts of Feckenham and time travel and the inhabitants of Shurnock Court.

There were a whole host of ghosts around Feckenham, but none at Shurnock and it appeared Shurnock had belonged to the church after the dissolution of the monasteries and to the Throckmortons before that but no Lady Jane appeared as an owner. The place seemed to have been empty for a while before 1606. Time travel had only one scientific reference based on Einstein and used travel into space. I was sure I hadn't done that. I had got nowhere with my research by the time of my next visit.

Chapter 2

The forecast on the next Saturday threatened heavy rain, although it started sunny. We did need rain after two months of drought but as usual, I wished it would only rain at night. As I expected an empty house, with Carole away, I packed waterproofs into my backpack plus chocolate, crisps, a sausage roll and a hot drink in my metal cup with its close fitting lid. Its easier to cope with rain on a full stomach. I was using quite a lot of energy hacking pyracanthus. I added a flapjack to help with the hill on the way home The cloud was beginning to build even as I flew down the hill and across the valley floor making the scenery look more dramatic. The swallows were busy nest building in the dilapidated Tudor farmhouse half-way along the valley. A buzzard soared on the updraughts caused by the mixing air temperatures. The lambs in the fields baaed at me, almost fully grown. How lucky I was to live and work in such a beautiful place, free from war and famine. We didn't even have poisonous creatures to worry about, except for adders. I felt the need to whoop with joy.

I had discovered the gate where the sweeping drive would have begun was not locked and I could push my bike across the field and approach the house as it once would have been seen. It certainly looked magnificent from here. The place felt deserted today. I was sure no one was home. I got stuck into that pyracanthus which lasted me a good hour and then had a quick go over the cottage bed, where weed seed had sent up new shoots. I was half glad, half disappointed that no one appeared from the past. I moved on to the forsythia and picked the tops off the undiggble brambles and nettles growing from under the forsythia roots. There was no sign of Lady Jane. I hesitated. Part of me wanted to see if I could time slip by the apple tree, my more sensible side told me not to be so stupid. I would walk round but not under the tree, I decided. I needed to see if there was any more bindweed popping up. I put my rucksack of tools on my back and gathered up my bag of clothes. The rain was beginning but was not yet heavy enough to put on those waterproofs. With ten minutes to go, I dead-headed the late spring flowers and packed up. I'd change into waterproofs at the gate. I walked round the house to admire the almost tidy beds. They looked good. I was passing the old willow, turning my head to the house to ensure no one was at a window when the world shimmered again. I stumbled and nearly fell, landing on one knee. My sight swam again and cleared to an almost black sky. A man in priest's robes was disappearing at a scurry around the house, his back to me. Rain hammered down around me and soaked me to the skin before I had a chance to reach for my cagoule. No point putting it on now. I staggered to my feet and squinted up through the waterfall of rain across my face. Now when was I? The kitchen wing existed but only as a single storey. I needed to get out of this rain but where had the priest gone? Perhaps it was better to just try to get back to my time. Shrugging my pack up on my shoulders I started with the apple tree, walking in all directions, trying to emulate my previous actions. Not surprised it didn't work, I moved to the water pipes, and was not too disheartened. The herb garden was well established, and a little neglected, I noticed as I hurried confidently on towards the door in the wall. The yard now included a barn and a few empty flower beds but the animals were gone. The door stuck at first but opened abruptly as I put a shoulder to it. I fell through it and caught my balance as I staggered on to the path. The path advanced, just an area of mud leading into a forest I had never seen before. There was no rose in its flower bed. I went back through the door and tried again without staggering, going slowly as I had the first time, but the forest remained stubbornly in front of me and the rain continued to drench me. I was getting cold. I crept into the barn, but it was empty, not even straw to snuggle into. I laid down my rucksack and tried jumping up and down. My attention was drawn to the front drive as I heard the clatter of horses hooves and a small covered cart swung round the house with the priest and another cloak garbed man hunched forward to protect themselves against the rain. They rumbled off down the drive and vanished, without spotting me in the shadows of the barn. I headed for the house and tried the front door, which was not yet the grand affair of my day but was more than the previous visit into history. To my relief, it opened into the hall entrance, with the other door opening to my left. I had an impression of building work commenced but not completed. Was it empty because the work was on going or because the work had been abandoned? My teeth were beginning to chatter. I needed to get dry. Thank goodness for my rainproof bag and those spare clothes. First checking the rooms were all empty, I threw off my wet clothes and climbed into my waterproofs and the long sleeved shirt I had put in in case the temperature had dropped. I half dried my hair on the wet T-shirt. It seemed that one room was going to be a bedroom and the great hall was for everything else. I found some hooks in the empty fireplace and hung up my sodden trousers and shirt. Lucky they were both made of lightweight, easy to dry material, I thought. There was no sign that anyone lived here. The floor was dusty and the ceiling was home to many spiders living in grimy webs, but it had been a hasty departure, with a table and chairs left behind, and beside the fireplace, a stub of candle and a contraption I had never encountered before. I thought it might be a flint for lighting fires. I remembered my hot drink and fished it out of the bag. Would it still be hot after time travel? Yes, it would. Well. I would get warm and dry, explore the house and wait for the rain to stop and then I would work out how to get home. I had done it before. I would do it again. I roamed around the house as I sipped my steaming drink, feeling relief as the warmth seeped through my body. Was it still June in this old century? The changes in the house wings told me I didn't always encounter the same year when time slipped. I hoped I was in the time of Lady Jane. No logic to this. It was somehow comforting to think she might be nearby. There were no glass windows. The few window openings were shuttered. I cautiously opened the door and peeped out. The rain still fell. I could see rough pasture where I expected the front flower bed to be, with trees scattered about. The leaves were thick and green. No blossom, so June was a strong possibility. I pulled the door shut and wandered back into the hall. There was a battered cauldron hanging from a bar across the fireplace. Nothing in it except a spider's web. Curiously, I opened one of the back doors and looked across at the other wing set at right angles to the great hall. I could see a door set low with steps leading down to it. A cellar? The rain stopped quite suddenly, as if God had turned off a tap, just the odd drip from the thatch above. My hot drink was gone. Time to find a way home. I packed up my gear carefully. I wouldn't be able to come back for anything I left behind. Feeling slightly guilty about leaving a door unlocked, I walked out of the oldest door, and through the herb garden, as Lady Jane must have done and looked hopefully for a hazy image of my forsythia bed, but there was just a ragged verge, small lawn, the moat and then the trees. It looked so different to the larger lawn and tennis court of my time with its truncated moat. Just in case, I retraced my steps and tried all the different paths through the herb garden. Nothing changed. Well, I thought, the door in the wall had always been the best time shifter so I'd try there next. The yard looked desolate without its animals and felt cold as well as empty. I walked to the door stifling any desire to put off the moment. Pulled it open and willed the rose, choisya, and viburnum to appear. The path led stubbornly into the forest. I stepped forward and then tried easing sideways with my eyes shut and the images of my day held in my mind. I could tell from the feel of the mud beneath my feet that it hadn't worked. I should have felt the firmness of paving slabs. I'd best try the apple tree, I thought, but my heart was beating erratically and my breath was coming short. I was scared. What would I do if it didn't work? As I scurried nervously along the herb bed I tried to think more calmly of a plan if I was stuck. I was trying to stuff the ribbons of panic back into a box in my mind but they kept oozing out of the cracks, preventing logical thought. I was nearly at the tree. I stopped, delaying the moment when I might find myself stuck here. My palms sweated and my lip trembled. I was almost in tears. I pulled in a deep breath. "Get a grip," I ordered myself. "No crying." I stood straight, fists clenched. "Just do it." I walked forwards, backwards, stood still and stepped sideways, turned my body and my head but nothing changed except that the black storm clouds gradually cleared leaving a blue sky and the smell of after storm Summer. Strangely, having taken the step and failed, I felt calmer. I was stuck for today but most of the times I had met people had been earlier in the day. Maybe it had to be the right time of day. I would try later just in case, but prepare to spend the night here and try again tomorrow.

The hollow feeling from stomach to throat was easing as I considered what to do about food and warmth and somewhere to sleep. The day was warming quickly now the rain had gone. The thick walled house wasn't exactly warm but I would cope by opening the shutters and doors on the sunniest side of the house until the evening. Thank goodness I had brought the extra food, today, and carried it with me into the past. I even had my loppers, saw and secateurs for cutting wood. I grimaced. No matches. I didn't have much confidence in my ability to spin wood or strike a spark with stones to start a fire. Lucky it was Summer. What if the churchmen came back? I felt they had just come for an inspection. The place was so bare. I walked over to the vegetable bed the gardener had been working on the last time I slipped. It was overgrown with nettles, dandelions, buttercups and several other weeds. There were hazel sticks with dead whitened tendrils of bean stalks winding haphazardly around them. They looked like they had been there at least a year. No beans, I thought, but suddenly my attention sharpened. There was a pea shoot sprawling across the ground. I took a hazel stick and gently wound the pea stalk around it. Someone might get peas later, even if it wasn't me. Was there anything else in this abandoned land? Stalks I had thought were grass turned out to be, hopefully, onions. Were those carrots? Well the leaf looked right. A bit early in the year to pull them yet. If only there were strawberries. I couldn't find any. I remembered the cellar. "Don't raise your hopes, Bish," I said, but found myself breaking into a hopeful run, anyway. I slowed at the steps which were mossy. A broken leg would be the end. Hanging on tightly to the wooden rail I traversed the six steps down and turned the iron ring to open the heavy door. It was shadowy in there. I opened the double doors wide. There were barrels against the far wall. The first was lidless and empty. The second had a tap near its base. Expecting it to be empty, I wobbled it and heard and felt the slosh of liquid. Water? Cider? Apple juice? Probably more like vinegar. I would bring my cup later. The next barrel felt almost full of something that rattled but I couldn't open it. The lid was pegged shut. Stifling frustration, I went back to the hall and turned my rucksack upside down. Had I anything that would open that barrel. I didn't want to bust the secateurs, stabbing it. I picked up the bow saw but discarded it, too hard to saw through, everything the wrong angle for the saw to bite. Loppers? Useless. The trowel might give some leverage. Thank goodness I rode a bike. I had a fork, and spoon to use as tyre levers and a real tyre lever. Carrying my treasures, I returned to the cellar. The tools slipped or wedged but wouldn't lever. I shouted in frustration but after stomping about and bruising my foot with a kick at the barrel, I thought to find a good sized stone and hammered the tyre lever into the crack. The lid creaked but remained solid. I tried again on the other side of the lid but it still remained firm. There was a crack where there had been none. I could get the handle of the spoon in there. I hammered the tyre lever in again and made a crack for the fork, then again and leaned on the lever and spoon together. The spoon bent, but I could now see there was a wax seal. I went to get my pruning knife and slid it round the wax. Laughing at myself to relieve the tension, I thought it'd be great if all this effort led to the release of something rotten and mouldy. Re inserting the tyre lever I levered again and the lid popped up. Hazel nuts. Treasure. A whole barrel of them. I wouldn't starve. Now for the liquid. I placed my cup under the tap and opened it. Sniffing the liquid, I thought it was vinegar, but a careful sip suggested cider. Pretty vinegary cider, but it was definitely alcoholic, hitting the back of my throat and making me cough, warming the surface of my tongue. I tried another sip and felt my lips pucker. I'd have to water it down but at least it was likely to be safe to drink. I had a whole moatful of water but was it safe to drink? Unless I could make fire, I couldn't boil it to be sure. There was no wood by the fireplace. Was there a wood heap anywhere? I searched cellar, house and barn but any wood that had been left must have been taken by the villagers. Thank goodness for the saw and loppers. Whether or not, I could make a spark, if I was stuck here, I needed wood and it would save me sitting worrying. I took my tools and found a plank bridge over the narrowest part of the moat leading into the trees by the door in the wall. I found a few dead branches scattered across the forest floor, dragged them back across the bridge, careful not to get another soaking by falling off the planks. I settled down to sawing and lopping and the familiarity of my actions washed the panic from my mind as the pile of logs grew. I fetched my damp clothes out into the sun and draped them across the lavender and rosemary bushes, amongst the busy bees. I was going to need them tonight as blankets. Occasionally, I looked around in case there were any people around but there was no one. Why was the place deserted? If the house was built originally in Tudor times, but the elaborate porch was built in 1606, we must be in HenryVIII, Edward VI, Mary or Elizabeth's reigns. I didn't think those churchmen were monks, so er did that make it after Henry? I wished I had had time to read more about Shurnock's history and the Tudor period. I remembered in Tudor times there were executions and beatings, burning of witches, and torture, hanging and drawing. I needed to know if I was supposed to be supporting the Catholics or Protestants and, if I met anyone I had to convince them I was neither a witch nor a tramp, but had a right to be here. Could I live off the land without anyone knowing I was here until I found a way home? I shuddered, remembering that people could be imprisoned or executed for poaching, especially if I killed a deer in the king's forest. What was the sentence for stealing timber, I thought gazing at my log pile? Were those trees Shurnock Court's or the King's? I dropped the saw and took the evidence inside, stacking it by the fire, then hid my bag of tools in the cellar's darkest corner. My watch said it was 2pm. No wonder I was hungry. I laid out the food, which had to last me.......how long? I ate the sausage roll and put the rest out of sight to avoid temptation. What now? I might as well do some work on the vegetable patch. I took the trowel and began to weed. It occurred to me that nettles and dandelions were edible. Nettles made soup.(I shuddered at the thought of my tongue being stung.) and dandelion roots made coffee. I vaguely thought the leaves were OK as salad. I was now fixated on food. What else could I eat? There were tree leaves. I nodded to myself – beech,, yes and hawthorn were OK. Weeding away, I felt more positive about survival. I didn't think I could kill animals even if I could catch them but I would survive on green stuff and nuts. If I was brave enough to meet the villagers, maybe I could get eggs, but then I needed a story to explain my presence. The great thing about gardening is that it soothes the soul whilst leaving the brain free to think. If those clergymen were here checking the property, it seemed likely it belonged to the church. Surely they wouldn't check it often if they came in a cart. I had until their next visit to find a way home (and please don't let it take that long, the emotional part of my brain interrupted). Perhaps I could tell the villagers I had been sent to manage the gardens and maintain the building until a tenant was found. It did sort of make sense. I could say I was supposed to find extra work to pay for supplies. I wasn't sure I was brave enough to try it. Too many things could go wrong but if I couldn't get back, I would need things like clothes for the colder weather. I looked down at my clothes. How on earth would I explain what I was wearing? I pushed the thought away. Standing, to stretch my back, I saw the sun was dropping beyond the house. It was getting on for late afternoon. I gathered some of the dandelions but left the nettles. No point getting stung until I had a fire to cook them on. I nibbled a leaf. Crikey, that was bitter. I wasn't going to eat too many of them if I could help it. I tried some more cider to quench my thirst. That was pretty awful too, but again, no coffee even with dandelion root, until I worked out how to use the flint. I picked it up and looked at it from all angles. Poking it gave me no clues. I put it down. Maybe I should just try to get home again. I didn't fancy a night on that hard bed with no soft warm blankets and sheets and no pillow either, except my bag or rucksack. I packed everything I owned up, including my almost dry clothes and set off round the known timeslip spots, going slowly, looking for the overlay of hazy future landmarks. The ground remained obstinately in this century. I walked the whole area inside the moat until I was tired and it was getting dark. I would try tomorrow. I still had some of my food left. It would be alright. My rucksack was rubbish as a pillow but I stuffed grass into my bag and changed back into my dry clothes, using the waterproofs and long sleeved shirt as covers. It wasn't comfortable, exactly, but I was tired enough to doze and eventually fall into a deeper sleep just before dawn. I woke to silence. No traffic noise in the distance. No background noise as the neighbours started their day. If I listened carefully, I could hear birds singing, but the thick walls muffled the outside world. The room, with its shuttered windows was dim and shadowy. What time was it? I twisted my wrist and squinted at my watch and sat up quickly. It was 7.45. No furry alarm clock padding across the blankets and purring in my ear. Was she alright. I hoped she would find someone to feed her breakfast. Would she be worrying about me? I had no time to sit there thinking. This was the time I had met the kitchen maid and gardener at the cottage bed. I ran out of the room. Paused, ran back and grabbed my waterproofs and shirt, stuffed my feet into my socks and shoes, ran to my bag and rucksack, burst out of the back door and sprinted to the yard, ignoring the spot where I had met Lady Jane. Going for the place which had worked best, before. It didn't work. I couldn't accept it and walked up and down the path, stepping sideways and racking my brains. What was I doing wrong? Was it something to do with what I was thinking? My mind had been relaxed, free from stress, but focussed on another task in the 21st century, but I had been stressed last time I succeeded in travelling forward in time. It was impossible to relax. Impossible to pretend I could focus on another task near the path and it might not even help. Despondently, I tried the other time slip spots but I didn't expect them to work. I had run out of ideas. I had no other methods to try. I thought of Bubble waiting for me to come home and ached with loneliness. Tears came to my eyes as I realised I might never see her smiley stripey face again, or feel her paws land firmly on my body as she leapt firmly off the window sill to wake me up, purring with cat laughter. As I stood, shoulders slumped, I thought of Mum waiting for my phone call this morning and worrying about why I hadn't rung. A blade of anger stabbed through me. I was not going to be defeated. I would find my way back. Someone, somewhere would know about the timeslips. I would try to find them, and twice everyday I would walk the grounds looking for that haziness leading into my time. Until it happened, I needed to work out how to survive in the here and now. I would be like Robinson Crusoe, making the best of what I had. The sun was already up and glittering on the lake where ducks, geese and swans splashed and swam. Beyond the lake, there were trees to the horizon, but inside the moat, there was grass nibbled short by a small herd of sheep. The sheep were standing in a huddle, staring at me in astonishment. I supposed they didn't see many people. Their coats were thick and looked in need of shearing. I froze for a few seconds thinking about an invasion of sheep shearers some time soon. Was that why the clergy were visiting? Would my story still work if I encountered them? I was thirsty and hungry, not a good state for positive and logical thought. I went back to the house and took a couple of handfuls of nuts. The cider didn't taste so bad. Maybe it was an acquired taste. It didn't really stop me feeling thirsty though. I daren't drink out of the moat. I had read that dysentery and other waterborne diseases were rife in Tudor times and there were no medicines in the cupboard to deal with a dodgy stomach. I eyed the flint. I now had wood. It was time to find out how to make fire. I thought back to those programmes on survival. I needed kindling. Thank goodness it was Summer so that the sun had dried the loose leaf and twig blanket on the forest floor after yesterday's rain. I took my emptied bag and filled it with dry grass, twigs and dead sticks. I wished I had a couple of newspapers and a box of matches. Arranging the grass and twigs carefully, I took up the flint. There was a stone and piece of slate in a frame to hold it steady. Perhaps I just had to slide them together. No spark. I changed the angle. Still nothing. Frustration came to my rescue. I struck them together aggressively and a spark flew. It landed nowhere near my neat pile of kindling, but I now had a better idea of the arc. I moved nearer the kindling. Leaning forwards on my knees. Three more attempts failed. No spark. Robinson Crusoe had had it easier. He had already been taught how to light a fire before he was shipwrecked. I wasn't getting the angle of strike right. My mind was almost bursting with frustration. Why hadn't those stupid Tudor people already discovered matches? I laughed at myself. Make that electricity, why don't you? And sterilised bottled water, or even mains water through a tap. I needed that laugh. My tensed up shoulders relaxed and my subconscious stepped forwards to show me how it was done. The spark leapt and landed on the twigs. I scrunched the grass into a tighter ball, took my pruning knife and a log and shaved off thin strips of wood, pushing them close together and then struck and struck and struck. Sparks flew and eventually a tiny curl of smoke rose. I crouched low and blew gently, willing a glow of flame. The grass began to shrivel and a spot of orange red appeared, spinning along a grass stalk. I tried not to tremble as I added more grass and shavings and the smoke thickened. I blew harder and, at last, a flame burst up and started to greedily consume the shavings. I added twigs and then sticks and finally a log. I sat back on my heels. I'd done it. I needed to boil some water. I picked up my cup and ran to the moat. I should have filled the cauldron I thought. I'd do that next time. Four cups of water would do for now. No, make that six, for a day's worth of water. Belatedly, I worried about the smoke from the chimney which would give my presence away. Where was the nearest dwelling? The main village of Feckenham was over a mile away so should be OK but were there nearer farms which might smell or see the smoke? Nothing I could do but sit tight with my story ready and see if anyone came to investigate. I looked at the dandelion roots. Did I have to grind them, chop them, roast them first or what? I didn't want to waste my water getting it wrong. I would settle for boiled water. I remembered there had been other barrels in the cellar that I never checked after the success of finding nuts and cider. I collected my tools and made another careful traverse of the steps. Another barrel sloshed but had no tap. I had seen people banging in a tap. Maybe that's what I had to do. Another barrel rattled, but was lighter. I got busy with my levers, and released dried peas. A smile spread across my face. Pea soup. A vegetable that was not bitter. I picked up a handful and took them into the house. I would have to soak them before cooking them properly so no peas today. I checked my supplies. Lunch would be crisps. What else could I do? More wood would be needed. I put another log on to keep the fire going while I worked and took my cagoule out to use as a sack as well as my rucksack . I wished I had a wheelbarrow. The house must have been deserted a while or all this timber on the forest floor would have been burnt. I was lucky to have supplies so close to the fire. I even found some fallen trees to saw into logs. It took me all morning, but I had a woodpile to do a week's burning. The water had boiled and I celebrated with a drink of safe water and the crisps. I put the peas in the cauldron to soak. After I'd eaten I walked around again looking for details that might link the places where time had mixed in case that might give me a clue as to why it worked or how it worked. They were all on paths but I couldn't see how to use that fact. Now what. The blue sky beckoned me outside and I thought I might work some more on the vegetable bed. I could plant some of those dry peas. It was a bit late in the year but I might manage to increase my crop for next year, or even eat some fresh. It would have been nice to have some potatoes but Walter Raleigh probably hadn't brought them back from America yet. When did we find tomatoes? I weeded more thoughtfully, putting aside flowers that were edible in some way, like violets and marigolds and plantain. I was going to get tired pretty soon of the same foods. I stood up stretching my back and remembered the herb garden that I had walked through without thinking so many times. There were my flavourings. Excitedly, I bounced back to the house and gathered handfuls of rosemary, sage and mint. I could make herb teas and pea and mint soup. I would start right now with my cauldron of water. The fire had gone out but the cauldron was still warm. With only my cup to hold water, I needed to think this through. Should I flavour all the water, which probably already tasted a bit of peas or should I scoop some water out for something else, like diluting the cider. I took out a cupful. I could always boil more but gosh it was annoying that I didn't have a dish or even a plate. I sipped the tepid water which did taste a little of peas. I didn't reckon it would improve the cider. When should I relight the fire? It would start getting dark about 8pm so then everyone should be back home and my smoke wouldn't show and it would warm the rooms a bit for the night. I hadn't slept well last night because I'd been cold, apart from the bed being hard. Could I improve the bed with leaves and grass. A straw or hay bale would have been useful. There was sheep's wool caught on the hawthorn twigs but not enough for even a scarf never mind a blanket. I could use it for string though. I'd collect that later. Cautiously, I crossed the plank bridge and entered the trees, looking for ferns or long grasses. I felt jumpy, afraid of meeting another gatherer. Was this Shurnock's property or the King's or someone else's? There were few tracks and what there were looked more like fox, deer or rabbit than human paths. I normally like a bit of isolation but this total aloneness was unsettling. It made me feel vulnerable. I found myself jumping at noises that I was making – the rustle of cloth against leaf or the snap of a stick under my feet. There was a whole world of birds above my head, the daylight changing as fluttering wings came between me and the dappled sunlight, and the shadows made dancing patterns on the browns and oranges beyond my feet. I moved slowly, looking back often, afraid of getting lost in this trackless tangle of bramble, nettle and tree, and tried to walk a more or less straight line to make returning easier using the sun. I was heading out west and would return east, paralleling the road to Feckenham which most likely existed following the old Roman road from Droitwich to Alcester, but I intended staying well south of that. The land was getting marshier, despite the trees. Ash, beech, hawthorn and oak were giving way to willow and alder. The leafy alder twigs might give the bed a bit of bounce so I collected a few armfuls, made my way back and laid them on the bed broken into small pieces. Then I took my shears to the moat edges and cut the longer grass the sheep hadn't been able to access and spread that on top of the alder. I hoped I wouldn't be sharing my sleeping space with too many insects. It was about afternoon tea time, I thought wryly, but I wasn't yet ready to light the fire. I took a cup of water out into the sun and sprawled by the moat. There was nothing else to do and I was sleepy due to my uncomfortable dozing the night before. The sun wasn't as hot as in 2019 in the clear blue sky. No global warming I decided, yawning, but it was perfect for snoozing in. Imperceptibly, I went from snooze to sleep. I didn't know what woke me, but I was suddenly awake and alert. I was lying on my back, looking at the sky but I could hear, some way off, talking. I rolled slowly over hoping, if I was in sight of anyone they wouldn't see my slow movements. Flat on my stomach, I raised my head and looked around. There was no one in sight. The voices were on the other side of the house. Should I hide? If they came round the house, sharp eyes would spot my blue T-shirt and black tracksuit trousers against the grass. Should I actually try to see who was here? If I could work out what was happening, I could add to my story of why I was here. I suddenly realised I had left my rucksack propped by the herb garden door. If anyone saw it, what would they think of those metal tools and the nylon and plastic rucksack? I had better try and look. I would be in trouble if they took my tools. It took an age to wriggle along the circumference of the moat but it was my only way to remain concealed. There was another cart by the plank bridge and two men and two boys throwing wood into it, while a mule waited patiently in the shafts. I felt indignant. They were stealing my wood. Not my cut logs, but my future supplies. My first instinct was to leap to my feet and tell them to go away but although the children were ragged and thin, the men were well muscled. A challenge might not be the best idea. It did give credence to my story of being there as a sort of custodian later. I was lucky. They were concentrating hard on filling their cart fast and getting away. When the youngest child tired and tried to slip away into the herb garden, one of the men called him back sharply, and he returned with a drooping body and head dropped down to collect more twigs and stack them to the side of the larger fallen trunks the two men were lifting. With the cart nearly full, the older boy was sent ahead to check for anyone on the road. Apparently it was all clear as he waved urgently to the men and boy waiting by the cart. One of the men lifted the younger boy into the cart and they walked the mule along the overgrown track to the out of sight lane. I trembled with relief as I realised I might have had the fire going with smoke billowing from the chimney, or I might have been in plain sight, working in the herb garden, which I had intended to do if I hadn't fallen asleep. These must have been villagers furtively adding to their wood supplies and I wasn't yet ready to pretend an authority I didn't have in challenging them. Feeling a little wobbly, I went into the house, picking up my rucksack where it had fallen over by the door, and barring the door behind me. What a good thing I hadn't opened the shutters to let the sunshine in. How lucky I had shut the cellar door and hadn't got around to clearing the moss from the steps. I hunkered down in a corner, belatedly hiding from a world of uncertainty and terrors. I laughed at myself again in a jerky fashion – bolting the stable door after the horse had bolted. Just luck I wasn't found. Once I had regained my nerve, I followed their wheel ruts stealthily to the lane. The ruts turned left, headed for the village. The lane was just a wide rutted track beneath tall overhanging trees. It was odd not seeing tarmac, even though I shouldn't have expected it. Somewhere under the mud, deep down, there could be Roman stone but the Roman's last used the road centuries before and battles had been fought, towns razed and rebuilt and many years of leaf litter dropped since then. The rutted surface spoke of a loss of skills and a lack of communal discipline or perhaps just a loss of knowledge, tools and organisation. I stood and dithered, unable to decide if I should go along the lane to look at Feckenham village and find out how close the next dwellings were, or just stay hidden in my bolthole. A glance at my watch told me it was 6 o' clock. Workers should have returned from the fields for their evening meal. The road should be empty.

Hesitantly, I set off West. Not far along, I came across another track and peering down it from behind the trees, saw some hens pecking at the ground and a chimney stack smoking above the thick track-side undergrowth. Its height suggested a one storey cottage. The lane was too dry to pick out the mule drawn cart tracks. I couldn't tell if this was the home of my wood thieves. I wasn't going down there, anyway and walked onwards towards Feckenham. There was another building just off the lane and then a wide track forked off to my right. The trees confused me. How far had I walked? That cottage by the road had unnerved me. If anyone looked out of the shuttered window, I would be in plain sight. Abruptly, I turned round and scurried back to shelter. I would explore just before dawn, hopefully before anyone looked out of their doors or considered unshuttering their windows. The sight of those hens had set off a craving for eggs. Ironically, I had money in my pockets but how could I pay with 21st century coins, no matter what the base metal? Maybe, if I was stuck here long enough, I could buy some hens of my own.

Collecting my gear, though, with not much hope, I explored the time slip posts but remained stuck in this time of basic survival. I had managed one full day in this old world and now found the silence quietened my mind. I was sad and lonely without the presence of Bubble and Mum on the end of the phone but the lack of technological complications was immensely soothing. It was time to relight the fire from the tiny red glows in the enormous grate, make myself a warm drink, eat some more nuts and sleep. I allowed myself only one log to heat the water, added mint and drank. It tasted good. The peas were not quite soft. By tomorrow, they might be edible. Real soup tomorrow night. I slept well and again the lack of a cat clock and daylight made me sleep late. When I got up and creaked the shutter ajar, the sun streamed in, bringing warmth with its light. I had missed my chance to explore.

I felt caged that day. There was plenty of space to walk and run. I could cut wood and weed and trim rosemary and lavender in the herb garden but the moat and my fear of discovery penned me in. By late afternoon I was desperate to escape. I had tried those timeslip holes lethargically, not even bothering to pack my gear. If it had worked I would have left everything behind. I had found a second plank bridge across the moat where the new porch would eventually have an arched ironwork bridge. I set myself the task of creating a path from there to the road. There were fewer trees here and the track I created was almost straight. On reaching the main route, I decided I would explore away from the village where there might not be any people, marched back to scoop a cup of pea water, and set off. If I walked purposefully, no one would question me, would they? Well, they might look at me oddly in my t-shirt and long trousers but I couldn't skulk forever. This was a practise run for my eventual visit to Feckenham. Even in my day, this was an uninhabited road. There should be few people on it today. I felt released, liberated, walking under the towering trees with their wide girths and listening to the tremendous whistle of birds. I walked fast to ensure no one walked up behind me. It was good not to have to worry about fast cars and raucous, rumbling lorries. I should hear a horse well before I saw it. I looked nervously at the sides of the lane. I was walking along the contours of a hill, the land dipping away to the south and climbing steeply to my left. The trees were thinning on my right. I could see a wide plain and a bump of a hill on the horizon. Occasionally I saw ditches running away down hill but they were all nearly dry. The downpour I got caught in must have been a one off. I had best decide how far I was going to go. I couldn't remember any side turns before the crossroads at Astwood Bank about 2 miles ahead. I passed a track on my left, the house again well back from the lane, lurking amongst the trees. I hurried by even though there was no sign of life. Below me, a half mile away, I could see people working in a field, hoeing in strips. It was odd to see the lack of hedges, just squares of bare land hacked out of the trees. It made it even odder that Shurnock was deserted. I dug into my brain trying to fit historical facts together to pinpoint the year I was inhabiting. The clothes were definitely those of Tudor pictures, but which king or queen? It could even be the Stuarts, I supposed, though no one so far wore the uniform of the puritans. There was a squeak of wheels from somewhere behind me. Without conscious thought, I leapt off the road, into the undergrowth, and slid, unbalanced into one of the ditches, scrunching on washed clean gravel, trying not to splash in the trapped puddles. Close to the road I was still in sight, I scrambled downstream, recklessly stinging my fingers on bankside nettles as I kept my balance with my hands. I half fell down a miniature waterfall and crouched behind fern fronds as the squeaking wagon passed. I put my hands under the running water to cool the biting stings. No chance of looking for dock leaves. I could hear the ferocious barking of a dog nearby. I'd better keep going. My feet were already wet, so I had no need to step with care. I rolled up my trousers and it occurred to me that they now looked more like the Tudor half knee shorts. The socks were wet. They might as well stay on. I could see the edge of a thatched roof and hear pigs and chickens. This was the dog's home. I hoped it was tethered. A dog bite could easily kill without antibiotics. I moved as fast as possible without breaking my ankle or a leg, tearing skin on overhanging brambles and thorns until I could no longer hear that ferocious bark. The banks were so bramble bound that I had no choice but to go on. Where would I end up? I tried to conjure up a map in my head. South east of Feckenham was what? I could only think of Inkberrow. I hoped I wouldn't have to go that far. The land was levelling out, and suddenly the brambles ran out and I could see the strip farmers. No good climbing out here. Grimacing, I got down on my knees and crawled along the damp ditch. The ditch turned suddenly to the right and I peered over its edge. I was next to another track. I climbed out, carefully behind a hawthorn thicket. Where did this track go? I looked for the sun to get my bearings. The track bent. I couldn't go north or I would be back at the field. I would have to go west. I would be too far south to hit Feckenham so somewhere I must head back north. My track suddenly bent south and reminded me strongly of a road I once encountered doing exactly this. I had spotted the water tower on the highest point of Redditch and used it to steer me home via Feckenham. If only I could have used that water tower now. Ahead of me a narrow, barely used path slid off the main track going about Northwest. Was this that same track? How stupid that I hadn't brought my shears or secateurs, not even long sleeves. I eased onto it, ducking and dodging briars and branches and internally jumped for joy. This was the path. I was sure of it. Frowning, I realised the path went right into Feckenham. Somehow, I must find another diversion to slip past the village. It seemed to take hours. It was getting dark. I was so utterly stupid to have strayed away from Shurnock. The land was rising and I was back in the trees. It was hard to be sure of the route because the trees were well spread with room for deer to be hunted from horseback and many tracks churned by horses' hooves. I hoped I wasn't going round in circles. The sun had disappeared behind the trees but still gave light to the sky. I stopped, feeling helpless and useless, totally lost, totally dis-spirited. I had taken more knocks than I could handle and wanted to just lie down in this quiet place and give myself to nature. The moon saved me, sending its calm glow glistening down through the trees. It lifted my heart and mind. I focussed on the next silver coated tree and realised I could climb it. Carefully, I raised myself through the branches and the world opened out below me. I could see the ridge to the North. My house would be built someday at the far end of that ridge. I turned South and looked over the vast plain of Feckenham Forest. I climbed higher and there was Feckenham not more than half a mile away. It was big. Sprawling to twice the size I had expected, stretching westward towards Droitwich and northward beyond the market square. There were sparks flying from what must be the Smithy on the eastern edge. Smoke rose from chimneys and I could smell stew cooking. My mouth watered. Above my head, stars sparkled, glimmered and glittered. So many pinpricks of light. More than I had ever seen before. It was beautiful. I felt awed and small and my problems became insignificant under that immense sky. I could see the path bending into Feckenham. There was a small track forking eastward close to a farm before the path reached Feckenham. I would go that way. I slithered back to the ground and was soon striding along the southern edge of the farm, following a bubbling brook, splashing across it and then, picking my way through the trees, I found the roof of Shurnock ahead of me. I felt the relief of home coming. It was 10 o' clock. I was too tired to light the fire. I drank, ate nuts and slept.

I couldn't believe it. I had overslept again. Daylight filtered in. Furious with my lack of self-discipline, I lit the fire, heated a day's water, first rescuing the softened peas, and roasted dandelion roots. I was ravenous. I ate the crisps. No more messing about. Tonight, at midnight, I would walk to Feckenham. Everyone would be asleep because it made no sense to waste fuel or candles. I would sleep in the afternoon to make sure I could stay awake all night. I felt so hungry it was hard to think of anything except food, I ate all the dandelion leaves and gathered hawthorn leaves which helped. Ate more nuts and drank cider. Feeling a little better, I gathered more mint and added it to the cauldron with the peas. Tonight I would warm myself with pea and mint soup before I went out. I was missing Bubble. I sent a message through the ether, telling her I would get back as soon as I could, that I loved her but she must find someone to feed her until I got back. I know cats are telepathic but didn't really expect her to pick up a message from four hundred years away. She was an unusually loyal cat. I hated that she would think I had abandoned her. I wondered if Mum would have alerted the police to my disappearance. Would they be searching Shurnock with dogs and scratching their heads over my scent trail disappearing half way across the lawn. My sense of humour rescued me, imagining the police force suddenly appearing in the 16th century, bewilderment on all sides. I tried again to get home. Still no shimmer of overlaid centuries. If I was stuck here, I would make the house more habitable. I gathered more branches off hazel trees, sheep's wool and nettle stems and made myself a broom. The dust was thick. I tied my waterproof trousers around my mouth and nose and swept out the dust, my eyes itching and watering as the dust rose and filled the air.

I sat in the herb garden waiting for the dust to settle and with the sun on my face and the background sound of bird song, felt at peace. I would get back but in the meantime I felt lucky. I had food and drink of sorts and shelter and warmth. There was no bad news reaching me from the outside world. No bills to pay, no technological problems to get frustrated about, no people griping or arguing. If I only had Bubble, I would be happy. I was surprised by the tears that fell at the ache of her absence. I wiped them away angrily. Crying never helped. I must find Lady Jane and ask her to help. I stood up determinedly and then sat again. One step at a time. I had to wait until midnight to check out Feckenham first, but I could develop my plan. In case it went wrong, I would leave a note somewhere at Shurnock where a serious search would find it but it would stay hidden until then. I wrote, "If you find this note after 2019, my name is Margot Bish. Please contact my mother." I gave her address, wondering if she would still move house with me gone. "It may seem crazy but I have fallen back in time and can't get back. I am healthy and safe. I miss those I love." I now had to find a good place to put it. It had to be somewhere that still existed unchanged in 2019 but dry and out of the light. I wedged it behind the skirting board near the old front door. It looked like oak and would probably outlast the wall. Tonight I would check out Feckenham, get a feel for the inhabitants and how I might fit myself in and earn some money. Then, tomorrow or the next day I would go and introduce myself. I sweated at the thought, and eventually I would find someone to ask about Lady Jane and then I would find her and find a way home. It might take a week or so. I would learn as much as I could in that time about how to live in this time of long ago and what the people were really like. I had a few hours to waste before lunch and then my afternoon of sleep. I would make something of the yard which should be a walled kitchen garden. I needed a spade and remembered the gardener's wooden spade. Mine wouldn't be as good as his. For that I needed, at the least, an axe. I wondered into the forest and found a fallen tree with a branch at the correct angle and sawed away until I had a shaft and rough semi circular blade with a point to drive into the ground and flat edge to push with my foot. Feeling creative, I sawed another circle for a plate and another to dig out the centre sometime to make a dish for my soup. Still nervous about that moat water and worried about the smoke created to boil it I considered making a water butt. I didn't have anything I could dig out the centre with. Then I remembered the empty barrel. I ran to the cellar and brought it outside. Should I try to catch water off the roof or would that be dirty from soaking through the thatch? I decided to put it on the edge of the trees where the leaves in a heavy shower would drip into the barrel. Then I moved it into the open in the centre of the herb bed, nearer to the house, with nothing to divert the downward drop of the rain. I couldn't work out the science of which was the better location but nearer the house seemed a good idea. I returned to my spade and tried to make a handle. It was a failure. I needed screws or nails or a drill to make a hole for a wooden peg. My wool and nettle bindings weren't strong enough. My plate was OK, though. I proudly placed it by the fire. I left the makings of the dish outside the door for later improvements. I took my spade and tried it. I needed the trowel to break up the surface but the lower layers were easier to dig and after an hour I had some useful looking beds ready for planting. I fetched some more peas and marked them with hazel sticks as I planted them. The back wall was perfect for fruit trees, I thought. Pity I didn't have a cherry tree or grape vine to plant. I paused. Hang on. I did have some fruit didn't I? I'd put it in the front pocket of my rucksack. I dropped my tools and trotted back to the house. The grapes were bruised and sticky, the cherries slightly flattened but still edible. No point trying to save any. I ate the lot, savouring every nibble. It would be years before the stones and seeds bore fruit of their own. I planted the lot, marking their positions with more hazel sticks and standing back realised I had subconsciously planted them where the vine and cherry tree existed in 2019. If they grew, they might confuse a few experts. My cherry stones were probably created from bees pollinating from varieties that didn't exist in the 1500's. Goodness knows where the grapes had come from. Hold on, I thought. Was it actually me that planted the vine and tree that existed in 2019 back here in the 1500's? Well, probably not the cherry. I didn't think they lasted that long, but maybe the 2019 cherry was a child of this 1500's tree. My brain cartwheeled at the thought of me being part of history's timeline. Could I change the future or was I already a part of what would happen? If I studied history's paintings, would I find me tucked into the crowd? What a way to show Mum that I had survived. I put the thoughts away. It probably wasn't a good idea to draw attention to myself to the extent of being painted in my odd, unfashionable clothes. I wished I had worn a long plain coloured shirt and a black anorak on the day I moved through time. I was losing track of the days already. How long had I been here? I counted on my fingers. Three nights. My watch gave me the date. I had my diary in my bag. I would mark off the days in that so I remembered when I had changed times. The sun, today was playing hide and seek amongst the clouds, but the air was still pleasantly warm. I might get some rain in my barrel later. I hoped it wouldn't be while I was exploring

Feckenham. It was lunchtime. The sun was at its highest point in the sky. Midday. It seemed a good plan to try to learn the time from the sun and then be able to use it for direction from its height in the sky which would give me the hour. How did Tudor people know the time and direction when it was cloudy or dark? I'd better not wear my watch when I went to introduce myself. More nuts and hawthorn leaves for lunch. I'd eat the flapjack for breakfast tomorrow to give me energy in case I managed to find work. I wanted to give a good impression. It was no good being useless due to to being hungry. Looking at my diary, I realised I had let down my Monday and Tuesday customers for the first time ever. "Sorry," I thought. Would someone think to ring them and say I had disappeared? Would they all find another gardener or wait to see if I returned? It was time to rest. Outside in the sun or on my bed? The bed was cold and still hard and if anyone did come to check the house, they would have me trapped in the room. I took my bag pillow and snoozed by the lake, close to the reeds for camouflage. I took my belongings, shut the doors and shuttered the windows. No one came. As dusk fell, with the sky showing pink, orange and red beneath the fading blue, I lit the fire and heated my soup, watching the changing patterns in the flames and feeling the warmth on my face. The soup was delicious. I put more peas to soak and added rosemary for a different flavour. Everything seemed to take longer in this time. I had at least thought to take the cauldron to the moat rather than filling it one cup at a time and boiled the water before adding the peas. It was almost time to go. The temperature was dropping despite the cloud. I added my long sleeved shirt and my cagoule, wishing it wasn't bright yellow, and also my waterproof trousers. If I walked fast, I might get warm enough to remove the rustling layers and wrap that bright yellow inside the dark blue trousers. I had to walk cautiously to begin with, afraid of twisting an ankle in the rutted track but gradually my eyes adjusted to the pinprick light from the stars and I picked up the pace, glad I had reconnoitred earlier and knew the beginning of the route. I passed the lane to the farm, no hens. There was the hovel, all dark, no smoke. Here was the track going off to the right. The moon appeared on the horizon, a half moon adding a half light and sharp shadows. The lane started uphill. I must be a half mile away. I came to another track on my left. I recognised it as one that, in 2019 led to a farm and a marshy nature reserve. I might go and look at that sometime. Not tonight. I reached the top of the hill. Warm now, I removed that luminous cagoule and the trousers with their whisper, crackle and swoosh as one leg brushed against the other, and tucked them into the undergrowth. My heart beat was speeding up and I felt quivery, with a fluttering in my stomach. I took a steadying breath. Everyone would be asleep. It would be fine. I passed the smithy. The forge fire was snoozing, not fiercely sparking and roaring but emitting a steady warm glow through the plank cracked shutters. It was good to know there was a kind of normality, a rhythm of life surrounding me if only I could find a way of entering it, of being part of it. At the bottom of the hill, I passed several cottages and then came to a T Junction. I had a strong sense of recognition at the sweeping curve. The inn was a different building but a sign still swung offering accommodation and a drink to thirsty travellers. It too was dark, no late night revelling by candlelight. I could see more cottages along the main road but turned right into the centre of the community. The village green existed with its gate to the church. There were three grand two storey houses and the ruins of a fourth around the green. A row of one room dwellings spread alongside the green with its water pump and trough. The lane was cobbled, the cobbles almost worn flat and polished from many feet. A small house stood near the church. The vicar's home, I supposed. Unusually, it had a garden with flowers as well as vegetables. It was overgrown and I had a strong desire to liberate the struggling plants. How odd it was, not having a notice board outside the church with the name of the vicar and the times of services. With a leap of the heart I remembered it was a crime under Elizabeth I not to go to church. What day was it? Had I missed a service? I hoped tomorrow wasn't Sunday. I assumed my watch wouldn't be showing the right day if the date was right. Unless I just happened to have found a year that was a twin of mine. I walked on through the eerily silent, sleeping village. More tiny homes squeezed together fronting onto the cobbles. The odd arch with a gate leading to the backs, big enough for a cart. There were two more huge properties at the North end of the village with cleared land around them. The first suggestion of enclosed farming. Was I looking at a field of hay? It was too dark to be sure. How many inhabitants lived here? It seemed bigger than the Feckenham of my time. Gazing across the cleared land, I could see more cottages and tiny one room buildings on the other side of the church and a small cluster of homes which might house people working for the big houses. There was no shop, other than the smithy, so even if I could earn money, where could I spend it? Well, perhaps I could just ask for food in return for labour. I really would love some bread, butter and cheese or an egg on toast. My mouth watered at the thought and my stomach gave a gurgle of anticipation. It was time to go home, sleep and wake ready to meet the villagers. I set off home at a brisk pace, relieved not to have woken any village dogs. My feet were becoming more confident and I found I no longer stumbled or tripped on the uneven surface. I collected my waterproofs from their hiding place but had no need to put them back on, feeling warm from the exercise. I looked around me as I walked, enjoying being part of the night. An owl glided through the trees, white and ghostlike, and screeched angrily at my presence. I felt exhilarated by its presence. A fox crossed the track and turned its head mid stride to assess me. Writing me off as of no account, it continued on its journey. It was large and sleek, confident in its ability to survive. I felt clumsy and incompetent in comparison with my need for props like knives , saws and spades. I was nearly home when I encountered the cat. Black and white and watching me with interest from the undergrowth. Another successful hunter, I thought, unlike Bubble who was sick if she ate a mouse. Was that evolution? "Good evening," I greeted the cat. He gave me a baleful stare. "Well. Maybe we can make friends another time," I suggested and left him to his hunting.

Chapter 3

Despite my afternoon nap, I slept well but finally managed an acceptable wake up time, just after six o'clock. I wanted to get to Feckenham early before too many people were about. I would feel vulnerable before a crowd of stares but felt I could more confidently talk to one or two early risers, probably busy about their morning tasks and so less likely to linger asking questions I couldn't answer. I drank the cold pea water, wanting a clear head and not yet organised enough to have put a cup of clean water aside. I took the flapjack, (only one bar of chocolate left from my hoard), and ate it en route. In my rucksack, I carried all my tools, except the spade, and my cup filled with cider. I rolled my trousers up and pulled my socks high to look like stockings, then wore my long-sleeved shirt inside out to hide the checked pattern and the buttons as best I could. It was the nearest I could get to a jerkin. The distance seemed shorter in the daylight and I had reached the smithy before being swamped with uncertainty and fear. My feet glued themselves to the earthy ground and my knees locked. I looked around helplessly. I couldn't do this. I turned and found my feet would un-glue facing away from danger. How stupid. I turned again to Feckenham and over-rode my toes trying to dig into the ground. "You'll have to do it sometime," I told myself. "You're nearly out of food." Still my legs tried to lock. If the smith was looking out, he would think I was a complete idiot, talking to myself and walking in circles. It was probably embarrassment that pushed me on. My steps were short and my breathing ragged as I went downhill. I came to another halt at the T- Junction but there was no alternative plan. A girl in long skirts and carrying a wooden bucket with a rope handle tripped lightly down the steps of the big house opposite the green and hurried over to the pump. An older lady appeared from the cottages and joined her. They chatted as the younger lass pumped water into both buckets and then returned towards the big house. She looked casually around the street as she walked and focussed on me. I had to move. Where could I pretend I was going? I knew no names to mention. The church was the safest place. I moved purposefully towards the green, giving her a polite nod as I passed. She half curtsied and I watched several emotions cross her face, confusion, doubt, almost a giggle as she looked at my clothes, quickly stifled and then blankness hiding whatever she thought next. The older lady still stood by the pump and gazed at me more openly, assessing. I nodded to her also. "Good morning," I tried. She frowned and put her head on one side. She returned my nod with a slow nod back, head up and meeting my eye. She spoke but the words were unintelligible. I hadn't considered the changes to the English language. Was she speaking English or did they speak Latin, or even French? I hoped they didn't speak Latin. I hardly knew any Latin at all, just the words that were now linked to English like, er Matins, or Benedictine, or er carpe diem. Seize the day. Had she said diem? I didn't think she had said Bonjour. I might have been safer pretending I was dumb, but it was too late now. Of course, with no television, it was possible people from different parts of England would not understand each other with different influences of French, Roman, Viking and Saxon all affecting words and dialect. I obviously wasn't local. I would have to come from southern England, but not London. The gentry here would know what Londoners sounded like. I fished around in my mind and decided I would have come from Weybourne Abbey near Farnham in Surrey. I had least seen the ruins and knew that Henry VIII had demolished it, giving me reason to be working elsewhere. Whilst working this out, I had reached the church grounds, and walked through the arched entrance. The grounds were marked with a low stone wall. To keep the dead in, or the living out? I wasn't sure. There was a stone path to the church door. Pulling the door open, I went inside and felt relief. The church looked almost the same as in my time. It made me feel safe, which was silly really. There were fewer pews and less inscriptions and the stonework was clean, not age blackened, the surfaces flatter and squarer, not eroded by time. I had never thought before about churches once being new. How odd. In 2019, I wasn't a religious person. My church was the outdoor world and I felt strongly that if there was a God, he would be quite happy that I was out there looking after the world he had created, but now I slipped into a pew and knelt to offer a quiet prayer asking for any help I could be given to get home. I refused to stoop to bribery about going to church more often if I got back. God knew what I believed in. It was no good lying about my intentions. As I rose to my feet, I heard footsteps and turned to find a black clad figure advancing towards the altar. He was only a little taller than me but exuded confidence and authority. He spoke kindly and questioningly to me and again I didn't understand a word he said. He saw this and signalled me to wait where I was while he went to the altar and deposited a large book on the nearby table, open at a page half covered in curly script. He returned and repeated more clearly what he had said. It was a greeting and a question, I thought. Almost good morning and can I do anything for you. I tried my English first. "Good morning. I am working at Shurnock Court, for the church and came to offer a prayer," I tried. The vicar's eyebrows rose in surprise. Then he frowned and shook his head, not understanding. I would try French.* "Bon jour, Je travais a Shurnock, pour l'eglise et je voudrais a visiter votre eglise pour dieu," I tried, not having a clue what the word for prayer was. The eyebrows rose again, but settled in more understanding. "Bien venue," he replied. "Quand vous etes finis, Venez vous a le vicarage, celui la." He waved in the general direction of his house. "Nous pouvons parler celui la plus comfortable," "Merci," I replied and he turned and left without further discussion, giving me a smile at the door. I knelt again on trembling knees, not sure if I would ever rise again. The story was begun but my French was a disaster. How could I possibly hold a conversation and make him understand I needed work. I did need his help and the church offered sanctity didn't it? I prayed more fervently for help and courage and left the church, turning to walk to the vicarage where the vicar waited on his *door step. A lady hovered beside him. "My wife," he indicated. "She speaks more dialects than I." Now I was committed, I felt less panic and found I could pick out words better. "Merci," I replied. "Thank you." The lady nodded and smiled. "De quelles ville etes vous?" she asked. "Guildford," I lied thinking of the nearest big town to Weybourne Abbey. " J'apprends sur les monks de Weybourne et puis j'ai travaiile a Evesham et Worcester dans les jardins. Je suis un jardinier et maintenant je travail a Shurnock jusque un tenant est trouve. Aussi les clergy dit je doit travail en le village pour tout les gentes pour les viandes." I hoped I had explained my presence* and also explained that I had to work in the village for my keep, but

---

*   See end of book for translation of the French

*

my French being rusty, I could have asked for a ride on a pig for all I knew. The lady turned to her husband and explained to him what she thought I had said. She turned back to me for confirmation but I nodded without having a clue if she had it right. They then had a private discussion which involved their garden and my hopes rose. "Eh bien," the vicar's wife said to me. "Peut etre vous au jour'd hui travail ici et nous vous donnons dejeuner, oui?" "Oh, yes please," I said, the relief strong in my voice. They had understood. She looked at my back pack and then waved at me. "Vennez ici," she led the way to a covered alcove and pointed at a spade with a metal blade. I smiled delightedly as I picked it up. She then led me to a vegetable patch in as bad a state as the one at Shurnock and left me to it. Not knowing what to do with the weeds, I piled them at the corner of the bed, working hard finding rows of baby carrots, tiny cabbages, peas, ready for harvest, and onions. There were other things in rows that I didn't recognise, possibly some cousins of beetroot and turnips, the leaves were right but the roots were not of the same size, shape or colour. I hesitantly separated the dandelions not sure if these were crops for salad and coffee or real weeds. There were brambles, but remembering the gardener's frown, I thinned the old growth and left the newer shoots. I would have to find something to tie them onto. I could see a congested apple tree further down the garden. That might yield some useful branches. Out of the corner of my eye, I saw the vicar's wife standing at the door watching me. Eventually she gave a nod of approval to herself and disappeared. It seemed I was working in an acceptable manner. As I worked, I was joined by four hens, clucking and chortling and dashing in to grab the grubs I unearthed, with a delighted cackle. One tried to eat my shoelaces. There was a more human chuckle behind me and I turned to find the vicar's wife carrying a wooden platter with a wooden mug and a disc of plate holding buttered bread and cheese. "You have earned this," she said and it was English of a sort I understood, if heavily accented. My smile was huge and full of gratitude. No payment could have been better. "Thank you very much," I said, taking the platter from her. "Thank You," she said, indicating the cleared beds. The mug held sweet apple juice. The food was delicious and filling. In real gratitude, I worked harder all afternoon and by the end of the day, three quarters of the garden was cleared, the brambles neatly tied in, the fruit shrubs and trees thinned of their rubbing branches and flowers blooming in delightful colours. The vicar came out and chased the hens around the garden, trying to get them into a coop. I was amused to find two were well behaved but the shoelace chaser and one accomplice gave him some good exercise. As the light began to fade, I realised it was getting on for 7 o' clock. I tapped shyly on the door and the vicar answered it. He looked in some wonder at his now beautiful garden. I pointed to the last area to be cleared. "Tomorrow?" I asked What was that in French? Was it demain or was that yesterday? "Dans le matin?" I tried to clarify. "Ah, Oui," he said. "Attendez." I waited and he returned with an egg and another hunk of bread. I could have hugged him but thought members of the church probably didn't do that sort of thing. I almost danced on the way home. If only the vicar would tell other people he had this idiot who could barely speak but was a genius with plants and gardens, I would be able to survive. I ate the bread while I waited for the fire to heat my soup and decided that actually rosemary didn't go well with peas. I would go back to the mint tomorrow. I whispered goodnight to Bubble as I fell on my bed and slept soundly until 6am the next morning.

I was not good at boiling eggs in a cauldron on a fire. The end result was rock hard but at least I wasn't hungry. I returned jauntily to the vicar's garden and set to work without fuss. The hens ran eagerly to join me and good naturedly got under my feet as I worked. The vicar's wife was seen to be laughing at their antics. She shooed them away but they soon returned. I was given another lunch of bread and cheese and lettuce from the liberated garden. When I was finished, I packed my tools and prepared to go home, but to my surprise, the vicar's wife led me across the green to the house of the lady I had seen yesterday. Without knocking, she opened the door and called and the lady appeared. They talked rapidly while I stood there unable to understand what they said. Then the lady nodded and took my wrist, leading me through the low roofed room, and out of the back door. Behind was a communal field, divided into strips. Some were tidy with rows of peas and the beginnings of beans, and root vegetables in other rows. My new customer obviously needed some help. The bean framework had collapsed and the beans lay sprawled across the floor. The peas were tangled and their support had half fallen on the beans and over the root vegetables, and tussocks of grass invaded the root crops and what should have been fallow land ready for planting. The room had been almost bare, just a chair, a table, wooden spoon, dish and mug, and a bed in the corner. I thought I would be working with my trowel, but I was handed a metal edged hoe. Almost new and a metal fork with thick prongs almost like a hay fork but stronger and blunter. With delight, I started work. It was satisfying working with such good tools and the silty soil covered with compost and manure was easy to dig. There were more hens here and a pig. It was hard to put together the tiny bare accommodation and the richness of the tools and land and make a logical scenario. The lady had so much confidence but so few possessions. She stood in the doorway and watched me work approvingly but we didn't talk. At the end, she handed me three eggs. It seemed like an overpayment and although I would have loved three days of eggs, I took one and pushed her hand closed on the others. She gave me almost an impish grin, odd on that lined face and handed another egg to me, in turn closing my hand on the two I now held. We shared a smile. "Thank you." I said. "Come tomorrow," she ordered. I shook my head and gestured at the field. "Its finished," I said. She shook her head and gestured at another house. "There," she said. It seemed I had another job lined up. "Thank you," I said. This seemed to be a word people understood. "Eight o' clock?" I held up eight fingers and pointed at where the sun would be at that time. "Huit heure?" "Yes," she said. I felt jubilant. I was earning. If only word would spread that I was worth employing for a few eggs I would survive. I carried them carefully, afraid of breakages and placed them by the fireplace with some relief. Lighting the fire with pride at my skill with the flint, I reflected that I had better start storing dry grass. I would never manage a fire with damp stalks and it was in the wet that I would really need a fire. I shuddered, thinking that I had better get home before the Winter. My clothes were too sparse to cope with low temperatures, my cagoule only shower proof. How could I earn enough for more clothes and where could I buy them, anyway? I reckoned there was a storm coming. The air was heavy, the light edging to purple as clouds rolled in overhead. A gust of wind rattled the shutters and made the fire roar as the wind burst under the door and presumably exited up the chimney. There was a flicker of light from outside the room. Time to get that grass, I thought and ran for the door. The sky was one eighth blue, with the sun creating a brilliant edge to the black clouds surrounding it. There was another flash of lightning away to the south. I hurried to the moat edge and hastily grabbed armfuls of grass, throwing them through the door, and then ran to the forest edge to collect kindling. As I ran back to the house, dropping a trail of twigs and sticks, the first drops fell. They felt as big as marshmallows and exploded as they hit the ground, sending droplets flying back into the air. I dived into the house as a ball of black fur blurred past me. I dropped the sticks by the fireplace and shut the door. Turning, I found the cat I had met the night before last sitting on the table and watching me carefully. The end of his tail flicked rhythmically in warning. "You don't have to glare at me," I said. "You're quite welcome to stay here out of the storm. Just don't expect me to feed you. I don't even have enough to feed myself." He gazed around the room as if checking I was telling the truth. Was he sneering at me? Laughing at my inability to hunt? Probably. You're welcome to share my fire, I told him, trying to assert my superiority in being able to create fire. He accepted the offer with dignity. I scooped soup into my cup and drank. It was still hot despite the rain but the soup was still comforting. Apart from the firelight and the odd flicker of lightning, the room was dark. The cat and I spent some time watching the flames but I still felt the need to ration my firewood, unsure of the rules on collecting wood from the King's forest so I let the fire die and, yawning, told the cat I was going to bed. He yawned in agreement. I snuggled as best I could into the ferns, twigs and grasses and curled up small under my T- shirt and waterproofs blanket in the cooler bedroom. Less tired that night, I dozed and woke and dozed again, only to wake in the dark as paws prodded my legs into an acceptable pillow for a cat's body. I thought of Bubble and whispered to her. " I'll be back as soon as I can but find someone else to sleep on for now if you can. I love you". If only she could know I hadn't abandoned her on purpose. My heart ached for my bossy little tabby with her big emotions and dramatic outlook on life. I looked at the shadowy ball tucked into the hollow of my stomach and legs and felt just a little comforted to have a him there, accepting life as it came and making the most of every situation. I fell fully asleep.

It seemed my visitor was an early riser, leaping from the bed before dawn and demanding that I opened the door so that he could go hunting for his breakfast. One up to me, I thought smugly as I cooked an egg, but now I craved bread and butter to dip into the yolk which was only partially hard today. I discovered boiling egg in pea soup changed the flavour of the egg. It was still good to eat. I looked eagerly into my rainwater barrel as the sky lightened. How much rain had we had? Maybe a couple of cupfuls. I could now drink water, cider and pea soup. How great to have a choice of three different flavours. I must find a way to soak the peas not in the cauldron so that I could experiment with herb teas. I thought both rosemary and mint should work if I soaked them long enough but that needed a spare container.

I was back in the village for eight, as promised. How did the villagers know what the time was? I knocked on the indicated door and waited. There was a shout from inside which I hoped asked me to enter. I stuck my head in and saw a man lying on the bed in the corner. His leg was bent at an odd angle but held in place with rough splints. His face was white and strained with pain but he tried to sit up as I stepped inside. Instinctively, I wanted to straighten that leg to get it to mend in the right position but it would hurt him terribly and presumably it had been strapped by a doctor. Perhaps I shouldn't interfere. He gave me a tight smile and waved at the back door. I went through and found another strip of land in need of help. I hoed away the weeds, sorting the various plants in case any were things the man would eat and set up the bean poles, trying to weave the stacked willow onto a strong framework as I had no string or twine. There were bean seeds in a wooden pot by the back door. The French words were unknown to ask if I should plant them. I asked in English with hand signals and got vigorous nodding from the bed. I dug holes at each pole and hoped the slugs would leave them alone. As I finished, the vicar arrived. We exchanged bonjours. I had noticed there was no food in the house. No hens and no pig. There were tools by the door. A pitchfork, a fierce looking knife and ragged shears. There was also a broken ladder. At the end of the strip of land were sheaves of thatch. The vicar pointed towards the inside room and then at the sheaves and then at the ladder and explained in words I was beginning to understand that the man had fallen while thatching and broken his leg. The vicar fished in his cloak and produced a coin. "For your work," he said and I understood the words. Either his wife had coached him to speak the King's English or I was getting the hang of the local dialect. I took the coin. It was lucky I still had an egg left, I thought because I had no way of using the coin for food. The vicar beckoned and led me around the end of the cottages instead of through the thatcher's home. Looking at the vicar's back, I realised I still didn't know what day it was. When did I have to go to church, and would I have to give this coin to a collection plate? So many things I ought to know but didn't. My heart jumped a few beats and I felt a prickle of sweat as I realised I ought to know all the prayers and hymns if I was taught in an abbey, even allowing for changes from Latin to English and the dissolution of the monasteries. As we returned to the village square, the vicar turned to me,"Will you be witnessing the court, today?" he asked, and I saw that the villagers were congregating on the green in anticipation of some event. As I watched, a carriage arrived and two men in sombre cloaks disembarked, one unloading several rolls of paper. "Excuse me," the vicar said, "I have duties," and he hurried over to greet the men and lead them into the church. The villagers watched but did not follow. Some of them peered along the road rather like someone waiting for a bus that was late. I looked the same way. There was the clumping of a horse walking on hard ground and then the echo of hooves on cobbles and a handsome black horse, expertly ridden, walked up the street, halted by a mounting block and the rider dropped neatly to the ground. He tied it alongside a chestnut horse I had not seen arrive, already tethered. Without acknowledging the crowd, he walked into the church, but it seemed this was who they had been waiting for because after a brief hesitation they began to file into the church. I watched until they had all disappeared and then, laying aside my bag of tools, and hiding them in the shadows behind the arched gateway, I joined the crowd, keeping as best I could at the back of the crowd and out of sight. The church had been laid out as a courtroom with three visitors sat behind a table and our vicar sat nearby. The man with the rolls of paper seemed to be a scribe ready to write down what was said at yet another table. Our vicar also sat with quill, ink and a huge book. The rider of the chestnut must have arrived while I was gardening. It seemed we had three judges and two witness accounts of the proceedings. The man who had arrived with the scribe looked like a clergyman. The other two exuded authority. They were the elite, the makers and interpreters of the law, the decision makers on right and wrong. Their mouths were stern and their backs as straight as iron rods. There was no give, no likelihood of lenience. I was glad I had not yet been caught breaking the law. One of the judges spoke and the scribe bent to his quill. His voice was clear so that I understood what was being said. "I open this court of Friday 15th June 1564. Witness to the court : Johannes of Feckenham, vicar of this parish and William Parson of Bradleye Greene. Presiding, Sir Nicholas of Throckmorton, Geoffrey Markham of Astwood Bank parish and myself, your normal magistrate, Sir John Throckmorton. Please step forward, the first petitioner." A young man stepped shyly forward, removing a sack hat which he twisted and kneaded in his hands nervously. "Your name?" Sir John asked. "William Carter" the man replied. "And your request?" I had no idea what William the carter required as his accent was too strong for interpretation and his voice too quiet. Even the magistrate requested a repetition. Johannes gently encouraged the young man to speak clearly and loudly. "Your request will be granted. It is your right." He said. I still did not catch the words, something about taking on his father's house and trade, but the magistrate nodded. "Granted," he said. "Next case." The lady I had helped with the land stood straight backed and stated clearly that she requested continuation of her widow's pension. The magistrate looked to Johannes who confirmed her right and that too was granted. She then continue to stand and said, "I also make a request for poor payment for Simeon the Thatcher who is unable to work due to a fall and for leniency in his tithe for the next quarter," The magistrate's eyebrows rose in surprise and then switched to a frown. Sir Nicholas smiled into his beard and I gathered his relative was not used to being challenged by a woman. She stood unaffected by the angry glare waiting peaceably for his decision. Sir John turned to Sir Nicholas for an opinion. "What is the extent of his injury?" Sir Nicholas enquired. "His ladder collapsed, and he fell and broke his leg," the woman stated. "You had best ask the doctor how long it will take to mend." "Is the doctor present?" John huffed. "I am," a man rose from a pew. " The break is bad. He might never regain his trade but should be able to walk within a month with a brace. From then on I would think he could act as a general labourer and thus earn his keep." "I would suggest, then four week's pauper pay and six week's tithe free." Sir Nicholas suggested. "Agreed," the magistrate stated. "Next case!" As the lady turned, I saw her exchange a smile with the vicar. It seemed they had achieved what they wanted for the thatcher. I wondered about that leg. Did I dare, with only my first aider's knowledge, try to reset it. It didn't look as though the doctor intended further action or surgery. I reflected that I couldn't make it much worse and it sounded as though the injury was recent. As other cases came forwards, I considered the date. Perhaps I wasn't even in Lady Jane's time. She had said Henry was on the throne but 1564 was too late for him. Something happened in 1558 which I associated with Elizabeth I, but my history was too hazy. I gazed around the church. There were few tapestries. Almost no colour. No stained glass. No Latin inscriptions. I must be in Elizabethan England, mustn't I. My attention was yanked back to the proceedings by a man falling to his knees and putting his hands together in an appeal for mercy. Sir John was reading a report. His face was serious and firm. Sir Nicholas was no longer smiling. "You were witnessed in the act of hunting in the Queen's forest. Do you have any defence?" " I c-c-c-caught nothing, Sire," the man trembled. "But you intended to catch what?" Sir John demanded. "Nothing," the man insisted. "I understand you were carrying traps," Sir John was impatient. The man looked at the floor and said nothing. Sir John shrugged his shoulders. "You know the sentence for poaching is execution?" The man's shoulders heaved in a silent sob and he rubbed a sleeve across his face. "My children are starving," he said. I wanted to leap up and defend the man but what could I say? That the sentence was too harsh? That the law should be changed. Sir John's look had hardened whilst Sir Nicholas's eyes had softened. Was that sympathy I saw? "Your family will receive benefit," he told the man. The man nodded but still sobbed and was unable to speak. I saw a woman put her hands to her mouth and her eyes fill with tears. Sir John was gruff. "You will be put in the hands of the bailiff as of now until sentence." he said. Another man stepped forwards and lifted the poacher to his feet by his arm, pulling him away. The woman cried out and ran to intercept them, throwing herself into her husband's arms they embraced passionately and the bailiff waited patiently and impassively. I didn't know how he could carry out his job with so little emotion. My throat ached and my eyes had filled with tears. The next case was almost as traumatic with theft of one hen being sentenced with a public whipping of fifty lashes. I felt sick with the barbarity of the age. If only I could change it but, without putting my own life at risk, I couldn't see how. Thankfully, there were no more cases and the court hearing came to an end. I stood with the rest of the villagers while the three judges and the two witnesses left the church. I mingled with the crowd as they left, trying not to be seen by these figures of knowledge and authority. There was a chance the villagers would think my clothes were London fashion. I was certain these

Throckmortons would know otherwise. I decided to sit in the shadowy entrance to the church until they had gone. Sir John mounted and left immediately. The silent judge from Astwood Bank, whose name I had forgotten left on foot. The scribe and the Bradleye Green churchman climbed into their carriage and were driven away but Sir Nicholas loitered, chatting to the vicar. "Are you home for good?" the vicar asked. "I know not," said Sir Nicholas, "But I hope so. My time in gaol in France was harrowing. I have lost my taste for diplomacy. I should be happy to spend time with my wife at Coughton while I recover and then a place in the queen's court would be fine." He paused, and then smiled. "And how are you doing with the tithes and taxes. Has your mathematics improved since we last met?" Johannes grimaced. "I am afraid not. The figures still dance to their own strange rhythms and give me the wrong answers." "Just two days until your masters come to collect," Sir Nicholas warned. "You know you will be fined if you are late," He swung on to his horse. "Perhaps you should employ a bean counter." He clicked his tongue and bumped his knee on the horse's flank. The horse wheeled and departed. I peered around the doorway and the vicar jumped. "I did not know you were there," he said. "Did you hear the whole conversation?" I nodded. "Do you know any good bean counters?" he asked. "I might try," I said hopefully, thinking that he had easily saved my life with his help and I owed him at least an attempt at counting his beans. "You are good at numbers?" he said, surprised but hopeful. "Let's see," I said. He took me by the arm, lifted his skirts and ran to his house, dragging me into a room with a heap of untidily stacked ledgers by a table close to the unshuttered window. The table held nothing but a quill pen and a pot of ink. He pushed me into a chair and opened the top ledger. He turned back some pages. "The beginning of the quarter is here. I have to work out a tenth of the quotas and change it to coins." he lifted another smaller ledger. "This is the agreed value of each animal or crop. We give the value in coins and they decide whether to reconvert to animals or crops or take the value in coins." He patted me excitedly on the back. "Carry on," He whisked out of the room and closed the door as if to prevent me from fleeing. What had I let myself in for? The swirling writing was almost illegible, the figures not in straight columns and all the animals and crops mixed up. I picked up the quill and looked at it. I didn't even know how to use a quill pen. I remembered I had a stub of pencil in my diary. I wasn't going to distract myself with the quill pen. I would make a table using the pencil and then try to write on the ledger the correct answers with the quill. I have always enjoyed number puzzles and became absorbed in the best way to solve this mess, ignoring who owed what and going for the totals first which was what seemed to matter here. How many pigs could I count, how many hens. I was stumped by the different measurements for crops, bushels and stukes, pounds of grain. Best to have different columns for bushels and stukes, I supposed and then? Well should I know the difference? How many bushels to the pound?. I'd worry about that later. Another problem loomed. How many pennies to the guinea? What was a crown? I could see the headings for each coin at the top of the column but value per animal seemed to be in pennies. I would stick to pennies. I was surely supposed to know the value of a guinea so couldn't ask. As I worked, I thought that I could look back at the last quarter to find the conversions from one measure to another, assuming the vicar had got it right last quarter and maybe also work out the value of guineas and shillings for the total figure at the end. It took me three hours to make my table and do the multiplication and then divide by ten for the tithe and several false starts to work out the conversions as the vicar had obviously made several major mistakes and apparently fudged the figures to make them balance. Eventually, I was mostly certain I had things right and sat back in the chair, rubbing my eyes. Just got to work out how to use the quill. I picked it up just as the vicar poked his head around the door. "How goes it?" he asked. "Done," I said, "Except for writing in the totals. Perhaps it is best if you do that in your handwriting." I was pleased with my excuse to avoid the quill. Johannes clapped his hands. "You are sure it is right?" "Well, almost sure," I replied honestly. He looked over my shoulder at my tables. "What a good idea to work in pennies all through," he exclaimed, "and to calculate the bushels separate to the sheaves. I never thought of that." I laughed internally. As I stood, he slid into the chair and grabbed the quill, writing with his tongue sticking out of the side of his mouth in concentration, like a schoolboy first learning to write and then flung the quill delightedly to the table. "Stay to eat," he said. I was hungry and there was only one egg left at Shurnock but I was afraid of my lack of knowledge of table manners. Supposing I was invited to say grace. I started to shake my head but the vicar insisted, once again taking my arm and dragging me through the house to the kitchen. "I still don't even know your name," he cried. "Margot," I said. He turned to his wife. "Marco is eating with us," he announced. "He has completed the accounts in just three hours and I do believe he has got the sums right." I opened my mouth and then shut it. My clothes were nearest those of a man, my voice middle range. I was doing the work of a man. I supposed I looked young enough not to have a beard or stubble and I realised that although short in my time, I was actually as tall as most of the men I had encountered. This was no time to come clean about being female. "To complete the introductions, my name is Johannes and my wife is Jacqueline." I nodded, unsure if I should bow or kiss her hand or anything, but then we had already met several days ago so the introduction was somewhat belated and therefore informal. Jacqueline smiled fondly at her excited husband. There was already food on the table. Competently, she collected another plate and a wooden mug, cleared a space alongside a bench seat and waved me to it. Who was supposed to sit first? Ladies, guests or the host. I hovered uncertainly. "Sit, sit, sit," my host instructed eagerly. Had he read my mind. It seemed the gents sat and the women served and then sat. I was relieved when the vicar gabbled a grace and then tucked in, waving me to do the same. I copied as best I could and saw Jacqueline smile quietly. She was incredibly intelligent and I reckoned she somehow knew I was out of my depth whilst her husband was so excited and relieved to have the accounts complete that he was unaware of my hesitation in every action. There were meats and cheeses and more crisp lettuce and bread and butter. I tried not to gobble, but my stomach was ecstatic. My mug was filled with cider and I sipped carefully for fear of getting drunk and over-talkative. In fact, it was a quiet meal and at the end there was another prayer of thanks. As we left the table, Jacqueline said, "I think Marco is quite tired. You really should let him go my dear," "Yes, of course," said the vicar. "I must pay you for your time," He hurried away and thrust a pouch of coins at me at the door. "You have been sent as a miracle to me," he said cheerfully as I went out into the dusk. "I expect you will have a day off tomorrow and I will see you at church on Sunday." "Yes, of course," I replied. I almost asked what time, but again, this was something I should know so I would have to arrive early and get my cue from the villagers. I walked back to Shurnock in a daze. My stomach was full and I had money to barter for food. The pouch felt full. How many coins would buy clothes. I dreamed of saving enough for a blanket for my bed. If those sheep didn't look out, I'd be stealing the fleece off their backs, I thought sleepily. The cat was waiting at the door. "Oh, you're sleeping here again are you? Well, I'm not getting up in the night to let you out hunting," I warned him, as he trotted over the threshold, "And I'm still not feeding you," I added. The cat paid no attention but walked into the bedroom and prepared his nest. I joined him and eased into sleep.

SATURDAY

It was useful, after all to have my new furry alarm clock. He woke me by cleaning vigorously, leaning on my legs. It was dawn, about 4.30am. I felt refreshed and decided I would go exploring. I wanted to see what Redditch looked like in the 16th century. I would save the egg for a treat tomorrow, and ate nuts for breakfast. Wondering if I smelt, I had a swim in the moat but wasn't sure if that also was smelly. I rubbed myself with rosemary and lavender as I dried off. I took my cagoule and trousers in my bag, and a cup of cider for lunch. Then added the purse of coins. It was possible I might find shops to buy a saucepan or other cooking container. I had noticed a tiny path heading North from almost opposite the newly cut access to Shurnock. I thought it might come out by Astwood Court and set off. The trees were thick and the land rose steeply so that the path curved to find the best way up the slope. I lost my sense of direction and there was no sun to use a compass. I came to a fork and hesitated. I tried left. I came to another junction with a bigger lane. Surely this wasn't the road to Astwood Bank already. It had to be right, anyway as two lefts would leave me heading either west or south. The contours of the surrounding countryside had a familiarity, but the trees instead of fields had me flummoxed. I came to another crossroads. As I hovered indecisively, a wagon full of cut timber appeared, a man leading the mule that pulled it and talking to the mule who seemed to be listening with interest. They passed from right to left, the man only giving me a cursory glance. I set off to the right, but my mind was wondering about the timber. Where were they going? I came to a Tudor house set in a large cleared area, with what looked like wheat or barley in a field and another field of corn. I recognised the house, with its right angled barn. I had taken the wrong fork in that track and bent myself back towards Feckenham. I decided to abort my exploration and try to find where the wagon had gone. He had been going at less than full walking pace. I ought to be able to catch him up. I turned and took the waggoner's route and found myself back in Feckenham, but now there were carts lined up on the green and around the square and busy people arranging goods on them as if for sale. The villagers were out and inspecting the produce. More people were appearing from the Droitwich Road carrying sacks and baskets. A smile split my face. It was market day. I went into the churchyard and found a quiet corner to study my coins. They were rough edged and several different colours but I had no idea of their value. It seemed like a lot of money but how would I know? I sorted them into different sorts and put the biggest back in the purse. They would surely be the highest value and I would offer them for something expensive and see if I got change. One man had a load of pots of pans. There was a stall selling cheeses which made my mouth water and some of the villagers had set up trestle tables with bread and vegetables to barter with or sell. Another stall had skins. I wasn't sure if they were sheep. They might have been goats. I wished they had prices up so I could get a hang of relative worth. The skins man saw me looking and asked me a question. He was probably asking if I wanted to buy but could have been asking if I thought it was a nice day. I felt a foreigner in my own country. Well, on foreign holidays, I had dived right in. Why not now? "How much?" I asked pointing at a skin that would just about cover my body as a blanket. The trader looked at me, assessing my wealth, I thought. " Ten pennies," he said. It occurred to me that the skin would be heavy and I had no bicycle to carry it home on. It would be silly to buy it now. I nodded and turned to walk away."Eight," the man shouted. I turned, hesitating. Perhaps I should try a lower price? I still couldn't carry it. I half shrugged unable to explain and moved on. The cheese monger was gathering together cheeses and calling out prices. I was definitely going to buy some cheese, but first I needed a saucepan. A lady in fine clothes was bartering with the pedlar for a large pan made of copper. I watched carefully as they agreed a price and saw the coins in her hand as she paid. I had similar coins but only wanted a smaller pan. I saw he also had wooden mugs and dishes and a kettle perfect for one person's drinks. I sorted out coins similar to the lady's and then picked up the kettle and the pan and a mug. I reckoned the price should be about the same. Indicating my items I handed him the coins, trying to look assertive and confident. He looked at my offerings and shook his head with a scowl. I raised my chin arrogantly and held his gaze. He looked at my intended purchases again, looked at the coins, then scanned his offerings. He reached out, removed my pan and offered me another with a dent in it and slightly smaller. It seemed fair to me. I took the pan and gave him the coins and we smiled at each other with mutual respect. I put my new purchases in my bag. My biggest coins were gone. Food was more important than the blanket, I thought, and headed for the cheese stall. He was doing a good trade. I watched and waited, trying to see which coins were used to cover which cheeses. He saw me watching and put his head on one side, assessing. Then he held up a wedge of cheese. "One penny?" He offered. I shrugged. I noticed people had bartered less here, accepting the prices offered so I proffered a coin, with a nod. He reached in his apron pocket and gave me some coins back with the cheese. So that coin had been, what? A florin, a sixpence maybe. These were probably pennies. Thinking about bread and butter, I absent-mindedly put the pennies in my trouser pocket and walked on. The villager's bread was newly baked and there were rolls as well as a loaf and tiny pats of butter. I studied my coins and thought that bread was about half the price of cheese, so a penny might cover the cost. I could see another man selling salted meats and pies. I would love a pie for lunch, but with no fridges and summer heat, how was he keeping the meat safe? I didn't want food poisoning. I would just buy the bread, I thought and dipped into my pocket for a penny, handing it over and then pointing out what I wanted. The woman behind the stall looked at my coin and turned it over in her hands, puzzled and I realised with horror that I had had modern coins also still in that pocket. She waved at me to wait, and I thought of just running away, but already her neighbours knew where I was from via the vicar and running would be highly suspicious behaviour. I couldn't leave Shurnock as it was the only place I knew where the time slipped into my century. I stood my ground and trembled and sweated while she talked to a man who was probably her husband. He, too, studied the coin. I thought it was a ten pence piece, big, silver coloured and shiny. He took it to another stall holder who also looked at it with interest but shook his head. How many other people would be alerted to my strange money? Would they think me a spy? I would have to convince them it was a new coin from London, and maybe I could get it back and offer a proper penny. Another man had joined them and seemed to be suggesting a solution. The first man came back. Looked at his wares and offered me two more loaves. I felt guilty. If he tried to pass that coin on, would he be in trouble or would it simply become part of the Worcestershire currency? The men had seemed to accept its value based on its size, colour and the ten pence engraving. No one had checked the date, or if they had, perhaps just didn't recognise it as a date. I didn't need all that bread. I pushed it back at him and instead lifted another pat of butter and indicated just one loaf. He nodded and tried to give me a penny change. I refused it. It was already going to be difficult for him to pass on. I wished I could take it back as someone with more knowledge might see it and start asking questions about the caretaker of Shurnock Court. The skins man had watched with interest. I went and sat beyond the church while I recovered my nerves, nibbling gently on my roll and sipping the cider from my cup away from prying eyes. Explaining my heat retaining aluminium cup with its plastic lid would be beyond me. I still had eight pennies and two more big unknown coins. The confident lady was selling purple carrots and eggs. I offered her the big coin for six eggs and three carrots. She shook her head, reached out and took the bread and extra pat of butter with a smile. We had successfully bartered, I thought. It was easier to fit the carrots and eggs in my bag, putting the eggs carefully in the folds of my cagoule and the carrots in the kettle. The bread and butter went in the saucepan. Could I carry that goat skin? The only other stall was the carpenter and his mule. He had originally gone beyond the market and offloaded a fair amount of his products elsewhere before coming back late to set up his wares. Spade handles, wooden rakes, wooden spoons and dishes. He had no metal blades for his spade or prongs for a fork. I supposed I might find those at the smithy but for now I would manage without. I returned to the skins stall and experimentally held out seven pennies. He accepted immediately and I thought I must have still overpaid, but if we were both happy, that was fine by me. Now I just had to get everything back to Shurnock. I was thirsty again. There was a man selling barrels of some drink. I took out my mug. Would he sell me one mugful for a penny? He shook his head but pointed to one of the cottages. I went where he pointed and held up my mug and the penny. My mug and the penny were taken and my mug returned, filled with a drink tasting of pears but with the power of strong alcohol. I coughed as the first sip hit the back of my throat and the nearby crowd laughed. I laughed, too, already feeling a little tipsy. I sipped more carefully and grew accustomed to the taste and the bite. It slipped down with ease and I thought it was time to go before I caused any more laughter or made any more mistakes with coins as a result of a fuzzy head. Waving, cheerfully at those I now knew, I walked a concentratedly straight line to the Roman road and headed for home, resting often and rearranging my purchases as they slid out of my arms. I could hear, after a mile, the rattle of wheels and the clump of hooves and soon the carpenter came alongside, this time riding his almost empty wagon. He indicated with his thumb and called "Jump!" I needed no further encouragement, throwing in the goat skin and my bag and clumsily climbing aboard, sitting with my legs dangling out of the back and watching the dust rise and settle as the wagon trundled along. I leapt off with a shout of gratitude at the entrance to Shurnock, grabbing my purchases as the wagon trundled on. The cat greeted me with a rub around the legs, surprisingly tame for a hunting farmer's cat. Studying his sleek fur, I thought he was also surprisingly clean and well fed. He invited himself to share my bread and cheese tea and I had no need to light the fire now we had a goat skin to share and cider and rainwater to drink. It was a pity I hadn't been able to buy a keg of ale but tomorrow I would start experimenting with herbal teas.

Chapter 4

SUNDAY

The pear perry and warm soft skin gave my my best ever night's sleep and it was lucky the cat woke me again at dawn. I had no idea when the church service would be so got up and heated water to wash, something I had skimped on until now, not wanting to waste water when I had to carry it from the moat and not having any soap. My teeth felt furry. I brushed them with my finger and wished there had been a cosmetics stall at the market the day before. I tipped out my washing water and added barrel rain water to boil my egg. I looked down at my clothes. Too late to wash them, I tried to brush off some of the mud and rolled up my trousers as before. The cat had watched my ablutions as if laughing at my feeble attempts to get clean, but now he stood up and wandered out of the door. He walked through the herb garden and as he reached the grass, he blurred, faded and vanished. He had time slipped. It took a second of disbelief and then I ran to follow him, but I couldn't get through. What had he done that I had not? I had found a sort of peace in working out survival here in 1564 and meeting the kind villagers but now I felt a surge of frustration and helplessness and homesickness. In desperation, I ran around trying the other spaces and shouted to the cat to come back and show me what to do. Nothing. I remembered the church service with a stab of panic. The punishments were brutal for missing a service. I hurried off to the village. How did the villagers know what the time was? I hadn't seen a bell to ring. I found people already clustered, chatting together on the village green. I was relieved to see that, although there were a few in fine clothes, most still wore work type garments and I was no more out of place than normal in rolled up polyester mix trousers and cotton shirt. I saw the vicar scurrying from his home. He slowed and walked more sedately as he reached the church and led the way inside. I saw there was a hierarchy with the more richly dressed entering first and the poorest dressed last. I mingled with the last stragglers and found only the better dressed had pews. The rest of us stood or kneeled on the cold stone floor at the back of the church, which suited me fine – less eyes to examine me and see that I didn't know the order of service, the prayers or the hymns. I found I was now attuned to the vicar's voice. The service was in English but there were still words I didn't understand. How amazing that our language had changed so much. At the end of the service, the vicar exited first and then the richer people so it was easy for me to sidle out with the crowd and disappear back towards Shurnock. The sabbath was supposed to be a day of rest so I thought it best to stay within the boundaries of Shurnock,.I was no good at resting so entertained myself, trying to dig out the wood from my makeshift bowl with my knife and the blade of my dismantled secateurs. I needed a chisel. Next market day, I would check the smithy and the carpenter to see if I could buy one, I thought, but I needed more coins if I was going to buy. Where else could I get work? I spent the afternoon partially watching the birds on the moat. Swans, geese and a type of duck I had never seen before, with smaller birds darting through the reeds. Occasionally I dozed and woke. And dozed again. The wood pilferers must have heard of my presence and did not appear. I felt lonely without the cat but ate my ration of bread and cheese and slept well, feeling more in balance with the land, surrounded by the natural noises of this world and free of the disturbing technology of the future.

MONDAY

With no cat, I slept late the next morning and decided to
have another attempt at finding Redditch. It occurred to me
that Bordesley Abbey existed in both times and had had a
turbulent time. Would that turbulence result in a shakiness
in time? Once again I packed a drink, but added bread and
cheese this time as well as my last coins. I carefully left
my modern day coins behind, hidden in a cranny of the
fireplace. As I set out, I looked round for the cat. No sign.
At the fork, I turned right and followed a path over the top
of the hill. I met just one man amongst the trees, gathering
wood, but he scurried away when he saw me. It reminded
me that I still didn't know if my fire was made from an
illegal hoard. Now I had drinking water in the form of rain,
I must be frugal with those fires. The land seemed empty.
No buzz of traffic. No rumbling tractors or hum of hedge
trimmers. I met a stag in a clearing. It assessed me as the
market traders had, slowly and steadily and then sauntered
into the trees. The track I was on branched and I shut my
eyes to visualise where the tracks might go. That big Tudor
farm I had seen on the Saturday to the left. Hopefully,
Astwood Court to the right. I set off right and soon came to
a hamlet, moated as Shurnock was but with a small
community attached to the big house. There were the usual
hens and pigs but the big house had a stable block and two
sleek horses sharing a paddock. There was a stable hand
unloading sacks from a wagon and a rotting pile of manure
in a corner. It felt affluent and alive compared to the
silence of Shurnock. No one paid me much attention. The
stable lad was busy at his task and no one else was about. I
found a grander bridge over the moat, leading to a road,
still rutted, but wide and hardened with passing traffic.
Another road led from my track straight on. I hesitated

again. The road must go to the Astwood Bank ridge as it did in my day but the straight on road was not there. I vaguely remembered a footpath. Was this road the Monarch's way? Soon to be used by King Charles in his escape from the Cromwellian army? If it was, it would go straight to Redditch. I would try it. I couldn't get very lost because the ridge to my east went right to the centre of Redditch, or at least the old village centre of Headless Cross on the top of the hill. Actually, I could get lost if I mixed that ridge with the east west ridge going to Bromsgrove but that was miles ahead. If in doubt, I would head east and uphill, I thought. I came to another clearing after what seemed hours of tree after tree after tree, my spirits drooping with the unmarked featureless miles. I had considered turning back but wasn't even sure I could follow the trail I had walked. On the flat Feckenham plain, I could get more confused than marching into the pincers of Redditch's two ridges. It was a relief to hear the rowdiness of other human beings. There was a house being built. The vast framework skeleton of precisely worked interlocking beams stood, immense and impressive. Two carpenters worked from rickety scaffolding, balancing on joists to erect the huge rafters. No machinery but cog wound winches. A death drop of over 5 metres beneath them. They were laughing as they worked, hammering timber pegs into holes to make the structure sturdy. That house is still there, in 500 years, I thought in awe. I knew where I was, even if my route was still uncertain. As expected, the land began to climb. |I was on the south-west edge of what would eventually be Redditch New Town. I came to a small hamlet, about six homes on the top of a sub ridge, the land so steep, the houses looked over the forest below. I gazed back the way I had come. Acres of forest, some dense trees and other areas partially cleared., more like parkland than forest. It was odd seeing no grazing sheep or cows, no fields enclosed with barbed wire or hedgerow. The villages could barely be seen, just the odd corner of thatch from one of the bigger houses. The top of the hill now showed above me but I had reached a crossroads. Straight on or right, I thought. The map I carried in my head was useless as none of those roads existed. I tried straight on but came to a headland with no obvious path, except to the west. Downhearted, I retraced my steps and headed east. The track zig zagged up hill and at last I arrived on the ridge top. I could see a river snaking through the valley to the east, with watermills spaced out and lots of open spaces. There were hillocks and a straight road with hamlets around the mills and along the road. The land was swampy looking with most buildings on the slopes and hill tops. The river disappeared behind the ridge I stood on to the north. That was where I would find the abbey, or at least its ruins after the destruction ordered by Henry VIII. There was a good sized village on this hilltop, with an inn and a baker's shop. If I had enough nerve I might stop here on the way back. I realised, I had little expectation of leaping forward in time from Bordesley Abbey, but I would still try to find it. There was a real road along the ridge. Rubble had been dropped in the mud of centuries and vegetation worn down to nothing by passing feet, hooves and wheels. My tiredness eased and I strode eagerly downhill. It was a shock to find Redditch didn't exist at all. Someone had laid out stone blocks in the shape of a church on a bluff overlooking the abbey remains, the river and a vast swamp dotted with pools of open water. A track led downhill to the abbey. It stood darkly silhouetted like black fangs from the swamp, tumbled blocks of stone, fire stained and forlorn. I hopped from tussock to tussock, looking up at the immense arches, all that was left of a structured community. Where were the monks now? I wondered. There were tracks built up high above the water, creating fishing pools and I followed these through what must have been outbuildings, and then onto a hay field above the marsh. The river running past the abbey swung downhill southwards and I thought if I followed it, I must come to the track running now past my house as a main road back up past the church site and onwards to the top of the ridge. I got my feet wet, and fell in the mud, but did eventually reach a track in the right place. There were no houses. Just scrub and trees and a fast flowing stream which ran from underground as a spring. I stood where my house would be built and felt further away from home than I had ever felt before. I had believed I would find Bubble on this spot, waiting faithfully for me to come home. How stupid I am, I thought. My energy drained away and I dropped to my knees in the gorse and grasses and wept until I felt hollow with grief. Was there any point moving? This was the nearest I could get to home and I was centuries away. I knelt in that spot until my body trembled and ached with fatigue and the declining sun made me cold. Out of discomfort, I pushed myself to my feet. It was, in fact, impossible to just give up. My instinct was for survival. I would go back to Shurnock and find Lady Jane or some other dewin and learn how to change time. I felt numb reascending the hill, with its bare headland, but on reaching the hilltop, I could smell cooking bacon and soup and I realised I had eaten nothing since breakfast. I was more than two hours from home. I would eat in the inn and save my rations for later in case I got lost on the last stretch to Shurnock,

The tavern was dark. I couldn't get used to the lack of glass. There were just two tiny windows with thick tinted glass held in place with thick lead edgings. Only the doorway let in real light. It shone on the bar counter and lit the man standing behind it. "Afternoon sire," he greeted me. "What can I serve 'ee?" I glanced around for inspiration. The place held only two other customers. Two elderly men playing shove ha'penny had a tankard each, but it was food I wanted. "Soup," I suggested, hopefully. The man nodded and vanished. I slid onto a bench adjacent to a long bare table and looked around at the sparseness. No pictures or photographs on the walls. No archaic ornaments to give the place character. This was a place to drink, eat or sleep. In this society, only the elders now unable to work had time for leisure, and I suspected grandmothers still babysat, and most men worked until they dropped. A harsher existence, or more satisfying and productive? The barman arrived with my soup, wooden bowl, wooden spoon, bread roll to dip. "Thank you," I said automatically. I handed him my last coin. He looked surprised and impressed. Dug around in his apron pocket and handed me a large number of coins, counting out as he laid them in my hand. How much had the vicar paid me for my accounting skills? It seemed an enormous sum compared to my gardening skills, but then, few people were educated in this time. Knowledge of numbers was rare and special. I had been lucky. The soup had vegetables and bacon in it. It tasted wonderful. I wiped the bowl clean with the last piece of my roll, hesitated about whether to return the bowl to the bar, but saw the barman advancing towards the table as I rose. I gave him a nod of thanks, made sure I had my bag, and left. Even from the top of the ridge, the sun was dropping behind the trees. It was going to be difficult finding my way back along the route I had come on. I had better go back along the ridge and then go back along The Saltway. It would add maybe a mile to my journey but getting lost in the dark with no recognisable roads to put me back on track would be terrifying. It was not as if I could just knock on a door and ask directions. In places, as I walked southwards, the trees thinned or had fallen and I had a view of the setting sun over hills far to the west. It was beautiful and familiar. The Black mountains and the Malverns still looked the same and gave me promise that the centuries were linked. They made the five hundred years of separation seem smaller and less difficult to bridge. The ridge dropped more steeply and I came to a fork in the road. I knew this place, but in my time it was a mini roundabout buzzing with traffic darting in all directions. Now, the simple choice was a road to Studley and Alcester, or to continue along the descending ridge to Astwood Bank, a shortcut to The Saltway and Droitwich. I took the right fork, but as the sun dropped lower started to consider taking another shortcut to find my route at Astwood Court. How obvious would the turn be? In my time, there was Dark Lane and Church Road. Did they both exist, even though the church was not yet built? It didn't matter which I took. They both went to the court. There were stars pricking into existence. More evidence of the vastness of time and the insignificance of human life. The moon appeared. I always felt comforted by its pale glow. Why a giant rock circling the earth and reflecting the sun's immense light should do this, I did not know, but serenity flowed out from my heart at its coming and washed the earlier despair from my body. I lengthened my stride and felt at one with the night. I found a right hand track, well used, descending into the trees. I took it. From its angle, I reckoned I was on Dark Lane, and as I descended, it matched its name. It was tar black. My stride became a shuffle, feeling carefully for trees roots, ruts and holes before every step. Perhaps I had made a mistake and should go back to the ridge, but I was tired and just wanted my bed. I shuffled on, thinking myself an idiot, wishing I had a torch, wondering now if I would know when I met the Church Road track and should swing left. Supposing, in this time, another track went straight on. I would end up in Hanbury! I stopped again and looked back up the steep almost invisible hill. Back to the ridge, or on? The hill was demoralising. Going back, a failure. I would go on. I realised I was talking to myself out loud, encouraging myself to continue one careful step at a time. It was dark because, as well as the trees, I was in a ravine, steep earth banks rising on either side. This would be a torrent in heavy rain. I could hear the odd tinkle of water close by. Mustn't fall in the stream, wherever it was. It took an age before the slope eased and the trees fell back. With relief, I came to a cross track and, swinging left found the moonlight dancing on the moat of Astwood Court, the set back buildings dark and silent in the night. A duck quacked, startled by my presence, and making me jump. My heart hammered and then eased. "Nearly home," I promised myself. I found the bridge and crossed, slowing again as I entered the more overgrown track beyond the hamlet, but the light was better, glimmer glow and shadow rather than the dense black of the ravine. Without warning, a tawny owl glided over my head and screeched as it sensed me. I felt wonder as the moon lit the swooping, silent shape navigating its way through the interlocking branches, no hesitation, no loss of speed. It made me feel clumsy, blundering, earthbound. I tripped over a root and sprawled, cursing as I got back to my feet. "Concentrate, stupid." I said fiercely. It was unnerving being the only human awake in all these miles of space. Then I wondered if there were poachers or game keepers about playing a game like blindfold chess amongst the trees, the penalty for a wrong move, death. I reached the junction of the track and stood unable to think straight. Which way? Was this where I had gone wrong on market day or had I not reached that point yet. My spirits had lifted with the discovery of Astwood Court, but now I just felt tired and wanted to be in my bed. Why had nobody thought of signposts yet? If I went left too early, I would end up re-climbing the ridge or on The Saltway but not knowing which way to go. If I went right and it was wrong (I raised a smile at the confusion of the English language) , I would find myself on the road to Feckenham. I went right, at least I would recognise the Feckenham road and not end up completey lost. I came to another junction. Same thoughts, same decision. Came out on the road to Feckenham. Well. I had done it wrong, but at least I now knew where I was. I turned left along this wider track, with the trees well spread, my heart lifting in the stronger moonlight and broke into a jog under the multi star studded sky. Another left on The Saltway. There was the track to the farm, and here was the track to Shurnock. I could see its shadowy form, not yet the imposing court it would become, but a smaller more welcome hump. I almost sprinted the last stretch in a surge of delighted energy and as I reached the door, a furry shape detached itself from the shadows and rubbed itself around my legs. A paw tapped at the door impatiently as I fumbled for the catch and we sprang into the room together. I still hadn't eaten or drunk the food I carried. I felt euphoric from my successful return. I started the fire, promising just one log and the cat sat on my bag by the hearth purring at the warmth. "I'm making you soft," I told him. He didn't care. Breaking my rules, I offered him a piece of my cheese. He took it politely, sniffed cautiously and gulped it down, licking his lips and cleaning a paw enthusiastically. I added a small amount of hot water to my drink and gulped it down, realising I was extremely thirsty. Leaving the fire to burn itself out, I went to bed and slept immediately.

Chapter 5

I had no reason to return to Feckenham the next day,
except to find more work, but how? I couldn't put up a
notice in the local shop, or safely knock on doors. The
villagers knew about me. I would have to wait and just get
Shurnock in perfect order. I set to, with my trowel and
makeshift spade. There was not enough money left to buy
a metal bladed spade. I looked at the fruit trees and carried
out a mid summer light prune, creating useful kindling at
the same time. I was enjoying a mid-morning cider when a
man appeared. "Good morning," I greeted him. I
recognised him as a villager. He was my height and
muscular, his clothes sack cloth but in good order. His
face was dirt shadowed but not grubby. "I have a job for
you, tomorrow," he said. The language was still strong in
dialect but not incomprehensible. I nodded, still shy of
talking in my modern English. "Meet us at the square at
dawn." I nodded again. I needed to know what we were
doing. But would he understand if I asked. The question
must have been in my eyes. "We need another man for
field work. There is sickness in the village." I hoped it
wasn't plague. So many other nasty question marks filled
my mind. Cholera, dysentery, tuberculosis, diphtheria,
small pox. I must check which way the water flowed
between Feckenham and Shurnock. For now, I would stick
to cider and rainwater and leave the moat alone. "You have
a scythe?" he asked. I shook my head. He scratched his
beard, puzzled, but said, " I'll bring Will's." With no more
fuss, he turned and left, turning again at the last moment to
introduce himself. "Richard," he said thumbing his chest
and turned away again, a positive man, something like a

site foreman, I thought. Intelligent, but not much schooled, not gentry. He had no arrogance but great practicality. I instinctively liked him and hoped we might be friends if I was stuck in this time for many more months. A little part of my mind rebelled against the thought, but much of it accepted the possibility and planned to live with it, day by day. There was little more I could do at Shurnock without seed. That was what I needed at the next market and it would be a late crop. June was late to be planting. I could do with a hen or two for my own eggs. How much was a pig or a goat for cheese? I looked at the sheep. How did one milk a sheep? How did I make cheese? Who did the sheep belong to? With no work to do and my appetite for adventure more than satiated, I snoozed in the afternoon. The cat came and slumped against me and snoozed, too. Scratching his ears, cautiously in case he retaliated with his claws for unwanted attention, I said, "How do you change time, cat?" I suspected he found it easy but wasn't saying. The day passed lazily. I was grateful for the warm sun, the food in my stomach and the roof over my head with its strong safe walls, barring wolves and human dangers. With nothing more to do, we ate early, a ration of cheese and bread, my first experiment of rosemary tea which was powerful and refreshing, and went to bed at sunset. I remembered I had meant to check which way the stream flowed. Tomorrow would do.

Chapter 6

WEDNESDAY

The cat woke me just before dawn to let him out to hunt and, in panic, I remembered I was supposed to be at Feckenham at dawn. I couldn't afford a reputation for tardiness. There was cloud in the sky. I shoved my waterproofs into my bag and another hunk of bread, drank rain water, scooped a cup of cider for later, ate bread and nuts as I ran to the village. The man was there on the green, leaning against two scythes, and also carried two wooden rakes laughing as I sprinted around the corner and panted as I halted beside him. "Good," he said. "Not late. Now we rouse the others." He led me north. The village was already awake with smoke from some of the chimneys, and buckets being filled at the pump by young women, chatting and laughing as they waited their turn at the pump. Another young man jogged over to join us. He gave me a grin, and swung his scythe onto his shoulder to walk more comfortably, the rake at his side. "You're Marco? I am Alan," "Pleased to meet you." I said, not having a clue what the correct greeting was. He gave me a doubtful look of non comprehension but said nothing. Our foreman had strode ahead and detoured to a hovel with a sack cloth hanging for a door. He pulled it aside and yelled "Up, up, you make us late!" A tousled head appeared in the doorway. "That's Gilbert," Alan informed me. Richard wasted no more time but led us further up the track to another waiting man, "Hugh," Alan said as he fell in alongside us. There were running footsteps from behind. Gilbert had caught us up, carrying his scythe. The field we were to work in was on the corner of the track I had walked in the night. Richard took us to the top of the field and indicated a row each. "We are one man short so we work hard and earn more," he announced matter-of-factly. It seemed we were clearing a hay crop. With no more discussion, we set to. I found the team were of varying abilities and styles. I sent a message of thanks to whoever controlled fate that I had volunteered on nature reserves where I had learned to scythe. I was taught by a master of efficiency. "Don't waste energy. Let the tool do the work," he advised and I learned the rhythm of the swing and twist, turning the scythe to cut in both directions of swing. Richard had the art down to perfection, striding forward, using his body as a lever and the length of his arms for a wide swing. Alan was precise and neat. Hugh, strong but uncoordinated, aged about eighteen, I thought he was still growing and unused to the length of his body. Gilbert, began slowly, still bleary eyed and not fully awake. Richard shouted at him as he lagged behind and he snapped more upright and increased his effort. The pace was fast and I found it hard to keep up, but was determined to pull my weight. I gritted my teeth and worked harder to use my body as a coiled spring, not fighting the scythe, but pushing it to increase momentum and then as it reached the end of its swing, recoiling hard to speed its return sweep. I had the row between Alan and Richard, I suspected this was to teach me what was expected and not be led by poorer examples. Hugh puffed as he worked alongside Alan, and Gilbert struggled to catch Richard up, his face pale above a skin and bone body. The field seemed enormous. I put my head down so that the size of the task would not daunt me. Were we going to do the whole field today? The first rows were cleared and Richard set us to the next section. I gazed wishfully at my bag and drink under the tree at the corner of the field, but it was clearly not yet a break time. This section was harder, working uphill I felt the sweat begin. Under my arm pits, across my forehead and down my back, sticking my shirt to my skin. My fingers and palms were beginning to tingle as the wooden handle rubbed against my hands. I changed my grip from right hand high to left hand high, thanking my lucky stars for a tendency to be ambidextrous able to guide that blade with either hand. Richard offered praise and admonishments, with no leniency for displays of pain or exhaustion and I admired his ability to bring out the best in his team. I could hear Hugh singing under his breath, the beat used to balance the rhythm of the scythe. We turned again at the top of the field, another row done, and set off back downhill, relieved by the pull of gravity, easing the ache in back, legs and arms. At the bottom, Richard glanced to the sun and led us over to the edge of the field. There were flagons sitting cooling in a running stream there. Lifting one, he uncorked it and took a swig, then handed it to Alan. I had been worrying about my unusual cup with its plastic lid. With relief, I realised we were to share whatever was in the flagons. Alan handed the flagon to Hugh who swigged and coughed, making Alan smile. Hugh caught his breath with a wheeze and a grin and passed the flagon to me. That wheeze suggested alcohol. What were we drinking? I took a swig but managed to control the reflex gasp. There was a heat and alcoholic burn behind the sweetness of honey and tanginess of fruit. Was this mead? I had never tasted it before. Thirst quenching, energy giving but probably dangerous to scythe users in large quantities. I handed the flagon to Gilbert. Richard gave Hugh a slap on the back. "You are working well, lad. I am pleased." he announced. He turned to me. "You work well for a student of numbers. I am surprised." There was a question in his voice. "The monks were disciplined," I said. "At harvest, we all pulled our weight." In my mind, I replaced the word monks with volunteers. On that reserve, we had all come from various backgrounds but had found great enjoyment and satisfaction in working as hard as we could as a team. I intended to do the same here. The flagon went round a second time and then we worked again. Another four strips as the sun reached its zenith and started its fall and the skin burned on my blistered hands. I risked a look at what we had achieved from the top of the field. We were three quarters done. The clouds now covered the sky and there was a sense of penned in heat, uncomfortable to work in. Richard studied it with a worried look. "It will be a short break for luncheon," he announced. "We must beat the rain. It will be heavy." At the base of the slope, we drank again and ate. Richard scrunched bread and then a juicy plum. Hugh and Alan had hard oatcakes which I had seen on the market stalls. Gilbert had nothing but the drink. I felt a beat of sympathy. Was the lack of food because he had overslept or was he in that vicious circle of starvation preventing good work which prevented good pay which prevented good eating which caused starvation and so on? Richard was driving him hard but he surprised me with an act of compassion, throwing a small pastry to Gilbert as he sat quietly resting and waiting to return to work. "Make sure you buy food with your earnings today," he said, not exactly ordering but as a statement of how things should be. Perhaps Gilbert was an alcoholic. I couldn't think what else he could spend money on. Finishing his last mouthful, Richard called us to our feet. Lunch had taken just ten minutes. I felt creaky and surreptitiously examined my throbbing hands. Those blisters were going to burst. Nothing I could do about it. The only thing I could do was pull my sleeves down over my hands but then I would wear out my shirt. I would have to boil water tonight and bathe my hands. "I think we must work to save as much of the crop as possible in case it rains, so, Hugh and Alan, start raking and stacking. Gilbert, Marco and me, keep scything. Go." Groaning internally, I picked up the scythe. Just two more rows to do. We worked uphill, the slight stiffness giving way to a persistent lactic acid ache. Richard marched on, impervious. Gilbert seemed galvanised by the food and drink and swung the scythe energetically. Determined not to be left behind, I gritted my teeth and blocked out the pain of tearing skin. My breath sobbed on the exhalations but I crept uphill. Richard was leaving me behind in his urgency as the sky blackened. He did not wait at the top but set off back downhill, concentrating on his task. I could hear Gilbert whimpering on each swing but kept my eyes on the scythe, blocking out the pain. I changed grip again and paused for one reinvigorating breath before setting off in Richard's wake. I was on the last stretch. Out of the corner of my eye, I saw Richard reach the bottom of the hill, cast an assessing look around and then run to get his rake. Oh no, I thought. We still have a whole field to rake. Hugh and Alan were working fast, faster than we had scythed. They were working in rectangles, a hayrick developing in the centre of each rectangle and had already covered our first swathe. Gilbert had caught me up. With pride as my spur, I scythed on, finishing almost level with the sobbing man. My face felt blank, my brain fogged, refusing to acknowledge the messages of pain, crying out for me stop while my body repaired itself. I didn't understand the urgency but the desperate raking at the far end of the field ensnared me and pushed me on. I took my rake but didn't know where to start. Richard saw my hesitation. "You and Gilbert start from that end of the field," he called. Gilbert had already begun and I joined him, raking from an imagined edge to the centre of a rectangle. Gilbert was an expert at this, no action wasted. I couldn't see how he stopped the wisps of hay escaping through the prongs. I felt useless. He glanced over at me, paused and watched and I put my head down in embarrassment. He came over. "Watch," he said and I saw how he raked across the line of the scythe so that each strand bound to its neighbours and blocked the gaps in the rake. I copied. "Good," he said and thundered back to his patch. There was a rumble in the distance. Thunder. Someone shouted. I raked harder. We finished the first rectangle and hurried up the slope. Richard had completed a rectangle in the same time as the two of us working together. Alan and Hugh were in the centre of the field, having completed another swathe on the far edge. The black sky made the ricks stand out dramatically like stones in a druids circle and dwarfed the running men. From the top of the slope, I raked endlessly, trying to find an efficient pattern to my movements that didn't increase the stickiness of blood on my punctured hands. There was a flash of lightning across the sky and a bang. I felt a rain drop bang onto my head and worked harder. We were so nearly there. Richard had joined us, raking frenetically in long sweeps. Two more figures arrived and we swept in an ever reducing circle as more drops fell. We were all panting hard, chests heaving as we arrived together, hair plastered to our heads with sweat , shirts sticking to our backs. We cheered as Gilbert raked in the last of the hay, and patted each other on the back. The exhilaration as high as a race won, a winning goal scored but I understood the difference between the sport of my day and the matters of survival in this time gone by. The skies let go their load with vengeance and we stood and laughed. The outside hay would wet and then dry. The inner core would remain fresh and undamaged. With the energy of success we trotted down to the field entrance, collecting our scythes. The stream was already running higher. The reduced exercise and the rain were making me cold. Richard retrieved the last flagon and the spirit warmth sent a spiral of heat through my body but I knew it was a false warmth. Once again, my waterproofs were useless. No point in getting them wet, too. The rain was sheetlike and hissed as it fell. Richard indicated we should run but it was hard to hear what he shouted against the pelting drops. The track was a river. If I ran down that road, I thought, I would be home, but I had to return the rake and scythe, Richard could not run with all those tools. I looked for a second at the way I wanted to go and then followed the gaggle of men the other way. Their boots thumped like clogs, except for Gilbert, who was hobbling, I realised on rag bound feet. Alan hopped occasionally and I reckoned his boots were rubbing. My shoes were sodden but the flexible soles were comfortable. It had been a long time since I ran any distance and I gradually dropped behind, puffing, my shins adding to the protest of my already exhausted muscles. When I reached the village only Richard was visible, standing under the eaves of one of the big houses. He took the tools from me, and handed me some coins. He gave me another thump on the back. "The master will be pleased. We will call you for another harvest, yes?" I felt like saying no. It hurt too much, but I needed the money and in a strange way, I had enjoyed the shared pain and the shared success, and I wanted to know more about grinning Alan, the growing Hugh, Richard's confident practicality and why Gilbert was as he was. "Yes," I said and felt a grin spread across my face. To keep warm, I jogged, walked, jogged and walked on the way to Shurnock. In true irony, the rain eased and stopped as I reached Shurnock's threshold. I pushed open the door, pulled out my waterproofs, stripped and used the T shirt as a towel again. Thank goodness for cotton, I thought. How else did people get dry? I lit the fire and set some rosemary tea to simmer in the kettle and set some more water to boil in the saucepan, feeling lucky. I could now boil my egg at the same time as making a drink. Such a luxury.

I hung my wet clothes on the chair and dragged it over to the fire, watching the steam rise and wondering how Gilbert was coping in his tiny hovel with no front door and no chimney, so presumably no fire. I stood looking out at the herb garden, drops of water sparkling on the leaves as the kettle came to the boil. The tea was warm, sweet and spicy. I looked at my hands. I must wash them, even though the rain had cleaned them pretty well. If they got infected, I had only the vaguest herbal knowledge to help me. I didn't even have salt to draw out the infection. I finished my tea and took the egg water, letting it cool while I ate the egg and then, gritting my teeth, stuck both hands in. My eyes smarted and the tears streamed but the sharp sting gradually eased with my hands immersed. I counted to a hundred before taking them out. The flaps of skin over the burst areas were white. No plasters. I had no gloves and didn't want to tear my clothes. There were only the leaves on the trees and the sheep's wool to bind them. At least the rain had washed the leaves clean. I put on my wet shoes and gathered some alder and hazel leaves, tying them on as best I could, even weaving a kind of bandage to slip over my palms. I looked at the coins I had earned. No grand coins like those earned at the vicarage but enough for food at the next market. I could afford a day off tomorrow to let my hands recover. I didn't sleep well that night, my body restless and aching, the cat was unimpressed and went to sleep on the chair by the fire.

Chapter 7

THURSDAY

I rose stiffly and found it hard to kneel to light the fire. I would have loved a hot shower to ease the aches. My hands were sore but there was no sign of infection. I smiled happily as I cooked an egg and mint tea. I was doing OK. I opened the door to see what sort of day we were getting and heard the thudding of a horse's hooves. There was no urgency to the hoof beat, but someone was coming. I looked around the room at the stuff I had acquired and the fire burning low on its way out. It was impossible to hide my presence. I only had time to try to time slip in the herb garden. Grabbing my rucksack of tools I hurried out, but only succeeded in running onto the tiny patch of grass. The cat watched, amused. "Its alright for you," I hissed, "You're not in danger." I couldn't escape, I would try to bluff out whatever came my way. The horse came into sight and I saw that the rider was Sir Nicholas. He dismounted onto a tree stump and I realised it was there as a mounting block. I moved forward uncertainly. He smiled and laughed. "No need to look so serious. I have been visiting your vicar and admiring his garden. I understand it is your labour." I nodded. "My brother has need of a gardener at Coughton Court. Our old gardener having died last Autumn. There is a boy, but he needs instruction. Are you interested?" I hesitated. To work at Coughton Court, even back in time would be a dream come true, but if I left Shurnock, I might never get home, and I wanted to get home to the people I loved, to a hot shower and an end to the endless dangers of deceit. Sir Nicholas was studying my face. "You need not decide now. I suggest I bring you a horse tomorrow and we ride over to look. You might consider it as a part time job in between duties here." Could he read my mind? I wondered. "Yes," I agreed, "That would be fine. What time will you come?" He was looking around absent mindedly at the herb garden as he spoke. "Oh around mid morning," he checked my face. I agreed happily. No struggling to wake at dawn. "How are you getting on with the sheep?" he asked interestedly. I didn't know how to answer the question. "Oh, they keep the grass short and leave all else alone. It's fine." "I expect my brother-in-law will be along soon with his shearers. He is itching to try local wool." "Indeed," I said, wanting to know more but again afraid of admitting my ignorance of things I should know. Sir Nicholas smiled. "I cannot make my mind up if he is a genius or a lunatic." He snorted, "Tapestry weaving. Where is the market for that?" I shrugged, feeling hopelessly out of my depth. Sir Nicholas smiled again and remounted his horse, turning it neatly, walking over the bridge and then moving easily to a canter. I hoped he wouldn't expect me to canter. My horse riding skills were extremely limited. Were church-taught children expected to ride horses? I had only seen pictures of them on mules or donkeys. Was Sir Nicholas playing with me? I decided to visit the vicar to find out more about Sir Nicholas.

It was almost as if he was expecting me. He smiled, standing in his garden. "I am hen chasing," he greeted me. "Two of them insist on pecking the peas." He pointed as my shoelace pecking friend and his compatriot. "How can I stop them?" "A bigger wired coop?" I suggested. "Hmm that would be expensive for four hens." He paused. "Perhaps I could get rid of some of them." "I quite like your rascals," I said. "Really?" he said. "Well, if you can catch them, they are yours. They are more trouble than they are worth." "Thank you." I couldn't believe my luck. "Have you had a visitor?" the vicar asked. Focussing his attention fully on me. I nodded. "Sir Nicholas," he said positively and looked undecided. He seemed almost surprised when he added. "Watch your step with him, Marco. He is powerful and fickle. Do not give too much away to him." My mouth opened and shut. How much had he worked out about me? " I was a bit worried," I said carefully. "Even though I have nothing to hide, he makes me nervous." "Yes. Follow your instinct." The vicar said. "But I think you will enjoy gardening at Coughton." I knew my face had lit up with excitement. "Yes. I think so, too." I agreed. The vicar turned. "I must go to speak to someone about a funeral, I will leave you to your hen capturing." His smile was sad as he left. I didn't know how I could carry two hens. I would have to take one at a time. They could run fast, despite their tiny flapping wings. I chased them all over the garden, the hens dodging even when I thought I had them cornered. I eventually trapped one against the wall and the apple tree and scooped it into my arms. The vicar's wife was standing in the porch, crying with laughter. She mopped away tears with her apron. "It's good to see laughter." I said, "Even at my expense." I laughed, too as I carried my prize away. The hen pecked interestedly at my fingers on the return journey to Shurnock, but didn't try to escape. I shut it in the cellar, apologetically. "I'll make you a coop really soon," I promised. I returned to the vicar's garden where my second hen gazed at me nervously, one eye at a time. "Come on you," I said, "You'll enjoy your new garden." I caught it surprisingly easily and chatted to it on the way home. They could live on grass and grubs until market day, when I would buy them some grain. I began to plan how to make a coop without wire. It would have to be woven hazel and willow. Four sides and a roof to keep them in, and nights spent in the barn. I had time to start this afternoon. I collected willow and hazel and tried to weave them together. At first the thing kept falling apart, but then I got the hang of sticking the hazel supports into the ground and weaving between them. It took a lot more lengths than I expected but I eventually had my coop, binding the rectangle together in an area of the vegetable patch which was not yet planted. I carried the hens over and released them. They look disgusted at their reduced freedom. "I'll let you out when you know I'm the food source," I said, " but I am not chasing you all round Shurnock Court every night to keep you safe from a fox." They gurgled at me and set to, greedily removing grubs from the grass. The cat watched with interest but did not interfere. Was he clever enough to know they were the source of eggs? The day was gone. I had missed lunch, absorbed in my weaving. I set the fire, boiling water and adding mint and peas to the saucepan water while the kettle water made rosemary tea and was used to clean the blisters on my hands after the day's work. I was terrified of infection. Seeing the thatcher's leg did not give me confidence in the doctor. That brought me back to sickness. I had forgotten again to check which way the water flowed. There were two sick field workers, a funeral being organised and the Coughton gardener dead. Was this normal or was their something infectious killing people and ought I to be staying away from the village? I toasted the last of my bread and ate it with the cheese and the last bit of butter. Night was falling. I went out and stood for a while under the starry sky, feeling a deep sense of awe and a wash of peace. My insignificance made my problems

minute. The world would go on whatever happened to me.
The cat was waiting for me to go to bed, ready to snuggle
with me in mutual warmth. Despite the itch of my mending
hands, I slept well, at peace with myself.

FRIDAY

I missed having bread with my egg the next morning, and
wondered how quickly my hens would settle and start
laying. Should I still buy more eggs at the next market? I
looked at my clothes. What should I wear to Coughton? It
was cooler today, and puffy clouds flitted occasionally
across the sun. My shoes were still wet. I winced as I
inserted my feet. Yuk. I pushed the waterproofs into their
bag. Could I ride with my tools in the rucksack? They
would put me off-balance, especially mounting. I decided
to take only the trowel, shears and secateurs, cushioned by
my waterproofs. My palms were sweating with
nervousness. I tried telling myself it was just another
gardening job but Sir Nicholas was no ordinary employer
and the owner of Coughton Court must also be a powerful
man. I was remembering that Coughton had links with the
Gunpowder Plot. Would I actually meet any of the men
involved? I could only remember Catesby and had no idea
of his Christian name. If I said the wrong thing to him,
would I change history? Were Sir Nicholas and his brother
protestant or catholic? The sound of hooves reached me
and I first ran to put the hens in their pen on a different
area of the grass. Then I hurried over the plank bridge,
nervous of having to guide my horse over it from the
saddle. As I reached the other side I realised I needed the
tree trunk to mount and retreated. I swallowed nervously,
hoping I wouldn't make a complete idiot of myself. Two
horses appeared and to my surprise, the lead rider was a
lady . As she came nearer, I saw it was Lady Jane. I smiled

up at her as she led my horse to the mounting block. She smiled, too but there was no recognition in her eyes. I felt confused, disappointed, unsure of what to say. "Good morrow," she said. "My cousin is busy and I was at a loose end, so you have me to be your guide. My name is Lady Jane." She was indicating her superiority to me, I thought, or perhaps giving me guidance as to the hierarchy. Did she know me but was pretending not to, or had we not reached that moment in time when we met? My brain did somersaults trying to work out if I could exist simultaneously in her time and mine. I half hoped I would be sucked back into my real time, but then, would I keep going round in the same cycle of time, unable to escape for ever? That would be a nightmare of epic proportions. She giggled. "Are you coming, then?" she asked and I realised I had been staring at her as I thought things through. "Yes, of course," I said. "I haven't ridden for some time so make allowances." I almost pleaded. "Indeed," she agreed watching me clamber onto the saddle. I was relieved to find my horse was a sturdy type, serious and plodding rather than skittish. Lady Jane led the way and my horse needed little encouragement to follow. She looked back with a laughing smile as we turned onto the main track and indicated I should ride alongside. My horse seemed to understand and caught up with her. "I have not been to Shurnock for some time. The new wing is impressive." "I think it will become more impressive still, some day," I said, thoughtlessly. "In what way?" she asked. "Oh, perhaps more height, an upstairs with separate rooms, and I think perhaps the porch has not yet been finished." I tried to shut myself up, but felt the need for information. "Do you know why it is left not complete? How long has it been empty?" "I used to come here when I was a child," she said. "It belonged to one of my uncles. He was imprisoned because he disagreed with the queen. I think that was when it was given to your employers, the new church." Her face gave no judgement. I had no clue to what she thought of her Uncle and his beliefs. "I'm sorry," I said and felt awkward. "I have a lot of Uncles," she said obscurely. She changed the subject. "You have good weather to garden in today. We had a most amazing mist yesterday morning. Witches' mist I call it. Low and thick. I wonder what makes it like that." "Warm moisture lifting from the ground and cold air above, condensing the moisture out into droplets," I replied. She was so relaxed that I found myself forgetting to guard my tongue, and she had such an intelligent interest in things. She glanced at my face and said, "You know the oddest things," She looked ahead at the gently winding track and said, "We can go faster from here." Before I could reply she encouraged her horse to trot. My horse responded without my intervention and I found myself bouncing all over the place, bumping the saddle as it rose to meet me. The horse rolled its eyes back and gave me a look of exasperation. I gathered my wits, and the reins and stood on the stirrups while I watched Lady Jane ahead of me as she rose and fell sedately. I tried to copy the rhythm of her movements and found things were better but my thighs soon ached with the effort. I saw her give a pull on the reins and her horse slowed to a walk. She looked back again. "Good," she said. I wasn't sure if she meant good that I was still in the saddle or good that I had kept up but anyway was too bumped about to reply. The track had narrowed and we walked one behind the other until we reached the ridge. Then she swung left. I was pleased to find my horse following without instruction from me. If it came to a battle of wills between me and the horse I was sure the horse would win. How could tiny little me have dominance over such a strong, large and graceful creature who could throw me off with ease if he so wished? The ears flicked enquiringly. Could horses read minds? If so, it was time to start believing in myself a little more. Lady Jane turned right onto a much narrower and steeper track and as my mount followed, I nearly slid forwards over his head. I managed to grab the saddle without dropping the reins. By bracing my feet against the stirrups, leaning back and pushing with my arms I managed to wriggle back into the middle of the saddle. The horse rolled its eyes again. I laughed internally and was glad Lady Jane had not witnessed my antics. The horses took their time on the loamy slopes, but after another right turn, the path widened again and levelled out. I sensed Lady Jane's glee as she nudged her horse into a trot. I was better prepared this time and bounced in a more controlled fashion, only nearly losing a stirrup when we swerved left across more open flat land. I saw Lady Jane's horse change its stride and accelerate. "Oh golly," I thought, but all other thoughts were erased from my mind as the ground blurred under us and the wind took my breath away. Was this a canter or a gallop? It felt like flying. I looked between the horses ears and held on with hands and knees. Adrenalin heated my blood and crazed my brain. I felt like whooping but hadn't the breath to spare. We crossed a road and entered another track and there in front of us was Coughton Court, but not as I knew it. There was more building yet to come. Even so,its three stories of height and turreted towers, spoke of money and power. Lady Jane accelerated again but I was going quite fast enough and tugged gently on the reins to say no faster. Thankfully, my horse responded and we arrived to find Lady Jane dismounted, flushed and laughing. She looked younger than I remembered her, but perhaps that was because of the ride. My horse knew its way around, taking me to a block to dismount and standing patiently as I dropped to the ground on trembling legs. Sir Nicholas appeared from a door as we crossed a moat bridge and walked under a portcullis into a yard, part stable, part house entrance. "I see my cousin did not manage to drop you into a ditch," he greeted me dryly. "I held on tight," I said with a high degree of truth. Wasting no time, he turned. "Come and see the mess we wish you to sort." he said. These people spoke a clearer English. There were undertones of French, I thought, in the vowels and softness of certain consonants like t and d, but I had less need of interpretation. The gardens began under another arch and formed a square surrounded on three sides by wings of the house. They were overgrown with nettles and buttercups and bindweed swamping herbs, flowers and vegetables but I had that deja vu feeling. I had been here before and knew how they would look in 500 year's time, and, my heart swelled with pride. I was going to create that garden of the future. Wow, I thought. I had halted to stare at the almost familiar layout. Sir Nicholas looked at me quizzically. I had no words to explain. "Tools?" I asked. "Ah yes. Over here." I was led to an oak doored narrow room with rake, hoe, spade, hazel switch broom and scythe. "William must have the barrow and pitchfork out," Sir Nicholas said. He led me on to a compost heap and a meadow where several cows grazed. To the right was an orchard. To the left, a river ran crossed by a foot bridge and a boy was running to the bridge from a row of tiny cottages, trying to shove his arm into the sleeve of a jerkin. My guide nodded in his direction with a curl of the lip, half grimace, half smile. "That, is, William. You will have to do something about his time keeping." "Mmmm" I agreed. "If I take the job." I was given a sharp glance, turning into an accepting wry smile. "And will you?" I felt we were participating in a fencing duel. "If the terms are right, yes." I said. Sir Nicholas clapped his hands together once. "Name your terms," he challenged. How could I? I had only been paid for my gardening in food. But, then, food was what I really needed. I could earn money for clothes by helping in the fields and even barter food for grain for my hens. I was going to be a head gardener, responsible not just for flowers but for much of the food on their tables. "Three days a week until William is well trained," I began, "Luncheon and three drinks provided, one pat of butter and, if you have a bread oven and grain, one loaf a week." "You drive a strong bargain, but I think you will earn it. I would agree, but I must check with my brother," Sir Nicholas said. "Will you wait?" I shrugged. "I might as well begin." "Such confidence," Sir Nicholas laughed. "Continue." He disappeared through the arch as William skidded breathless around the corner. "Sorry I'm late," he stammered and ducked as if expecting a blow. "Go and fetch the barrow and pitchfork," I told him. "We have hard work to do." He vanished at a run. I went to fetch the spade and hoe and dumped them and my bag next to the first bed. There were raspberry canes under the bindweed and the next bed held ripening strawberries amongst the nettles. I cut quickly along the base of the bindweed with my secateurs. Were they supposed to be in existence yet? I didn't know but best not to draw attention to them yet, then took my shears and sheared off the nettles as William returned at the gallop with the barrow. "You unwind the bindweed and put it straight in the barrow, like this." I demonstrated, afraid he may not have understood my strange accent. " I will dig out the nettles from the strawberry bed, over there." I watched him start, fingers trembling in his haste, knocking the odd young fruit to the floor but he was doing his best. "Good," I said and walked to the far end of the strawberry bed so that I could work back towards him and watch what he was doing. Gradually, he settled to his task and became absorbed and I settled to mine, using my bag to collect the nettles as I weeded. We met in the middle aisle. "Excellent," I said. I emptied my nettles onto his bindweed. "Now take them to where things are burnt. Not the compost heap. Do you understand?" he nodded. "Then go to the kitchen and ask for a big bowl for the strawberries." I mimed and pointed as best I could to demonstrate my words. He grabbed the barrow handles and trotted off. I started working on the bindweed roots with my trowel, digging as deep as I could. Some of them would grow back but they would be much weakened and would be too late to damage the fruit crop. William returned, puffing with two wooden bowls. I laughed internally at my expectation of Tupperware. "Good. Pick the red strawberries and put them in the bowls. Then take them to the kitchen." I put a stern frown on my face. "No eating them." William actually grinned, and I grinned back. He knelt to his task. Finishing the bindweed, I moved to the long bed. The herbs were planted haphazardly, not like the knot garden of my day. Did I dare change it? The opposite bed was bare but it should have been a reflection. In any case, the herbs needed clipping. They were growing one into another. I picked up my shears and was soon absorbed, enjoying the herbal scents as I clipped and concentrating hard on achieving perfect symmetry. William had vanished with his bowls. He returned quickly. "Now you can tie in the canes," I said, showing him how to twist the sheep's wool I had collected and pocketed between the frame of poles and the plant to stop rubbing and then tie a bow. He got it wrong twice but I showed him again and then again and he had the technique right. "Practise," I said gesturing to the long row of canes. I liked the look of concentration that came to his face. We would work well together, and I felt a pang of regret that I might leave him before I had taught him everything he needed to know. I collected the clippings and planted them in the empty bed as the knot garden would be. There was no box but that could come later. As I stood back to check the pattern, there was a chuckle behind me and I jumped. It was Sir Nicholas, standing watching me. "You work fast," he approved. "My brother's wife will be pleased. My brother will not notice. He sees only horses, deer and money." He was watching William now. "You have got William working well." "He's a good lad," I agreed. Sir Nicholas made no comment other than a noise at the back of his throat. "Luncheon is almost ready. You will dine with us. My brother wishes to meet his new gardener." I was sure this was not the correct protocol. What game was Sir Nicholas playing? I was going to refuse but then thought of Lady Jane. I still was not sure if she was pretending not to recognise me. After all, crossing time was a form of magic or witchcraft. Some time around now, weren't witches burned or drowned? She would be careful about admitting what had happened. I needed to see her again. I looked down at my dirty clothes, and at Sir Nicholas' tidy appearance. "I'm hardly dressed for it," I said. Sir Nicholas considered me. "I have some garments that might fit," he said, "and you can keep them as they no longer fit anyone else, here." Again, I felt suspicion at his motives, but I needed more clothes and also needed to not stand out in a crowd to be safe. "That would be fine," I replied. William was standing, open-mouthed. "William," I said, "When the canes are done, take the barrow to the burning pile, then have a break but be back in half an hour and start digging that bed. All the green bits to go on the compost heap." He nodded and bent to the canes. "Will he remember all that?" Sir Nicholas asked as he led me inside and up a spiral staircase. "I don't know," I replied. "This is an experiment,." The chuckle came again. I had a moment of panic. Would Sir Nicholas stay while I changed my clothes? Could I claim shyness in changing alone? First I would have to work out how to put them on and second, I couldn't let on that I wasn't a man. At the top of the stairs, he led me into a dressing room alongside a bedroom and pulled out a drawer, shifting things about and pulling out selected items. I fidgeted, part of me wanting to run away before my deceit was discovered. I needn't have worried. He handed me the garments. "Down the stairs, turn right and second door on the left," he instructed, and went away. My legs gave way beneath me in relief and I let out a breath I hadn't realised I was holding. I looked at the clothes. Stockings, breeches, a jacket and a thing like a ruff, even stiff leather shoes with leather laces. I stripped quickly and experimented with the clothes. The jacket was obvious, although the leather lace fastenings instead of zip or buttons were fiddly. The stockings were wool and itched. How did they stay up? I found more ties and that the ruff also had laces. It felt draughty compared to my trousers and also clumsy. The leather breeches were creaky and stiff. How did one sit down? I supposed I was allowed to feel uncomfortable. Monks wore long cloak habits, and who knew what underneath and I had been brought up, theoretically by the monks. There was no mirror. I looked down at myself and felt around but had to just hope it looked right. I stuffed my clothes into my bag and left it at the bottom of the stairs, following instructions to the dining room. I could hear voices as I arrived at the door and hovered nervously. "Just in time," Sir Nicholas drew me in. "Marco, this is my eldest brother, Sir Robert, and my wife, Anne, my cousin, Jane, you already know. This is my sister-in-law, Elizabeth and this is my brother's second son, George. They all studied me with interest and I nodded politely to each in turn but felt so sick with fear at the mistakes I could make at this table that I wondered if I could eat anything. I followed them to a long table in this vast, cool room with windows at each end letting in patterned light, dappled by the thick lead framework. A man servant stood ready to serve. I was dining with the top aristocracy and felt sweaty and unintelligent, right out of my depth. It seemed the ladies sat at one end of the table and the gents at the other and it felt odd that I was sitting with the men. "We have a clergyman at the table." Sir Robert observed. "You may say grace." I hadn't said grace since I was at primary school, nor paid much attention to it then. Thank goodness, we were not required to pray in Latin. I put my hands together, shut my eyes and was surprised to find the babyish words coming to my lips. They would do. "Amen" I finished. Sir Robert clapped his hands together. "Short and sweet," he guffawed. "I approve of that." He waved the manservant forwards and as the man spooned soup into bowls, reached forward and broke off a hunk of bread. The ladies were silent and ate daintily. Robert's son looked to be about nineteen and ate fast, darting curious glances at me but saying nothing. I was served last of the gents and was able to then copy Sir Nicholas, dipping the bread in my soup and sucking the thick broth and then scooping up the vegetables once the liquid was gone. There were meats, pickles and cheese to follow. I began to feel sleepy, not having had so much to eat for so long and found it difficult not to yawn. The goblet of cider didn't help. Sir Robert belched, almost as a signal to end his meal. He sharpened his gaze on me. "So. Where did you train as a gardener?" At least I had already answered this question. "Weybourne Abbey and then I worked under the monks at Evesham." he nodded approval. "You will have self discipline. That is good, and good knowledge, too of herbs and vegetables." "Yes, sir," I agreed. "It will be good to improve our food supplies. There were failings last year." Sir Robert said. I had no way to reply as I had no idea what the weather had been like or whether he meant because the gardener was in ill health." "God willing, and with good seed and soil nutrition." I said. "You priests," Sir Robert mocked. I ducked my head, not wanting him to read my reaction of denial. "I would like to discuss religion with you, sometime. My brother and I are in disagreement." There was a hiss from the ladies' end of the table but the eyes were all downcast. Lady Jane, or Sir Robert's wife. Someone thought this a dangerous topic. "For now, I should prefer to concentrate on the gardens," I suggested. "Yes, of course, You may go," Sir Robert said. I stood up and hoped it was correct to bow to the gents and then to the ladies before leaving. "Good manners," I heard Sir Nicholas say pointedly as I left the room. I had a full stomach and had not been accused of witchcraft, spying or deceit. It was good to go back to the simple gardening and greet William who was already digging. I glanced stealthily at my watch and saw it was just 25 minutes since I left him. Of course, he had no way of judging half an hour. I would have to create some sort of sun clock for him. I left him, and walked to the apple trees in the orchard. The branches were thick and tangled needing much work to remove all those crossing branches and the overlong shoots. I would do a gentle Summer prune and then a harder prune in the Winter but for now I cut off a twig and planted it at the edge of the vague shadow caused by the sun. That would be the end of lunch break. I took another and walked round 45 degrees – morning break. I walked 30 degrees the other way from the centre stick. Make that afternoon break. I guessed William should normally work until near dusk but I would have to leave earlier as I would never find my way home in the dark. Would he feel resentful, working on alone? I returned to the beds and, using my trowel and the hoe, matched William on the opposite long bed. He was surprised when I gave him an afternoon break. "We can work faster after a short rest," I told him in case he thought I was soft. He nodded thoughtfully. I liked his silence. It was restful. We worked on for another hour, finding onions, chives and carrots amongst the tangle of weeds, William now learning the difference between weeds to burn and weeds to compost, and he taught me about weeds he would take home to eat, putting them quietly in a separate pile. He retrieved some of my nettles and added them to his pile. Sir Nicholas appeared. "What a difference!" he exclaimed with genuine delight. "You may finish, now. Our stable lad is ready with your horse. He has instructions to lead you to the ridge and then return. You gave us three days. I presume you will return tomorrow. You can borrow the horse. There is food attached to his saddle." I felt disappointment that Lady Jane would not accompany me, but swallowed it. I turned to William. "You have worked well. Finish your bed, tidy away the weeds and then you can finish. Tomorrow, begin throwing all the rotted compost that I showed you on the weeded beds, but do not bury the plants or knock off the fruit." He nodded. There was no resentment. He seemed proud to be allowed to work on his own. "Good boy," I said and meant it. "I have never seen servants led by kindness before," Sir Nicholas said musingly. "Really?" I said. " I believe it works more than nine times out of ten." "Hmmm" he replied. A lad of about thirteen, stood holding my horse, another horse waited patiently, saddled and bridled. I climbed stiffly and clumsily into the saddle. The boy looked contemptuous, and with me mounted, vaulted from the ground into his saddle, showing me how it should be done. He set off along the sweeping drive, raising dust in the dry weather, My horse decided to follow. How was I going to make it keep going when we reached the ridge and the boy turned back? I hoped he wouldn't laugh at my attempts. He was a brilliant rider, and broke into a canter with ease. I concentrated on staying in the saddle and let my horse decide its own speed. Competitively, it caught the horse in front, and I tried not to look down at the blurring ground beneath their hooves. The boy looked startled to find me alongside, not knowing it was not by choice. He pushed his mount a little harder and I tugged a little on my reins, telling my horse this was not a race. It seemed aggrieved, but nevertheless, allowed the other horse to get ahead. We raced across the flat land, and slowed to climb the ridge, with me trying to mark in my mind the path I must take alone tomorrow. At the top, the lad jinked left and then pointed to the turn I must take for home, reining his horse in. My horse stopped too, snorting as it caught its breath from the climb. I gave it a moment and then gave it a nudge with my thighs and knees, shaking the reins hopefully. His eyes rolled back at me as a question and indicated that the other horse hadn't moved. I repeated my commands and to my relief he hesitantly walked forward, ears flicking, questioning. I pulled the right rein lightly and saw him focus on our route. He understood. I heard the lad wheel his horse and set off back to Coughton. My horse hesitated, wanting to follow, but he was already on my track and could not turn amongst the trees. With reluctance, he walked on, but, like William became engrossed in his task, carefully placing his hooves to avoid slipping on the steep slope. I braced myself and hung on, trying not to tip over the horse's head. Luckily, the route was obvious from this direction and my horse needed no guidance until we reached the entrance to Shurnock. He seemed to recognise it and was happy to turn as I pulled the left rein. There was some discussion about standing by the mounting block. I was glad no one was watching as we danced around getting into position. But I was not going to try sliding to the ground, afraid of getting a foot stuck in the stirrup and being dragged around by a frightened horse with my head banging on the floor or twisting under the horse's hooves. We managed at last. I led the horse to the grass, the sheep baaing in surprise at this newcomer. How could I stop him straying? I held the bridle rope, considering and eventually led him to the edge of the trees and tied the bridle to a branch. I heaved the saddle off with difficulty, my arms tired and my shoulders objecting. I needed to get his food to the barn, then take the hens in. I wanted a shower to ease the aches and clean off the mud. I looked at the moat. I was going to risk a swim, I decided. But finish the work first and light the fire, I admonished myself. I managed it more easily knowing I had the reward of a swim to follow. I stripped and waded in. It was surprisingly warm. The ducks quacked, objecting to my invasion of their territory, and swam into the reeds, regarding me balefully. I turned onto my back and looked up at the blue sky. No storm tonight. How odd we humans were to hate getting soaked in the rain but then immerse ourselves in water when it wasn't raining. How fickle. I laughed out loud. I was still stuck in this time but I had food, work, shelter, and even a warm bed to sleep in. I felt lucky. I kicked lazily around the small lake, staying clear of the reeds I might get tangled in. Eventually, I waded ashore, used my T-shirt as a towel again and forced my damp arms and legs back into my clothes, before eating a light meal – the lunch had been plenty to keep me nourished. I took the hens and horse to the barn for the night. The cat materialised. Who knew which time he had spent his day in? We slept through the dark night and woke ready for another day.

SATURDAY
 The hens and horse greeted us as we opened the barn door. I set up the coop in an area of the vegetable patch and left the hens to pick out the weeds and grubs. This was a fallow area so no danger of losing my food crops. The horse had munched his way through his food rations. I took him to the moat to drink while I sorted out the saddle and my tools. It was odd not being able to listen to a weather forecast, but then I hardly had a choice of clothes. I took my new set for lunch and the waterproofs for just in case. The weather forecast was unnecessary. I hoped the horse would know his way back to Coughton. Putting the saddle on the horse was difficult. There seemed to be an awful lot of straps, and the horse wasn't keen on the saddle and even less keen on the bridle, refusing to take the bit. I got annoyed eventually and the horse sensed this and gave in, thank goodness. I hadn't had time to check the timeslip places but I was looking forward to the challenges of Coughton and wasn't too worried. I led the horse to the mounting trunk. He played hard to get, snorting and dancing about. I suspected the cat was close by laughing at me but had no time to look for him. "If you don't keep still, I will have to tie your legs together," I said in exasperation. The horse stood still, as if understanding he had gone too far. I hurriedly climbed aboard and turned him to the bridge. "Take me home," I said. The ears turned back,

turned forwards, then back again and forwards. I gave him a nudge. "Home," I said. "Not too fast." I laughed at myself, trying to hold a conversation with my mount. The horse moved forwards, carefully over the bridge, and obeyed my command at the entrance as we turned onto the track. Did I dare risk a canter? No, I didn't. We walked sedately all the way to Coughton. I was relieved that the horse and I agreed on the route. I met Lady Jane and Lady Anne walking on the driveway to Coughton. We greeted each other. I wished Lady Jane had been on her own. I desperately wanted to talk to her. I told myself to be patient. The horse knew he was nearly home, and refused to stop, in fact picking up the pace so that we arrived at a canter. The stable lad looked impressed at our speed, not realising it was the horse's decision, not mine. It skewed to a halt at the mounting block and rolled its eyes, impatient for me to dismount. I dropped, stiffly to the ground. The stable lad took the bridle as I removed my tools. "Are you wanting the horse again tonight?" the lad asked. "I would think so," I said. He looked uncertain. "Yes," I said. My ear was acclimatising to the words I heard but my speech was still wrong, I thought. It was lucky there was no radio or television so people here did not know what people in another part of the country should sound like. Only the gentry travelled and I might arouse suspicions with the Throckmortons who seemed to travel widely. I would speak as little as possible and listen a lot. I walked through the courtyard and under the arch and there was William already at work. He looked up and gave me a shy smile. I smiled back. I brandished my tools. "We have a new job today, I told him. Just finish emptying that compost on the bed, then follow me. Bring the barrow. I'll be in the orchard." I pointed. He hurried to finish his compost throwing. I walked to the apple trees, laying down my loppers, secateurs and bow saw. I considered the tree with its many rubbing branches, poor thing, I thought. I checked I could climb it without a ladder, needing to feel confident in front of my apprentice. William bumped the barrow over the rough ground. "Do you know how to prune apple trees?" I asked him. He shook his head. "You will by the end of today," I promised him. "Now, usually we prune in the Winter, when the tree is asleep, no leaves, but these trees have lots of rubbing branches which are hurting them so we will start now. Do you understand?" He shrugged. I tried again, with actions to imitate the cold of winter and the falling of leaves and then pointed to some of the rubbing branches to show how the tree was being damaged. His smile spread, laughing at my actions, but also relieved that I wasn't berating him for not understanding and then happy because he did understand. "I'll do this tree to show you. You will do the next tree." He looked horrified. "I will watch and tell you what to do." He nodded again. I took the saw and loppers up the tree and cut out several branches, careful not to drop them on William. I tried to demonstrate the space I was creating and how I was cutting to reduce bleeding of the sap, cutting to buds or back to another branch forking off. He watched carefully. I came back to earth and then took him to the next tree. "Start with the loppers," I said, "while I cut some of this wood from the last tree. Then I'll show you how to use the saw safely." William climbed as easily as a squirrel, crouching in the tree and following instructions as I pointed to the branches to cut. While he lopped, I cut the branches on the floor into more manageable sizes, thinking about the house fires. There must be a log pile or two or three around somewhere to give me an idea of log size. William finished lopping and dropped down to the ground. I showed him how to start a cut without the saw slipping and how not to cut his fingers off and how not to get the saw trapped or tear the bark on a cut branch. He practised on the branches on the floor, naturally practical and sensible. He had the solemnity of a much older man, only his nervousness giving away his young age. There was none of the cheekiness, or loss of attention that I expected in a fourteen year old. I showed him which branches I wanted cut and where, and went off to find a log store to check the length of log required. There were three young children playing with a ball on a rough cut lawn, accompanied by a stiff backed lady – nurse, or tutor, I couldn't be sure. They were solemn faced, concentrating on perfection as they threw the ball one to another. Their clothes were smart and made of good cloth. I found a vast pile of logs and used my arm for measuring their length. When I returned, William was down from the tree and cutting the wood as I had done. "Now into logs," I said, "About this size." I cut a length with the loppers. "Use this as a measuring stick. Then put the wood in the barrow and take them to this year's wood pile." I started using the secateurs to tidy the kindling as William sawed the larger logs. I, as usual had become absorbed in the task and had forgotten about a mid-morning break. It was Sir Robert's wife, Elizabeth, who appeared to study our progress and inform me that Sir Robert required me to change for luncheon. She had none of Lady Jane's bounce and bubble. A thin, tight mouth, sad eyes, clasped hands, giving little away. I nodded and said I would come straight away. She returned to the house. I looked quickly at my watch and glanced over at my time sticks. "You are doing well, William. If you finish filling the barrow, you can then stop for lunch. Start work again when the sun's shadow reaches this stick and put the logs on the wood pile and I will be back about then, yes?" He understood. I got a nod and a grin. I guessed lunch breaks had not been permitted before. I took my new clothes to the same dressing room and changed. My hands were dirty but there was no water to wash with. How impolite was it to arrive at the table with dirty hands, or did no one notice? I took a few deep breaths to steady my nerves, reminding myself to keep my conversation short, especially on the subject of religion.

The family were waiting again with similar expressions. Sir Nicholas looked amused. Lady Jane looked worried, as if trying to warn me of a tricky situation ahead. Sir Robert gave the grace that day in Latin. No one commented but Sir Nicholas looked disapproving, Sir Robert's wife worried. Lady Jane caught my eye, indicating I should say nothing. I had no intention of objecting but I had a suspicion that use of Latin was against the law. There was more soup and meats and I felt relief that I knew how to deal with these foods and tried to drink as little cider as possible to keep a clear head. With the meal finished, the ladies rose and left as if at a secret signal and the man servant stepped forward and refilled our goblets with a bitter wine. I tensed. This was what Lady Jane had been warning me about. "Do you have a problem with a grace in Latin?" Sir Robert asked. Sir Nicholas began to speak but Sir Robert turned aggressively to him. "Let the boy speak," he said furiously. Sir Nicholas took a breath as if to argue and then subsided. There was a turmoil of unspoken emotions and words there, like water over barely concealed rocks on a coast of wrecked ships. I surprised myself, speaking from the heart. "I think the language is unimportant. God knows what is in our hearts and in our minds. This matters more than our words." "Ah, a diplomatic reply," Sir Nicholas said, reaching for more wine, from the flagon left on the table by the manservant. Sir Robert sat back in his chair. "You do not consider the Pope's teachings important?" I understood the fear and hidden warnings of the ladies. This was the talk of treason. Did I need to prove myself Catholic to keep my job? But if I did, would Sir Nicholas report me to my theoretical masters in Worcester? "I consider the Pope a good and important man," I began and felt Sir Nicholas's eyes, hard upon me. "But we are ruled by our queen and I know not why God has chosen to bring a split between her father and the Pope. She tries to be loyal to her father as all good daughters should be. I believe God looks to our actions in order to judge us. To be good to our neighbour, to teach goodness over evil, not to steal, or do harm. Both our queen and the Pope teach the same message and it is not for me, a lowly gardener taught by two sets of churchmen to judge the political rights and wrongs. The important message is that of honouring all men before God." The brothers looked at each other as if they were both reassessing their beliefs. "You have a complicated mind, Marco," Sir Nicholas said. "No," I said. "I have a simple mind that looks for the facts and not the detours and diversions of those who wish for control and power. The important facts are bedrock in the quicksand of politics." Sir Robert actually laughed. "I like your style, young sir. Return to your gardening. We will talk further another day." I rose on shaky legs, bowed to each man and left. As I changed into my gardening clothes and returned to the safety and simplicity of the garden, I thought about the relationship between Nicholas and Robert. Robert was older, the landowner and he and Nicholas plainly did not agree on important issues so why was Nicholas at Coughton and why had he backed down to Robert when he clearly had wanted to argue? Were he and his wife at the mercy of his brother in some way? I wished I had read more of the Throckmortons when I had visited Coughton Court in my time. The afternoon passed easily, the trees released from the friction and self imposed imprisonment of the tangled branches. The end result that William and I stood and admired were six trees of neat shape standing proud and a huge log pile to help keep the family warm in later Winters. I felt a shiver as I thought of those cold months ahead. How could I possibly cope? The church would one day discover me at Shurnock and I could only short term bluff with insisting I had been employed by a different sector of the church with a lack of communication creating confusion. I didn't even know the names of the churchmen I could mention. I shook the thoughts away. One day at a time. "Well, William, I will leave you the saw because I am not now here until next week. You are in charge, You can now prune the plum trees and the pear trees the same way and finish spreading the compost and I will see you next week." William had looked, first shocked, but then proud and he stood with his back tall and his shoulders high. He looked enviously for a second at the loppers and looked away. I laughed. "I need these for my other work," I said. "You can use them next week." He looked sheepish that I had read his mind. I gave him a half wave as I left him. "Work until the sun shadow reaches the stick," I said. "Then go home." I packed away all my clothes and returned to the courtyard. The horse was ready to go but looked unhappy to be leaving his stable. I mounted and the stable lad led him over the moat and gave him a slap. The horse started forward with a snort. Once in motion, he kept going and I concentrated hard on following the right tracks. I still had a fear of getting lost in the maze of unfamiliar tracks, all looking almost the same but leading in very different directions. It was a little like feeling my way through the maze of minds, Sir Robert, Sir Nicholas, Lady Jane and where did the vicar and his wife fit in, now preaching an English spoken service but originally trained by the Catholic church, giving me warnings to be careful with Sir Nicholas. I felt like I was swimming in a sea of hungry lurking sharks, mixed with more harmless dolphins. Even the dolphins had a hierarchy and could not step out of line . So far the dolphins were not bothered by my presence, welcoming me in, but would I raise their suspicions by aligning myself with the Throckmortons? I pulled myself back to finding my way to Shurnock. I had just gone the wrong way, hadn't I? Yes, missed a left turn. With difficulty, I turned the horse. Trampling the undergrowth and nearly losing his back legs in a ditch, making myself sweat at the thought of the horse falling, breaking a leg and me crushed beneath him. "Concentrate!" I told myself fiercely, and ferociously kept my mind on my direction until we crossed the ridge and had only a straight route home. I had to stay at Shurnock as long as possible and I had to keep working for the Throckmortons or I would lose my contact with Lady Jane and she seemed to be my only chance of finding my way forward to my time, unless the cat could show me, I supposed. How long had I been here? I had lost track of time again. I counted on my fingers and realised today was Saturday. I had missed the market where I had intended buying more bread and cheese and a keg of perry and eggs. Now how did I get more food? Sunday was going to be a hungry day. Back to the nuts and dandelions. I should have left Saturdays free of Coughton. I would reorganise my days next week, I thought. Monday I would go back to Coughton and eat there. Tuesday I would keep free. My eye ran beyond the turning to Shurnock. Droitwich was about seven miles. I would quite like to see a Tudor town and I could get some provisions there, couldn't I? The horse was happy to be directed into Shurnock and obediently halted at the mounting block this time. I wondered if he had a name. Did Tudor people name their animals or just think of them as tools? "I'll call you "Midnight," after your colour," I told the horse. He made no objection. "Come on then Midnight, come and have a grass snack while I sort your hay in the barn." The hens glared at me. Oh bother, I had promised them grain on Saturday and now I'd forgotten. "Sorry hens," I apologised. "I promise I will bring you grain from Droitwich on Tuesday. Just two more days of grubs and grass." They gurgled at me and looked reproachful. Hens are smart creatures. I reckoned they understood and were not pleased. I took them into the herb garden and barricaded the paths so they had more space to roam and rummage. I was tired. Thought I would manage without a fire tonight, eating nuts and drinking cider for my supper, putting the animals to bed, bone weary, before falling into bed and dropping into immediate sleep. No cat tonight. Perhaps he was sleeping in 2019.

Chapter 8

SUNDAY

I woke from a confused dream in which I dreamt I was in 2019 and dreaming of falling backwards in time to 1500 and was startled to find myself at Shurnock when I woke. Had I only dreamed I'd woken up? No, I was really here, and it was Sunday and I was going to be late for church unless I ran, right now. I ran and just about managed to attach myself to the last villagers entering the door, sweating heavily and struggling not to puff loudly as the vicar opened the service. Did someone make a note of which villagers weren't here? If you were ill, were you excused. I didn't know what Will looked like. Was he better? Was he here? No one looked particularly ill and the thatcher wasn't here. The service washed around me and I knelt and stood with the rest of the congregation, mumbling along with the prayers and hymns. My immediate neighbour seemed as ignorant of the words as I, which was comforting. He was stoop backed and held his head as if finding it difficult to hear. As before, the vicar left first, then the pew occupiers. Much to my surprise, Lady Jane was there, sharing a pew with another well dressed lady who seemed to have a mass of children but leant on Lady Jane's arm as she left the church. Lady Jane gave me a grave nod as she passed. I had to wait for several more well dressed parishioners before I could leave and when I finally got outside, I couldn't see them anywhere. I hung around hoping they would reappear but there was no sign. As the other villagers dispersed, I felt conspicuous loitering alone and frustratedly left the square. A man joined me. It was Richard. "We need your help, next week." He announced. My diary was filling up, I thought. "I've another client for Monday," I apologised. "No matter," Richard said. "I was wanting you Wednesday. Lord Sheldon is wanting his sheep rounded up. Something to do with removing their coats." "Shearing?" I asked. "Aye, that's the word." he agreed. "I don't know how to shear," I said. "Nay, nor do I," Richard laughed. "We are to be sorters and catchers. We start at Shurnock and then go to Mutton Hall by cart." I aimed to remain casual but my brain was whirling. Who would come to Shurnock? Would the churchmen come to host this event? How would they react to me? Or was it presumed by Lord Sheldon that I was a nominated host? I had a strong desire to run away and hide. "Will Lord Sheldon be there?" I asked. "He's waiting at Mutton Hall," Richard said. "Ah," I responded, "And how many shearers are there and what time do they arrive?" "We begin gathering the sheep just after dawn and wait. It is the first time I have done this so I do not know how it works. We will find out on the day, huh?" "Yes," I said uneasily. He waved and moved off to talk to someone else. It seemed I was now considered part of a labouring gang. I walked back to Shurnock, deep in thought. There was a chance that I could hide my occupation of Shurnock by acting as Richard's labourer. I would tidy everything away and hide the hens in the forest. What about Midnight? I didn't know if the shearers would want to use the barn so I couldn't hide him there. He would have to go into the forest, too, or should I leave him at Coughton when I worked there on Monday? It would take maybe two hours to walk home and then two hours to return on my next working day, but it would be safer. I didn't want word to spread that there was a valuable horse for the stealing at Shurnock. I had been concentrating so hard on my thinking that I was walking over the moat bridge before I became aware of my surroundings. I detoured to try the time slips on the way to the house. Nothing. I sat down under the apple tree to think things out. Would I end my life here? It was a strange existence, lonely, isolated but peaceful when I wasn't struggling with my ignorance of day to day life. Once I had the laws and etiquettes sorted out, I might enjoy this tough but simple life. My thoughts were accompanied only by the sound of ducks, moorhens and coots squabbling on the lake. No noise of motors. I smiled to myself thinking of the lack of diesel fumes but the air was not exactly fresh – horse manure, body odour, bad breath, and wood smoke. The herb garden was an essential part of Tudor life. A movement caught my eye near the house, making me jump. I got slowly to my feet, in the shadows of the tree. Should I hide, run or investigate? As I hesitated, Lady Jane appeared, coming from the barn and looking around, searching. I stepped forward. "Good afternoon," I greeted her. I was pleased to see her but also wary. Why was she here? She advanced across the grass and accepted my lips on her gloved hand. "I came, today, to look at Shurnock because my uncle is the magistrate for Feckenham and he has nowhere to stay when he holds court there. He complains that Coughton is too far after a long day of judgements. I was going to suggest that he rent Shurnock. Can I look round?" "Of course," I replied, mentally reviewing my possessions for giveaways and thinking only my lack of bedlinen would be surprising. "Go on ahead if you like. If you would like a drink, I can offer you herb tea, water or cider." "Perhaps I shall explore first and then we can talk. I should like to try your herb tea." I nodded. "I was just enjoying the shadows under the apple tree so I'll go and stoke up the fire to boil the water and then wait here." We walked to the house together and while I went to the fireplace, she looked around the room and then went into the other room. I filled the kettle with rosemary and water, giving her time to explore alone. I was aware of her exiting the house and peering into the well and then disappearing around the house, pausing to look at the apple and pear trees before disappearing around the next corner. My brain leapt. The Well! What an idiot I had been, carrying water from the moat all this time, taking the well as an ornamental feature as it was in 2019. It was a real water source, right outside the door. I ran to it and peered down the deep hole. There was even a bucket on a chain. If it came from underground, was it fresh and safe to wash in and drink? I wasn't sure. I stood, pondering and then began to think about Lady Jane. How did I begin a conversation involving time travel? Then I realised I had a more immediate problem. Only one cup, other than the one made of aluminium and where should we drink? I hesitated, not sure of the etiquette of offering a drink to a lone female when I was thought to be a man. The water was boiling. I filled the cup thinking I would have to say I wasn't thirsty. Holding the cup, I opened the old front door to see where Lady Jane had got to and put my head out. She was just beyond the herb garden and as she turned and saw me she swayed and turned pale as milk. She half turned back to her original focus and then back to me and staggered. I ran towards her, thinking she was ill but she backed away, her eyes wide. She was stuttering, incoherent. "Lady Jane," I cried. "What's the matter?" She took a breath and tried to stand straighter. "Y-y-you! How did you do that? Are you a warlock? I-I-I saw you just there, and your clothes were different and you asked me questions and then I turned and you were over there by the door and now I look down at the ground and the water cover has gone." I stood dumb and at first uncomprehending. I had been nowhere near her. Who had she seen that she was so sure was me? I was shaking my head in denial when the picture clicked. The me she had seen was the me in 2019 who asked her who was king and did she know Shakespeare and Francis Drake. Automatically I put out my hand to steady her swaying figure but she pulled away, still staring. "Are you really a churchman, or a demon? How did I trust you and become attracted to you?" It was my turn to feel shock and step backwards. I had felt that she liked me but attraction could have been a disaster. I held my hands out in a gesture asking her to stop and let me explain. "Please!" I exploded. "Let me try to explain. I won't touch you, but you have had a terrible shock. Let me get you a seat and you can have a drink and I will sit a safe distance away and tell you all I can." She was breathing fast, her face distressed, trying to get a grip on her reeling emotions. She put a hand to her mouth as if to staunch an escaping sob and nodded. I put my cup on the floor by the door, and I ran back in to the house, grabbed the bench chair and placed it outside against the house wall. She stumbled to it and sat, head back against the wall, eyes shut and face towards the sun. "Here's your drink," I said and heard the tension and solemnity in my voice. How could I explain what had happened in a way she would believe when I hardly believed it myself. I sat almost at her feet and took a deep breath which escaped in a sigh as I considered the task ahead. "I think," I said hesitantly, "That I will give you the facts and you must judge as you think what you must do, but please believe me, I am not a magician or wizard or warlock or a demon, just someone who has got caught up in events and is unsure how to put things right and I really need as much help as I can get but don't know who I can ask." I stopped, fighting my own fears and sense of panic, more difficult to deal with now I had put it into words and heard the stress in my voice. "You probably won't believe this, but I actually live about 400 years into the future." Lady Jane gasped and paled again, shaking her head in refusal. "I don't quite know how to prove this so let's leave that for a moment and go on with what happened. Is that all right?" Her eyes were still wide and she searched my face constantly for clues as to my honesty but she nodded. "About four weeks ago, in my time, I was walking along that path and I met you as, I thought, a sort of ghost who did not know she was a ghost right on that spot where you were today and we had the conversation you just told me about and you were, in fact, in my time. I told you about the mains water system and asked you about the king and everything because I was curious about the time you came from, and then the moment flickered and you weren't there and I carried on with my job, which is to look after the garden in my time for a lady called Carole. I thought I had seen someone from the past but didn't know how it had happened and I went home thinking about you and whether we would ever meet again and I was fascinated by you and how we had come to meet. I should add that I had already experienced a brief meeting with a man I thought was a head gardener and a maid over beyond the barn on two different days where we could see each other but neither of us came out of our time zones and I thought there must me some kind of time slip between my time and yours but I didn't, and still don't know what causes it. Several weeks after we met in that spot, I was over by the apple trees and I stumbled right into the time of the head gardener, which I think must be just a short time before now, but somehow, by walking around by the barn, I slipped back into my time". I gave a small smile, "and scared the living daylights out of my employer's son who was just walking passed when I appeared. Then, a week later, I stumbled into your time but nothing I have tried, and I have tried so many things, sends me back to my own time so now I am stuck here trying to survive and I had been looking for you because you were so composed asking about the water cover and I thought you might know the secret of the time slip". My voice cracked a bit as I added, "but now I know that is untrue and must just keep surviving in your time until I can work out what makes the time change". I paused and licked my lips which were dry with fear of messing up my explanation and finding myself on trial as a witch with death as a likely penalty. Lady Jane's face was blank. I guess I was looking at shock and the process of trying to absorb too many unbelievable facts. She was still concentrating hard and not outwardly denying what I said. I took a deep breath and gave a half shrug. "I have lied to everyone out of fear because I thought no one could believe the truth and I would be killed, like you said, as a demon or an agent of the devil, so I told people I was looking after the property while it was empty for the church because I saw two clergy walking round here on my first day of being stuck and then they went away and I thought that I could then tell the truth about being a gardener and have a roof over my head, at least until they came back and talked to the vicar at Feckenham." Lady Jane's face was less frozen now and I could see a frown creasing the skin between her eyes as she thought furiously. I swallowed convulsively. What did she see as her duty as a Christian ? To help a victim of circumstance or to report a time shifting demon to the church? "I'm sorry to have been deceitful to your family but I couldn't find an honest way to survive, and I thought if I worked hard for you for an honest wage, well, we'd be doing each other a favour. Oh, how can I convince you that I mean no harm and just want to go home?" The frustration vibrated in my rising voice and my open hands slapped against my thighs. Lady Jane's eyes were gaining focus and she reached out a finger and placed it across my lips. "Hush now," she said. "Give me some time to think. Your story is so strange, I think it must be the truth, but my head is full of fog and question marks and I need to find some order." She lifted her head and looked around her. "I came to Feckenham today to look at Shurnock and to go to church with my cousin Katherine, who is recently widowed, but in all honesty, they were excuses because I was curious about you. You were different to everyone else I ever met, more respectful to the view of a woman, knowing so much about the world but not with arrogance. I wanted to know your background, and now I do but almost wish I did not, and I have been away longer than I should have been on a Sunday so I must go." I jumped to my feet. "You won't bring the police or the church or soldiers in the night?" I asked anxiously. "Please, at least give me some warning if you are going to have me arrested." She shook her head. "My head is in a whirl. I don't know what action I will decide to take but no decision will be made tonight and I will tell no one of this conversation until we have spoken again. You can sleep safely tonight, I promise." "Thank you," I said with the deepest relief and gratitude. She turned and hurried through the house, pausing to look back and wave as she opened, and exited through the front door, closing it behind her." I stood, as if frozen on the spot. What should I do? I had an afternoon and a night to escape and go somewhere else, and I could use the horse to get further, but then, that would be stealing which would make me look even less trustworthy and I thought you could be hung for horse stealing so if I fled, I'd be better without the horse. Where would I go? Wherever I went, I would be on unknown territory and friendless. I slumped down on the step and rested my head on my knees, briefly shutting my eyes. I was already exhausted from the week's hard labouring. I really could not run tonight. I needed to eat and have another drink and sleep. I needed to buy more food. I found myself yawning as I raised my head and found the cat at my feet, gazing thoughtfully at me. I reached out a hand and rubbed his cheeks. He leaned into me, pushing back and purring. I remembered I had thought he had been gone through the time slip."You came back again," I whispered wonderingly. "How do you do it?" The cat walked against my legs, rubbing his body firmly against me and then headed into the house. "Oh. I see. You might tell me if I feed you first, huh?Well. Let's see what we've got. I think there is just one last piece of mouldy cheese we can share" The cat flicked his tail up in approval. We ate companionably and I found the tension easing from my body in acceptance. I had done what I had wanted and explained the thing to Lady Jane. I was no longer alone in my awareness of the time slip. It was a secret shared between me, Lady Jane and the cat. Tomorrow I would try again to escape back to my time and then go to Coughton if I could not. The day had slipped away as I thought through my options and the air had cooled as the sun disappeared behind the barn. The moon rose to take its place. I couldn't just run, I thought. Tramps were whipped until they left and returned to their home area and I had no home area to go to, except for Shurnock. I had to hope Lady Jane would keep our secret and maybe even find someone who could help. For now it was time to say goodnight to that reassuring moon and it's escort of stars and go to bed. The cat watched with approval as I organised my bed and leaped up beside me to share our cocoon of warmth. He hadn't shown me the way home, but maybe tomorrow.

Chapter 9

MONDAY

I ate nuts for breakfast, my stomach protesting against the lack of starch. Patrolling the garden, I remained glued to the 1500's, but felt no surprise and only a twitch of urgency to get away. There were things I had started in this century and I wanted to complete them before I left. The cat had abandoned me at dawn to catch his own feast for breakfast. I released the hens into the herb garden, barricading them in and saddled Midnight in the barn. The weather was grey and moody. I hoped I would not get caught in another storm while we worked. Putting on waterproofs in front of William seemed selfish and perhaps dangerous with any member of the family able to come to view our work, although I supposed they wouldn't come out in the rain. I did at least have a change of clothes now, regardless of how strange and uncomfortable they felt. Midnight understood we were going back to his favourite stable and behaved well, other than having a tendency to trot and canter in his eagerness. He sensibly eased to a walk as we climbed the ridge and descended the other side. I needed to make a decision about walking or riding home that evening. The stable lad would want to know. Keeping Midnight reduced my journey time to Coughton by about twenty minutes and gave me an option to go further to escape capture, but then I would have to stick to the main tracks to avoid being knocked off or knocked out by low hanging branches, and anyway, I couldn't ride well enough to escape other horse riders, whilst, without a horse I could hide in ditches and clamber along streams and I would have to feed the horse which would use up my money fast. I was enjoying riding Midnight, and liked his rolling eyed company but tonight he could stay in his own stable. As if understanding, Midnight broke into a delighted canter, with me still concentrating on remaining in the saddle. The stable lad must have heard us coming and was ready to steady the horse as we arrived. "I will be walking back today, so you can stable the horse," I told him. "Yes, sir," he said, eyebrows lifting in surprise. "I might want him again on Thursday." I said as I removed my tools. Midnight harrumphed. "He seems pleased about that," the stable lad commented, patting his nose and looking into his face. "I think he's pleased to see you," I suggested. The lad smiled, and reached up to stroke the horse's ears. "We're good friends," he said leading the horse away, to walk him around, cooling from his canter. I walked through the arch and found the beds all composted and William up a plum tree in the orchard. There were two ladies walking along a path, in earnest discussion. Sir Nicholas's wife and Sir Robert's wife. When they saw me, they waved me to join them. We said our good mornings and I gave them a bow, feeling slightly embarrassed. It felt theatrical and melodramatic, not yet a habit. Sir Robert's wife spoke first. "Anne has seen some gardens at the Queen's palace. We would like to duplicate them here. She waved a walking stick indicating the sides of the path. "Roses here, and a honeysuckle arch and then Chinese shrubs here, and then cherry trees along the path to create a blossom walk." She looked to her companion as if to check she had explained correctly. Anne gave her an approving nod. "You want us to prepare the ground?" I asked. "Indeed, and plant everything, too, obviously." Where was I supposed to get the plants from? No mail order catalogue, no garden nursery down the road. "Madam," I said. "I can prepare the beds now, but it is better to plant in Autumn or Winter so the plants can get their roots settled before they lose water through their leaves and need energy to flower," The ladies looked at each other, one seeking guidance from the other. Anne put her head on one side, considering, and then nodded. "That is acceptable," Sir Robert's wife agreed. "There are gardens, too at Charlecote Manor. The gardener there has been instructed to create new plants for us. Please advise us on quantity." How could I when I didn't know what shrubs he had? "May I go to Charlecote to discuss?" I asked. "I can calculate roses and trees but need to see the size and shape of the shrubs." I wondered about money. Coughton was not long built and must have cost a fortune. How vast were the family's funds? I normally discussed a budget with my clients but as I had no clue to the price of plants, perhaps I was better to let the family sort out the money side of things. "You may." The ladies approved. "If I mark out a rose garden and a shrub bed, would you approve or tell me what you want to change today?" I asked. Their eyes shone with excitement and humour. I didn't know why they were laughing. "Yes," they said. "We will visit after luncheon." They returned slowly to the house. There was such a difference between the nonchalant step of these ladies and the urgent hurry of the villagers where no minute could be wasted, their lives consisting of working, eating and sleeping. Only Sunday was a rest day, and market day a change from their essential lifestyle, their patched, handed down clothes and intent survival. In my day, almost everyone had time to play or rest in front of a television, even take a holiday. The difference was less marked. The priority of the villagers was to survive. The priority of the aristocracy to find ways to waste their time, impress their peer group and waste their money. It was a strange place to be, caught between the two classes. There was, as yet, no middle class. I felt, with my physical work, and management skills, lunching with the gents, I was creating one. I hoped William would learn my apparent confidence and one day converse with the aristocracy as an equal in respect and specialist knowledge, if not wealth. I walked the path, working out proportions and ratios, marking views of the house, and even views of the house still to come, and places to frame views of the distant hills and access to the river. Then I took one of William's sticks and began to draw beds, making use of the natural contours of the land, thinking about winter flooding, and planning the moving of soil where necessary to create a rose garden gently sloping to the river flood plain, with square beds and symmetrical paths. I longed to plant ground cover beneath the roses for a longer season of colour but this was not yet the fashion and I could not rush history. I tried a more curving path through my intended Chinese shrub garden, but suspected I would be instructed to revert to symmetry. I went to fetch William. "We have serious digging to do today," I told him. This is to be a path through a rose garden, a cherry tree walk and a shrub garden. Lady Throckmorton has not fully approved the layout but we definitely need good planting soil and no weeds all the way along the path on both sides. He stood, looking along the path, pushed out his bottom lip and blew air upwards so that his long fringe whirled upwards and fell dramatically. "Yes. It's a long way but we will take turns with the spade and the scythe and not look too far ahead to get demoralised. In fact, we will work to complete small rectangles and congratulate ourselves on every completion." My words were too long and complicated. William looked blank. "Let me explain, again," I said. I showed him how we would divide the path into sections. "For every bit completed, we will feel happy," I said. "Just ten bits to do." He tried to hide his feelings but he thought I was daft, I knew. "Go fetch the spade, the hoe, the scythe and the barrow," I said. He went. I took my shears and began to clear the nettle tops, brambles, grasses, small trees and dock stems, putting them in piles of edibles, burning and compost. I had realised the nettles would be an evening meal for William. I took first go with the spade while William scythed the long grass. Using his own initiative, he had also brought the rake, and cleared the scythed materials as he went along each section, understanding now how working in sections gave each set of muscles a rest and gave satisfaction with each cleared area. For now, I left the rose garden and Chinese garden untouched. I began to think ahead, I needed to leave William with enough instructions for work through two days while I wasn't there. We needed manure for the rose garden. Was there a large pile of horse droppings and straw somewhere, rotted down and ready to use? I hadn't found any remnants in the vegetable and fruit garden. "Your turn with the spade," I called to William, having completed the first section. I left him digging and went to explore the stable area, taking the barrow with me. I found an enormous heap behind the stable yard, too new for use. It would burn the plants. There was another more rotted pile of good crumbly nutrition beyond it. That would keep William occupied. I loaded the barrow several times, wheeling my loads to their various destinations, enjoying the total reuse ethos of Tudor Britain. Nothing thrown away, because there was nowhere to throw it and it was all useful. How had we lost this brilliant philosophy? It was Lady Throckmorton who called me to lunch. She ran her eye over the work in progress. "And where is the rose garden?" she asked. I explained my stick markings. "Is that acceptable?" I asked. "I think it is," she said. "And how many trees and roses?" I had the answers ready. "We can be flexible, but I would say twenty one roses and fourteen trees." I saw the first spontaneous smile. "My husband may be apoplectic," she said and turned. "I will tell him at luncheon." I hoped she wouldn't. I did not want to be embroiled in a marital argument. "Break time, William," I told him. "You know when to return." He pointed to the tree with the time sticks. "Right." I was filthy from the digging. How did earth get in my hair? I used my fingers to comb it out, and went down to the river to wash my hands and face, hoping the water was in fact clean and not filled with nasty bacterium. I wondered whether I would have to meet another cross-examination or whether the subject of costly plants would obliterate the intended conversation. I changed and hurried down. As before, I was last to the table. The grace was in Latin again. Who knew what I was "Amening"? I filled myself with soup and bread. There were strawberries from the garden as well. It looked to me as if Lady Throckmorton was summoning courage for her announcement but by the end of the meal had changed her mind. The ladies left the table quietly. The goblets were filled and I took a steadying sip to fortify my courage. "And what do you think to my horses?" Sir Robert asked. Sir Nicholas snorted. "I'm afraid I'm not an expert," I replied, "But I enjoy riding Midnight very much. He is well trained and intelligent." "Midnight, eh?" Sir Robert laughed. "Yes, a good name. I believe the stable lad calls him Blackie." He looked amused. "I have only, otherwise seen the horses that the stable lad and Lady Jane rode. They are all very handsome." To me, all horses are handsome, even the giant plough-horses and stocky cobs. Sir Robert looked pleased. "You are the first churchman I have known able to ride more than a mule. My brother expected you to fall off." I glanced at Sir Nicholas who had hidden his face in his goblet. "I thought he might," I said dryly. "Sorry to disappoint," I added. "I am going to walk home today, though because there will be many visitors to Shurnock this week for sheep shearing. Your horse is a great responsibility and I would not want to lose it." "You will walk back?" Sir Robert seemed startled by the idea. "Yes, I will leave some of my tools with William to reduce the weight of my sack but it is not such a great distance." It seemed, even in the sixteenth century, people were getting lazy about walking, getting on their horses, or into coaches, wagons and carts for more than three mile walks. It was only that fewer people had access to these modes of transport. Sir Robert shrugged. "As you like, and when will you return?" Heaven knows, I thought, but said, "Thursday and I will then work Monday, Thursday and Fridays if that suits." "As you like," came the reply. "You may go," I left with a bow. As I bowed to each brother, I noticed how much thinner Sir Nicholas was than his brother. Would Lady Jane or Lady Anne tell me what had happened in his recent past? I sensed he had seen more turmoil than his brother, had been in difficult situations and coped calmly and effectively. There was terrible knowledge hidden behind those eyes, never to be spoken of again, unless in sleep, when torment escaped the shackles of secrecy.

Once again, I changed clothes and worked with William, now marking each bed and path in the rose garden and the Chinese garden and explaining how I wanted the beds level in one plane but sloping towards the river and that the paths must be compacted to avoid becoming slushy in wet weather. I emphasised that the rose garden must be perfectly symmetrical. I took William to the manure heap and showed him the difference between ripe and rotted manure. "I won't be here again until Thursday," I said so you are in charge of making the new gardens perfect." William shook his head, afraid of the responsibility. "You are a good gardener," I told him. "One day, you will be a head gardener, in charge of all of this." He shook his head harder, frightened by the thought. I nodded emphatically and held his eyes. "I will teach you everything you need to know. You will do well." He looked back into my eyes, taking strength from my certainty. "For now," I laughed. "I am the head gardener, and telling you to dig those gardens so that there are no weeds, keep the lines straight and get the manure laid before I come again." He was still happier with orders. I left the tools I wouldn't need for survival at Shurnock. It was time for me to go. I had seen Lady Jane only at lunch and she had avoided eye contact. I needed to know what she had decided. Was she avoiding contact because she was going to have me arrested? The thought was terrifying. Perhaps I would just head South from here, aiming to get lost in a big city somewhere. I had a sudden idea that I could teach at Oxford University, my knowledge would make me appear brilliant. Or would it appear heretical? Or magical? No, better to keep my head down, unknown and safe. I would wait at Shurnock for her decision. I felt lonely and vulnerable leaving Coughton on foot. Everything seemed bigger, the buildings towering above me and the driveway stretching to eternity. There were deer in the adjoining parkland. I had never noticed them, dealing always with a horse moving faster than I liked on this stretch. Were they wild or bred for Royal hunting parties? I reached the end of the drive and strode out, glancing at my watch to time my journey home. The sky was still gloomy, but it had dropped no rain. I had been lucky. It gave the looming ridge before me a purple tinge and increased the illusion of great height caused by the tall trees on its slopes. I reached the top, out of breath, but enjoying the exertion and the sense of achievement as I crossed the ridge. The path down seemed less steep on my own feet with no horse slipping and sliding beneath me, head lowered for balance. I walked it with ease, trying to identify the occasional bird song and becoming aware of the thunk of axes off to my right. It was a sound I associated with charcoal burners although I couldn't remember where I had ever actually encountered it. I was sifting through my memory as I descended and peering vaguely through the trees to see if I had identified the sound correctly when suddenly several men erupted from the trees and surrounded me. I had no time to react before one pushed me hard to the ground and another sat on me, putting a knife to my throat. I had had the breath knocked from my body and couldn't make a noise. The knife put an end to my furious wriggling to get free. I froze. There were four of them, muscular but thin, and they were for some reason furious with me. The man with the knife snarled a question but his accent was thick and in my panic I couldn't understand him. I just looked back at those rage filled eyes, wondering if they would be the last thing I saw, and if it would hurt if they slit my throat. Please let the end be quick, I thought. Don't let it hurt. The man shouted his question again, spittle landing on my face. I automatically raised an arm to wipe it away and another man grabbed my arm and pinned it to the floor. He said something to the knife-man which I still didn't understand. My breath was returning, the muscles controlling my ribs heaved as they tried to pull air into my lungs. The weight of the knife-man felt suffocating. If I moved, the knife would cut, if I didn't I would asphyxiate. The two men holding me down were having an argument. I presumed they were discussing whether to kill me or question me. I was slicked in sweat as I lay beneath them. In desperation, I tried to roll sideways to dislodge the weight on my chest. I felt the knife cut in but the man's weight had fallen sideways and I kept rolling, until he fell clear. The other man still held my arm but I was rolling towards him and simply kept going, cannoning into his shins and knocking him off-balance. He let go to save himself on the slope and I tucked my feet under me ready to run. Another body bounced into me from behind and I half sprawled, turning the fall into a roll, tucking my head in, legs going untidily over my head. What had I stumbled into? I found my feet underneath me almost accidentally and levered upright. My rucksack was gone in the original attack but I wasn't stopping to find it. It would only slow me down. I ran. The trousers I kept rolled to my thighs were dropping down. Tough, I thought, Disguise right now was irrelevant. I just ran downslope through the bushes, the path lost in my tumble and roll. I could hear thudding feet and smashing branches. Twigs and loose stones rolled past me, racing me downhill. Adrenalin made me agile, gazelle-like I bounced over the leaf strewn ground, somehow avoiding breaking limbs, converting the slipping feet into forward motion and dodging the trunks of trees as they loomed in front of me or tried to trip my dancing feet. I came out onto a clearer track. Which way? Was this my track or a track to someone's shack. If they chased me on the main track, I thought they would have more stamina and catch me. Would they keep chasing? Should I just hide? They might just spread out and comb the area. It depended what I had done, what I had disturbed. How frightened were they that I might bring arrest to them? They had acted stupidly in alerting me to their presence. I would have ignored their activities if they had left me alone. Would they keep being stupid and chase me or would the fact they had frightened me off be enough for them. It seemed I had stood at that junction an age trying to decide what to do. CHOOSE, I told myself. I went right, trying to go fast but make no noise. They might not know which way I had gone.

I had been too slow. With a shaking of bushes, one of the men slid onto the path in front of me and shouted, his arms out barring my way. I looked hopelessly behind me as another man came cautiously along the track behind me. I lifted my arms in surrender and stood still. We were all puffing. "I don't know what I've done wrong," I said desperately. "How have I harmed you?" I was gabbling, my voice high with fear. My two captors looked at each other, not understanding and unsure how to react. They had caught me but still didn't know what to do with me. I realised they did not want to murder me but didn't know what else they could do. I spoke more slowly. "I am no danger to you. I am not interested in your business. I am just walking home. Please let me go." I was talking like some victim in a film, I thought. The other man had arrived. I was not going to be able to run this time. They hemmed me in and I thought any show of violence from me would result in a severe beating. The rules of survival had no room for fighting etiquette. I might be able to use my elementary judo if they attacked one at a time and make a space to escape again but why would they do that. The knife had disappeared. However I went, I wouldn't be stabbed. They conferred and one of the men pointed up the track. I wanted to shout, "Just decide, will you, I can't stand the suspense." I nearly laughed at myself, but it came out as a sob. The men agreed on something and manoeuvred me along the track by simply hemming me in and walking me along. We came to a shack. One of the men called out and another man appeared. The two other men held onto me, an arm around my neck, a hand on my arm. They talked and I still had no clue what they were saying. The man from the shack studied me and then snapped at the men. This was the leader and he wasn't pleased with his men. They wilted under his tirade. I could have run with their attention diverted but waited. This man could think, I might be able to discuss my way out. The men knew the forest better than me. If I ran again, I would be caught and I just might try their patience too far. The leader turned to me and asked me a question. I didn't understand and found tears coming to my eyes. Fear? Frustration? Anger that I had unleashed this danger so unintentionally. I wiped them away, furiously. My voice croaked as I said again. "I am no harm to you. I don't understand what you are afraid of, what harm I may be to you." The man looked at his team, and they discussed what I had said. Then the leader waved at his men to let me go. "Leave," he said. "Allez" he made a pushing gesture with his hands. Still, not really understanding, I took a step backwards, waiting for retaliation. There was none. The men stood clear. I took another step, then turned and walked back down the track, not looking back, feeling my body shake uncontrollably. The tears fell in floods and my breath came in wooshes. I was lost now. I arrived at the place where I had slid down the slope but it looked too difficult to ascend. It was hard to believe I hadn't broken my neck coming down it. I walked on along the track and with relief came to the main track home. I actually recognised it. What of my rucksack? I needed those tools. No other way of replacing them, I had to go back. I gritted my teeth and felt my muscles stiffening as I approached the hill where I had been ambushed. Was this stupid, to go back? My feet wanted to turn tail and run, but I really needed those tools. I pushed myself on. The slope was deserted. No sound of axes. My trowel had fallen out. I hunted around, found it, still weeping with released tension, put it in my bag with trembling fingers and wriggled into the straps. There was blood on my shirt, and on the ground. I felt my throat with my fingers. I was lucky. I let out a shaky laugh. That was not the right description. It was amazing, but I was still alive. The knife had scratched deeply but by pure luck, the man's balance had shifted away from my throat and not towards it. The scratch had bled considerably but was now scabbing over. I wiped at my eyes angrily and told myself to get my act together. I set off for home, jumping at every noise at the sides of the track. I looked at my watch as I arrived at Shurnock but the time was irrelevant. I had taken an hour and a half on the journey but had no idea how much time the attack had taken. I felt bruised and ached everywhere as the stress gradually eased from my muscles. I couldn't stop weeping. My breath still shuddered, my teeth chattered. It took me an age to light the fire, my fingers refusing to co-ordinate. I was unaware of the door opening or the presence of anyone else in the room until hands reached and took the flint from me. I was too exhausted to react, except to weep more. It was Lady Jane. I felt stupid, embarrassed at my inability to pull myself together. She lit the fire expertly and filled the kettle, disappeared into the herb garden and shoved a handful of sprigs into the kettle, then picked up my saucepan and added more water and more herbs. I sat numbly on the chair and watched. Couldn't think why she was here. She crouched beneath me and looked at my scratched, bruised face. Her face was solemn, but quiet. She reached out and touched the scar on my throat, gently and with silent sympathy. I again wiped away the tears, feeling six years old, receiving comfort after a tumble from my bicycle. The tears welled again. I wanted to be back in my time. Too much self pity, I admonished. Deal with it. She left the room and returned with a handful of leaves. Taking the saucepan from the fire, she used the leaves as a cloth and cleaned the cuts, pressing the liquid gently on the bruises. The throbbing eased. "Witch hazel," she announced with a smile, "is best but we are out of season so we try these other herbs," "Why are you here?" I asked. "To tell you what I have decided," she said. I wanted to stop her talking, too afraid to hear bad news but at the same time I needed to get the moment over with. She took the leaves outside, threw them away and returned to the fire, picking up my cup where I had dropped it, she looked at it with interest and then filled it from the kettle. She brought it to me and wrapped my fingers round it. "Drink," she commanded. "If I had honey, I would add it to deal with the shock, but the herbs have sugar within them. They will help." I sipped and the warmth gave me comfort while the sharpness of rosemary brought control back over my shaking limbs. I noticed for the first time how dirty my clothes were. I would have to wash them before going to Droitwich if Lady Jane was going to keep my secret. She knelt before me. "All last night, I could not decide what to do, and then, today, I watched you work with William and I thought how good you were to him and how hard you worked, and how careful to make things exactly right and I could see no wickedness in you, so I believe your story and think I must try to help you home, but I must not get involved directly for I have family honours to uphold and am already in debt to Robert for allowing me to stay at Coughton with my sister, while I work out what to do concerning my husband." I didn't understand all that she said, only focussed on the reprieve she had given me. My voice was husky. Too many emotions washing through me to explain. "I don't understand how you can help if you can't be involved." She sat back on her heels. "There are people of great knowledge of the past and the future here in the forest. One of them may know of your timeslips, but I dare not ask them nor ask any servant to contact them on my behalf because Robert already treads a thin line with the queen and his insistence on retaining the Catholic faith and so we are watched. Nicholas also holds high position with the queen and has recently returned from France where he was imprisoned for treachery against France. He was so ill when he returned but is now nearly recovered and will no doubt be given more work as a diplomat if I do not dishonour his name, but he has enemies that will be watching him and us to bring him disfavour if they can with the queen. It seems she can change her mind like quicksilver and will have executed those she distrusts." I had felt hope but now I felt as if I was tumbling into another abyss. "So how can you help me?" I asked. She sighed, weighing things up once again in her mind. "There is a lady I met once along the Droitwich road who gave me warning of the future and proved to be right. She lives in the forest near Himbleton. Most people think she is a harmless crone who has lost her mind so they leave her alone. If you can find her, she might help you." I had been to Himbleton a couple of times, cycling the country lanes to Worcester. How I would find it with so many unmarked tracks through the forest, I did not know but at least it was a door to knowledge unlocked. I would have to find a way to open it. "Well, thank you," I said. I glanced out of the open door. "It's almost dark. Will you be able to get back safely?" She stood up, still agile. "Oh yes," she said. "This horse and I used to wander in the moonlight often when I was younger. I miss him now that he is no longer mine. It is good to ride him again while I stay at Coughton." She hesitated again. "One last question. Do you know who hurt you?" I shrugged. "Four men with a knife and axes near the ridge. I'm not sure but they might have been charcoal burners." She nodded, angry. "Such stupid men. Brutes with no brains. I will send them a warning that they will be imprisoned if they harm you again." I wasn't sure if that was a good idea. She read my look. "It will be unofficial, but sincere," she said. I swallowed. "Thank you," I said. She wasted no more time, but hurried out, climbed neatly into the saddle and was gone, at one with her horse. I poured myself another drink, the shivers of terror nearly erased, but my body still felt sore and battered. I eased myself out of my blood stained, soil encrusted clothes and put on my new outfit. Picking everything up, I took it to the moat and dropped it in the water,rubbing and squeezing the fabric until the exuded water ran clear. Then I rubbed them all over with lavender and hung then in front of the fire. I sat cross-legged and watched the pictures in the flames, letting the heat cleanse my body of the dramas of the day until I felt drowsy enough to sleep. It was dark now. Bother. I thought, the hens are still out. I stood stiffly. Tonight they could sleep with me. The cat was elsewhere. Luckily, the hens were keen to explore the house and were not difficult to herd into the great hall where I created an enclosure against one of the walls. I threw one more log on the fire to help dry my steaming clothes and went to bed, sleeping instantly but waking every time I moved in my dreams, my body creaking as I turned and then slept again.

Chapter 10

TUESDAY

With no cat, it was the chicken's gurgles that woke me later than normal. It was nine o' clock and I felt awe at the villagers that they could maintain a rhythm of living without the use of a watch. I rolled, groaning wimpishly, out of the bed, rubbing my face carefully and wincing as I touched the swollen and skinned areas. I felt like spending the day in bed, but the lack of food drove me on. This was the only free day I could get to Droitwich. I ate nuts, gulped cider and considered what to wear. Comfortable almost dry clothes that made me stand out in a crowd, or uncomfortable dry clothes that allowed me to blend in? It was the bruises that decided me. It was better to blend in and be as unnoticeable as possible. Only my shoes looked strange on my stockinged feet. The Tudor shoes too uncomfortable to walk in. I refilled my cup and took more nuts. There were no pockets in my clothes. I stuffed the last of my money in the bag, and stuffed that in my rucksack and set off along the track to Droitwich, up Feckenham's hill, down the other side, and peeped into the main street and square as I passed. The smith was using his hammer on white hot metal. I wouldn't stop to talk to him today. There were tiny children kneeling in the road, playing a game with small stones, their hair long and tied back in loose pony tails. I had never thought, before of the difficulties of hair cutting before rivets were invented. There were no men about, and the women I could see were bustling and busy. I walked on unnoticed. Seven miles should take about two and a half hours. I'd be there for 11.30, have lunch. Shop and aim to get back for half past three.

It was odd having no hedges to mark the boundary between track and private property. There were areas of dense trees where in my day there were rolling fields. There were small hamlets with their stink of goats, pigs and woodsmoke, another forge with a small boy working the bellows, and a tinier sister looking on. Every now and again, the trees were cleared and I could see men working on strips of land, the occasional oxen or plough horse being led as they ploughed the land. I found my stride and enjoyed the light breeze blowing in my face, taking the heat out of my bruises. |I was glad no one I knew would see me until they had had at least one day to fade. Most of the damage was from branches and twigs whipping into my face as I had run down the slope. The men had pushed and grabbed rather than thumped. I would heal. Thank goodness I had not broken a leg on that treacherous ground. I passed several tracks, peering down them and wondering which one led to Himbleton. I tried to picture the map in my mind. Which side of Bradley Green was Himbleton? Even with a map, I had got lost on my way to Worcester. I kept thinking I could use the canal to orientate myself but of course, there was no canal yet. I seemed to remember a really straight road. If I was right, was that a Roman road and would it therefore be quite well used and so more obvious? My mind flitted about, freely as I walked. The land became less densely planted as I neared Droitwich so I could see a long way. How odd to not be able to use the radio towers at Wychbold to judge distance and direction. I had seen the blob of hill with Hanbury church showing above the trees, another link with 2019. Churches always seemed to absorb history. Were they possible timeslip points, if one knew the trick? No good asking a vicar, I supposed. The area approaching

Droitwich was treeless, just bare stumps in the denuded landscape. Some men were pic axing out the stumps, the first bare topped torsos I had seen. Their bodies shone with sweat. A man stood beyond them, holding a whip. He saw me watching and I looked away, hurriedly, afraid to show my feelings at physical punishment. One of the torsos had shown scars of recent whipping. Was this criminal labour or criminal punishment? The edges of Droitwich had the Tudor equivalents of a shanty town but no corrugated roofs or plastic curtained walls. Everything was woven hazel and willow or grass thatched roof. I dodged the ashes of burned out fires. Grimy children all skin and bones and big eyes sat in the gloom, staring at the world beyond their shelter. There were mothers with babies at their breasts. Apart from the paleness of their skin, I could have been in the slums of India. So much famine. There was nothing I could do to help. I put my head down and walked on until buildings replaced the rickety shacks and I raised my head in wonder. So much was recognisable. The High Street had no written name boards but the black timbered buildings and cobbled road felt the same. If only I could walk out of this street and see the modern structure of Droitwich library and the lido and a supermarket and buses ready to take me to Bromsgrove and another bus from there to home, except I didn't have enough money with me, I thought. The windows were different. Less glass and more wooden shutters. Glass was still expensive and plate glass not available. What windows there were, were small with thick glass that bent and coloured the light as it entered. Beyond the street, there was nothing but a vast area of salt workings. Men loading large blocks of salt onto wagons, their skin chafed and their eyes red from the stinging, abrasive salt. I turned back and studied the picture signs above the shops. A quill pen for a scribe, to write letters for people, or to read them. Then I supposed the next shop was a tailor. I looked through the door to the dim interior. I would like more clothes but there were no prices advertised. I had no idea what I could afford. I could smell food. Their was an essence of tea, not coffee, how odd. Then meats like bacon and sausage but spicy and salty. Then vegetables – carrots, peas, sweet corn on the cob, all laid out on barrows outside an open fronted shop. I could smell bread baking and my mouth watered but I was bewildered by the lack of written prices. Of course, paper was only just invented and very few could read.. Was I supposed to just barter? The next shop sold kegs and were marked with pictures of pears and apples and grapes. OK. Here were cider, perry and wine. I walked the whole street getting my bearings but lacking the courage to enter and show my ignorance. I found a corner behind the shops, next to the church and crouched down to drink, eat some nuts and look at my coins. I had brought my modern money. After all it was a valuable metal and should be accepted for its worth if I needed it. I would walk the street once more and prioritise my purchases. I made a mental note in my flustered brain of grain for the hens, perry for me, real tea (although expensive coming from China), a metal bladed spade, half moon shaped but bigger than an edging tool, and a new shirt and breeches. There was a cobbler. Should I get shoes? Then there was a dairy place with cheese and butter and milk. The green grocers also had grain and oats and the bakers had oatcakes as well as bread. There was very little fruit. Just raisins and currants and dates, oh and , wow, cherries. I reached the salt works again. I must not walk again down the street without entering a shop. People would notice. What were the most important things? And, I must not forget I was going to carry this stuff seven miles home. No bus, no bicycle. I should have kept Midnight after all. I checked my money again, trying to relate it to my market purchases. I still had that one big coin. Was it a florin? I had about 15 coins that I thought were pennies. Then I had four of my modern pound coins and three ten pence pieces, stating clearly that they were worth ten pennies. So, the most important were bread, cheese, grain, oatcakes, bacon, eggs and vegetables and cherries. I couldn't carry a barrel of perry. I needed a smaller container. No plastic or glass bottles. If enough money was left, I would buy a shirt. My own shirt was ripped and despite washing, stiff with dirt and sweat. It was also lightweight and if I was still here come September, I would need more layers. I started at the bakers, keeping most of my money hidden and offering pennies for the loaf and oatcakes. Just two pennies spent, I bought cheese and milk more confidently, remembering the cost at Feckenham's market. I selected beans and carrots, cherries and grain, raisins and radishes and discovered wooden pots of stiff honey. I felt excited and lucky to be able to buy these things that now were luxuries because I hadn't had to grow them. I was amazed how much I could buy for a penny. I still had my big coin. I went to the tailors. There were woollen shirts and was this silk? There were also jackets like body warmers made from skins. Too hot for now, but most likely more waterproof than my cagoule. They were heavy, though and I would not be able to carry one. I turned to the tailor, pointing at the shirts. "How much?" He looked at the clothes I wore, assessing my worth and pointed at the silk shirt. "One sovereign," he said firmly. That sounded a lot but then, silk had to come from China, overland by wagon or right round Africa by ship. "And this one?" he fingered the wool thoughtfully. I reflected that sheep farming was new. The wool back dotted landscape I was used to did not yet exist. Wool was special. "Also one sovereign," I shook my head emphatically. I didn't actually know what a sovereign was but it sounded a lot. Was it more than a pound? My new pounds were not very big in diameter, but thick. It was a risk, but I was tempted to try offering one. On the other hand, I still had the other big coin. I needed to work out what it was. I still also needed to buy bacon and my drink. I decided to buy them first and come back. I turned to the door. The tailor pulled at my sleeve and offered a lower price. I laughed internally. Twice now my uncertainty had been misunderstood as hard bargaining. "I will come back," I promised. He removed his hand. My rucksack was full and getting heavy. I used the last of my pennies buying a lump of bacon, then went and looked again at the barrels of alcohol. There were pottery jars on a shelf, with corked tops. I picked one up. It was pretty heavy. I could only manage one. As I turned to pay the hovering shopman, I saw there were wooden mugs also on the shelf. I picked one up and offered him one of my ten pence pieces. He turned it over, curiously and took it out into the street to look more carefully in good light. "Ten pennies," I said, pointing to the number. He frowned, considering. Then nodded and swiftly put it in his apron pocket. I was getting no change. I thought I had probably been overcharged but on the other hand, I would have needed a pound at least to buy this in my time, and I still now had money to spare. I returned to the tailors. I would offer the big coin. I pointed to the wool shirts, lifted one of about my size off its hook on the wall and handed over the coin. His eyes widened and he fished in his apron pocket, removing scissors and stiff thread before sorting coins. I had change. How much had the vicar paid me? Was his inability to add affecting his ability to calculate what to pay me? I was grateful but it seemed wrong that the field workers received so little for their work in all weather, risking their health while I had received a small fortune for sitting in relative luxury adding figures for a few hours. I would give back in some way if I could. My purchasing was done. I would not be able to carry another thing. I walked past the shanty town, eyes down, feeling guilty to have so much. These must be the families of the salt workers, another low paid job. Once clear of the town, I sat in a cleared space where it looked like carts might pull in to pass each other and uncorked my bottle, glugging a little liquid into my new mug. I sipped cautiously and coughed as the alcohol burn hit the back of my throat and warmed my oesophagus as it descended. It left a taste of pears. I sipped again, more prepared for the sting and licked my lips. I liked it. I ate an oatcake, feeling already a little tipsy. Standing up, I was relieved to find I still had my balance and set off for home, feeling an urge to sing. I often did sing when I walked but had so far kept silent as I knew no Tudor songs, except, perhaps Ring a ring of roses – the plague song, Oranges and Lemons – the execution song, London hadn't burnt yet, and perhaps Greensleeves, Was there a context behind that, which I didn't know? I shrugged and sang songs by The Carpenters which fitted my mood. Most people didn't understand me. They wouldn't know what I was singing about and who cared if I changed the history of music? I paused at the turning I thought went to Himbleton and noticed a noose hanging here from a tree, a kicked over tree stump off to one side and remembered the sentence of execution. Was this where it would take place to warn other would be criminals? Or would it be a public spectacle in Feckenham itself? I felt nauseous. How could people stand and watch someone die? I hoped no one would ask me to attend, tucked away at Shurnock. My rucksack was rubbing on a bruise to my collar bone that I had not even noticed getting. I stopped, changed the load around, putting more in the bag that I carried, strap dangling from my hand. A mile on, my arm ached from the weight in my bag. Another twenty minutes and I'll have a rest and another drink, I thought. I should have brought more water. It wasn't a really hot day but the weight of my shopping was making me sweat. I could hear a cart rattling along the track, coming from Droitwich, wished I had a cart, too. How much did it cost or did everyone make their own? Did everyone have the skills to plane wood and make pegged joints that wouldn't fall apart on the first time of use? Did they pay a wheelwright to make wheels or could they do it themselves? I felt awe at the lost skills of these people who couldn't read, write, or pass an examination in maths but could make all the tools they needed within a tiny village, or at least by using a nearby town. I stood aside and the cart rattled by, the driver dressed in clothes of sacking, his load, salt. I had half hoped for a lift but the cart was full, the donkey could pull no more weight, but plodded stubbornly along. The driver paid me no attention. I walked on, resting often and beginning to wonder if I had bought too much and would have to dump some stuff, hiding it amongst the trees and coming back to fetch it later. I would get nearer, first. I sat after a while and drank again, eating a handful of raisins and relishing the new flavour on my tongue. The alcohol dulled my negative emotions and I managed another two miles before shifting my load again, back to the rucksack to ease the ache in my arms, one carrying the pottery bottle, one the filled bag. I was passed the turn to Bradley Green, and Hanbury church had been seen and was gone. I was over half way. Another wagon appeared, this time empty, but heading back to Droitwich. How disheartening. I managed to stop singing as he passed. However would I explain The Beatles,or Simon and Garfunkel? Even the piano was not yet invented. The church at Feckenham was in sight. I dropped my load and stretched out my fingers which felt moulded to the curve of my strap grip. Just one more mile to go. As I reached the turn to Feckenham, I saw a small crowd approaching the church green, their heads down and their step despondent. This had to be a funeral, though not everyone was dressed in black. There were no smiles, no laughter. I walked on, sad for someone's loss but feeling isolated and not yet part enough of the community to mourn with them. The hill had become steeper. My legs complained now as well as my arms. If only I could show the smith how to make me a bicycle, life would be so much easier. The chain would be difficult. If I put the pedals on the front wheel? Was a tricycle easier to make? How would you make a collar from the frame to the handlebars so that the handlebars and front wheel turned with wood and minimal metal skills? But they could make waterwheels. I had seen a derelict waterwheel at the abbey. It should be possible. "Bugger history," I thought as my conscience butted in with warnings about the history of mechanisation. I needed transport. My attempted visualisations of the science of bicycles had got me home. As I walked through the herb garden, I almost fell over the cat who appeared at my feet, and I had a sense of time shifting but it was gone too fast. "Crikey, cat!" I exclaimed, would you not keep doing that. If you're going through time, take me with you, dammit." The cat ignored my tirade and led me into the great hall, rubbing round my deposited food supplies and sniffing my rucksack with interest. As I unloaded my food, I heard another horse approaching. Not the churchmen, I thought. I'm too tired to deal with them. I walked to the front door and stood there watching. It was Sir Nicholas. He swung to the ground in his effortless way and saw me watching him. He was grim faced as he approached and studied my bruised and grazed face. "My cousin was upset last night. I insisted she tell me why. I see the damage is bad." He paused, considering. "They must be punished." I had almost forgotten the bruises and how bad they might look. There was no mirror here. I wondered what the shopkeepers of Droitwich had made of the damage. No one had commented. "No," I said. "Most of the damage is from me running into trees when I ran away. I think their leader will have already explained the folly of their actions" Sir Nicholas was angry. "You are surely not defending them." I swallowed. "I do not know what crime they were trying to hide from me and if it was murder or other violence, I don't condone it but if it was a crime for survival, I don't want their blood upon my conscience. Some punishments are harsher, I think than are acceptable." There was my tongue running away with me again. I had nearly referred to the difference between punishments in my time and the now I was living in. To reduce the impact of my comments, I added. "We in the church are taught to forgive and to turn the other cheek. I cannot unlearn those teachings." Unreadable emotions flitted across his face The diplomat, hiding his true feelings and not speaking until he had rehearsed every scenario. "I will speak to them myself," he said. "No physical retaliation but a warning for the future, yes? And if I find a serious crime of violence in evidence, there will be executions." I flinched, understanding but wishing the violence could be reduced. "I have been buying supplies in Droitwich," I said. "Would you like a drink to show my appreciation for your concern?" He laughed. "Marco, you amaze me. How could you walk so far? Or did you get a lift?" I smiled. "No, I walked. I am used to walking, although I bought more than I intended and would have welcomed a ride home." "So, let's see what you bought," he said, walking round me to lead me into the hall. He knew his way around, no hesitation. I filled my new cup with the perry and added a drop more to my other wooden cup for me. He sipped his drink, and laughed again. "You have a taste for quality, there." He looked around, noticing my drying clothes and then focussed on my bag. His eyes lost focus, looking inside his head. His forehead crinkled in a frown. He refocussed, started to say something and then stopped. He walked around the room and ended, looking into the herb garden. Then he turned again. "I wish to talk to you, but I want you to walk with me outside." I put the cup down slowly. I had never seen Sir Nicholas so uncertain of his actions. The positive words veiled a vast sea of indecision. "Where are we going?" I asked. "To the apple trees," he said. He turned to the door and exited, looking back to check I was following. He knew that something was not right, I thought and was going to challenge me but in what way and what would follow? We walked, one behind the other to the tree, he certain in his stride now his plan of action was decided, me hesitant, afraid of what was coming. He swung round, his cloak billowing and swirling and looked me in the eye. Then, leaving me beneath the first tree, he stepped over to the second, judging distances,. He nodded, confirming something in his head. "A long time ago, when I was nine years old, I visited this place and climbed this tree." He patted the trunk of the tree he stood beneath. I was hiding amongst the leaves when the gardener came past and I watched him wheel his barrow to the vegetable patch over there and when I looked back, you were standing beneath that tree, just as you are now, but wearing your other clothes, with their close weave and the long legs to your breeches that cover your stockings." He paused. My mouth had dried. He had been playing with me all this time, known my secret and said nothing, waiting for me to make a mistake.......and then what? I didn't know what to say, so just stood quiet. Sir Nicholas ran his tongue around his lips. "I saw you walk across the lawn and slid down the tree to stalk you. I thought I must be dreaming. You walked around in circles by the herb garden and then into the farmyard and I saw you open the door by the byre and vanish." He stopped talking and gazed at me intently. "I want to know who you are, and how you did that and why you seem no older now than then. Are you a spy? I have watched you carefully and see you have not the ways of a normal church- learned boy. You are too aware of the world, but I do not see you as a spy because you are not clever enough to fit in neatly, to remain unnoticed except by the likes of my brother who notices nothing, as I have said, but horseflesh." He had removed a small dagger from his belt and was cleaning his nails with it, looking at me in short glances between digging at each finger. I watched his actions with a kind of fascination. He was standing, balanced and careful. I had a feeling that if I ran, I might feel that dagger in my back. How far and how accurately could he throw it? He was older than me and if I dodged the dagger, I was sure I could out run him in his heavy robes, but then what ? I would have left my tools, my money and my clothes behind. I would have no food. He was playing with me, yes, but I could survive if I stayed and would almost certainly die if I ran. I sighed. To reduce the tension, I folded to the floor, and sat, ankles crossed, knees pulled up to my chest, back against the tree. "Its a long story," I said. There was no point trying to lie. Sir Nicholas was intelligent, a traveller, a diplomat. No tales of London would fool him. He had been there, advising the queen for goodness sakes. He knew both foreign and English coinage and all the ways of the church, both Catholic and Protestant. "Do you wish to sit?" I asked. "I can bring you a bench." He gave his throaty chuckle and himself sat on the floor. "I have not done this since I was fifteen years old," he said, "but my bones will still allow it. Now, tell me all." I told him the same story as I had told Lady Jane and he concentrated hard, assimilating facts and storing them for future use. When I had finished, he was again silent for some time. "Marco, you are the best chess piece I could ever hold," he whispered. "It is no matter that you cannot explain the time slip. You know the future and you can tell me what I should do to keep our queen safe and our country prosperous. I have seen your clothes and your tools and you can teach us how to make our steel strong and always sharp. Those metal pins that hold the blades so that you cut with ease." I frowned. "Do you mean rivets, or bolts?" I asked. He barked a laugh. "You tell me," he said. "My brother- in-law of the tapestries will want to know how you weave the fibres of your clothes so neat, so tight, and how you make the wool so thin and strong." I interrupted. "Its not wool. It's cotton, from America, or it might be India." He studied me carefully, pondering. "And where is America?" he asked. "Near China?" History must be falling apart around me, I thought. Too many things about to be invented too soon. The dagger was still out. I could refuse to tell but my value was in my knowledge. Oh God, what was I doing to the future? I tried to think clearly. In fact, drawing maps of the route to America wouldn't change much. Columbus had already reached the West Indies hadn't he? Cortez? Had he found South America by now? So, by the time the English had built their ships and accumulated stores and got lost a few times, it would be about the right time for the English to get there. As far as metalwork went, I could draw things but had no actual knowledge of how to build a furnace or create a metal foundry. I would only be pointing them in the right direction and giving them certainty that their experiments would succeed. I realised, with a surge of hope, that I might already be part of history. The things the Tudors designed and created were huge steps forward in science. Perhaps it was because I had shown them the way. I released the tense muscles around my jaw and looked Sir Nicholas in the eye. "Its a huge country, to the west. It blocks the way to China, but yes it is near China." Sir Nicholas was looking disbelieving. He tipped his head to the side, reminding me of the hens. "You would not try to fool me, Marco?" he asked suspiciously. "You are telling me the world is round, not flat? That it joins up on the other side? I had heard a tale that the Portuguese believed this but I thought them wrong." The dagger flashed in the sun as he raised it almost casually. I raised my chin. "I don't lie to you." I said. He quirked an eyebrow and I remembered all the deceits of the past two weeks. "Except to survive," I added. He snorted. "I can't help but like you," he said. "The world is truly round?" I nodded. "England will lead the world in exploration but I dare not tell you too much because I, well, I …." I did not know how to explain. I gave up and shook my head. "Its all too complicated." Sir Nicholas studied his dagger blade again and then switched his eyes rapidly to me. "You will tell me what I wish to know." he rapped out, and I jumped, his tone so certain, so threatening, so commanding. "I….daren't," I said, hoarse voiced, almost a whisper. "I could have you burnt as a magician," he threatened. "I know," I said, "But if I change history, I may never have been born," I said, "Nor my family exist." "Your pain will be the same," he said. I met his eyes. "I will tell you many things and perhaps I may try to avert the damage man does to the world in the time I live, but that will be enough to satiate your greed." Sir Nicholas recoiled. "I do this for my country," he said. I believed him. He had such a sense of honour. I understood that every point at which he had appeared devious was to protect his queen and the country he loved, and in this time, deviousness was required to match the demonism of the enemy he grappled with and I was sad for the world of men who never through time seemed able to live in harmony together. " I will tell you what you need to know to keep your country and your queen safe," I said. He held my eyes again, looking for my true beliefs and feelings and I didn't flinch beneath his gaze. We had found firm ground on which to deal. He nodded. "Tell me about America," he said. I found a stick and drew in the dirt, a picture of the world as best I could and how the North star and the sun could be used to find direction as well as time, which he already knew. "There are amazing plants there," I said. " For a new drink, which I call cocoa, and underground tubers for eating called potatoes, but the leaves are poisonous so don't eat those, and the cocoa can be used to make chocolate which, with sugar cane will rot all children's teeth and become an addiction". I didn't mention tobacco. Sir Walter could discover that for himself. Sir Nicholas was walking about in his excitement and his eyes gleamed. "There will be wars over this," I said. "With The Netherlands and Spain." He made a throwing away gesture. "Already, we have wars with Spain," he said. "Sir Francis Drake will be an important man," I said and stopped. He glanced at me, sensing my refusal to give more information but not knowing what lever to pull, what question to ask. "Tell me about rivets," he said. "I can't," I replied. He glared. I shook my head. " I only know you have to heat the metal high until it melts and then mould it or roll it to the right shape as a bar and then chop it and bang the end hard to flatten it. The key is in the temperature to make it soft and malleable but in our society all the jobs are separated, like apprenticeships and I was never taught how to make metal, only how to hit it with a press to make a constant shape. I think your smiths will be able to work on this instead of me." It was getting dark. I yawned, tired from my walking and the stresses of the afternoon. Sir Nicholas walked another circle. "I must go," he said. "Marco, you must tell no one else of this. I will be gone to London to see the queen's advisors," he paused, "Or at least those I can trust. I will send you ink, quill and manuscript. Will you redraw your map? And show your tools to the smith at Coughton when you go." "Do I still carry on gardening?" I asked. "Indeed you do." said Sir Nicholas. "I should be back by the beginning of next week."

I had another restless night, worrying about the information Sir Nicholas would try to extract from me and how I could avoid the science used in world destroying weapons like bombs from aeroplanes, tanks and automatic guns with their deadly spray of bullets. I was less worried about the atom bomb because I truly had no knowledge of the subject. What about electricity, or even gas lights? Could I, or should I mention them? I fell into dreams where I destroyed the world, and woke sweating, only to sleep again and in my dreams refuse to tell, facing torturers who threatened the rack and fire and the touch of molten metal.

WEDNESDAY
By morning. I was exhausted. Today was the day of sheep shearing. I was tempted to abscond and go in search of the

old woman at Himbleton but I still needed to live in this time and might yet need the villagers' help. I needed to earn their respect by working hard alongside them. I made the fire, yawning, poking gently at my scars and bruises to see what still hurt and ate a magnificent breakfast, saving the bacon, but eating cheese and eggs and milky porridge, feeling stronger than I had for weeks. I longed for coffee and couldn't wait for America to be discovered and the beans brought home. I had a sudden vision of the Red Indian tribes of America living their lives in tune with the land and being suddenly invaded by men with swords and knives and guns and I shut my eyes and sent them a message of apology hoping the future violence against them was not my fault, wishing I could change just that part of history so that we learned to live in peace with them and learn their ways of living with the land instead of in destruction of the land. I shook the thought away. I was a water droplet in a vast ocean. I would try a message of peace but I thought it would be swept away in the tumult of discovery. I remembered that I had intended hiding everything away in case the churchmen came. All that food. I did my best, hiding some in the barrels in the cellar and some in the wood. I changed into my familiar clothes, even the ragged shirt, thinking that chasing sheep would be dirty work. Packing the unwanted clothes in my rucksack,I took that to the forest, leaving only my bag with me, with my new cup and supplies for lunch. I tucked my tools behind the cellar barrels and finally remembered to move the goat skin from the bed, rolling it up and hiding it in the barn. The HENS! They knew now where the food was, I had given them grain for breakfast. I let them loose, and hoped they wouldn't stray far. I looked around, moving the chair to its original location. The ashes in the fire were still warm. I had forgotten the saucepan and kettle. I ran with them to the wood, piling twigs over the glinting metal. I couldn't remember what the log pile had been like. Hoped the clergy wouldn't remember either. They might not, I thought hopefully. Richard and Alan were walking down the track towards me. If I had forgotten anything else, it was hard luck. Alan waved a hand and gave a shout. I waved in reply. They carried woven panels, which had made them sweat with the bulkiness rather than the weight. "Just us three?" I asked. Richard looked worried. "Everyone is sick," he said. "Everyone?" I said, aghast. "Not plague?" "Not the whole village," Richard amended, "But the men I normally use." Not plague, then and not the well water, but an infection or an illness caused by sharing something while they laboured. "Are you both well?" I asked. "We are." Alan said. "Lets get those sheep. We have to pen them near the barn, we're told. I hope they are easier to herd than hens." I had my doubts, but led them round the house to where the sheep grazed, I wished I had been feeding them. Sheep come to the bang of a bucket if they associate it with mangold or swedes but run from everyone else, in my experience. They lifted their heads and eyed us suspiciously, then took flight, baaing loudly as we advanced. We spread out, me in the middle, spreading my arms wide, the other two using their woven panels. We had them almost cornered against the moat when they broke sideways and streamed like grey white water in both directions along the moat and then back into the centre of the field. "Well, they're nearer the barn now anyway," I said cheerfully. Alan gave me a worried look. Richard spat disgustedly. "We need more men," he said, "We need a plan," I suggested, "Do you have an idea?"Richard said hopefully. "I was just thinking that the path between the house and the moat is narrower on the herb garden side, so if we force them to run that way they will be easier to control. Also, if we put one of your panels to block off the plank bridge, they will have to turn towards the barn and we can stand the other panel beyond the barn to stop them running past it. It won't be wide enough to fill the gap so maybe one of us will have to run round the house to head them off. Richard rubbed his beard. "We'll try it," he said. It was difficult to wedge and stake the panels firmly. The sheep baaed at each other as if discussing their own plan and watched us between mouthfuls of grass, chewing with their heads up. "If we miss a couple, just concentrate on the main bunch and don't get distracted." I advised as we walked around the moat so that we could come at the sheep from the right angle, "and that big lady with the droopy ear is the boss, if all else fails, catch her." We walked in cautiously, arms spread wide. The sheep milled around, not sure which way to run and getting in each others way. "Alan," I said, "Try shouting to get them running. They should bound towards Richard and then curve towards the house. Alan yelled incomprehensibly. The sheep scuttled towards Richard who waved his arms aggressively. The herd swung right, and we ran to close in and stop them breaking around the wrong side of the house. Two split away but we ignored them and got the rest pushing through the gap between the moat and the herb garden."Run round now Alan," I yelled, and he raced away. One sheep ran into the herb garden in panic, but the rest galloped along the track, bumping each other as the moat forced them to curve right, "Hang back," I called to Richard. "Go slow, We don't need to panic them now.." The sheep slowed, looking for a way round us, but forced to step on. We heard Alan call."I am here, Ready." We stepped forward, our hands almost touching and the sheep moved uncertainly on. As they reached the open space beyond the house, they ran in all directions around the yard area, but Richard and Alan yanked up their panels closing the ends. We edged forward until the leader of the herd ran into the barn and the others followed. Running to the doors we swung them almost shut and then Richard produced some sort of string to tie the panels making the barn into an open pen. We were breathless but triumphant. "What about the other three?" Alan panted. "We'll encourage them gently," I said. "If the matriarch is calling them, they should come to the barn on their own. We just need her to decide its safe in the barn." "Lucky she doesn't know about the shearing," Alan commented. We waited a while, and then herded the sheep from the herb garden first. The other two took a brief canter around the lawn, and then, suddenly seemed to give up and trotted obediently to the barn where we opened our makeshift gate and let them join the herd, We turned to find a group of men watching us. Two carried short, sharp knives, another two held leather straps and the last man, well dressed, held nothing but authority. "You have done this before," he stated positively. "Well, no." I replied honestly, "But I have seen it done by others." I didn't mention that it was on television and it was dogs doing the running. He turned to his team, "Continuez" he told them. They climbed over the panels and seized two sheep, turning them neatly and cutting away the wool. They were experts, It took longer than with the battery shears I had seen sheep shearers use but soon there was a pile of dirty wool by each sheep and the holders released the shorn sheep, gesticulating to us to take them out of the pen. The shorn sheep were panicky and shaken and not easy to catch with no wool to grab hold of but we managed it without trampling the shearers who were on their next sheep, turning our bare skinned captives loose, Alan herded them back to their grass pasture. We were handed sacks to pack the wool in, leaving a coating of lanolin grease on our hands, and fluffy bits of wool in our hair. Looking at Richard and Alan, I was glad I had no beard. It took two hours to get the small flock sheared and then we all climbed into the back of a wagon, with the sacks of wool. One of the shearers and the man in charge drove the two horse team. The rest of the shearers opened woollen bags and removed food and drink. Richard, Alan and I copied them, although probably less thirsty. "How is Will?" I asked. Richard's reply was terse. "He died," The funeral, I thought, was Will's. There was pain as well as acceptance in Richard's face. "I am sorry," I said inadequately. Richard shrugged, not able to speak. I looked at Alan. "He had the fever and the wasting. We wished it otherwise, but it was expected," he said. If I knew what was wrong, could I help with my modern medical knowledge? Are the others the same?" I asked. "Yes." Alan said and his jaw hardened to block off emotion. I said no more, not wanting to raise false hope, but if it was dysentery or influenza, I knew about boiling water and rehydration and the need for body salts. I would try to save a few lives. The horses had picked up speed. I held on tight as the wagon bounced and rattled so that conversation was impossible against the noise and the rattling of the teeth in my skull. We arrived at a Tudor house undergoing expansion, carpenters raising the enormous beams and labourers plastering laths between the beams already standing. Not a hard hat in sight, I thought. We clambered down and the shearers led us to a field of sheep. An area was made up as a shearing pen. The shearers smiled and waved us on, sitting down as if ready for entertainment. There were woven herding boards lying ready for our use. For the first time, I saw hawthorn hedges, neat, well laid, keeping the sheep in this one field, "Do you have another plan?" Richard asked. There were about twenty five sheep.

Hesitantly, I said, "I suppose we only need to catch a few at a time to keep the shearers shearing, I think we can push the whole lot towards that shearing pen, but when they break, just concentrate on the middle four or five. The others will run to the other end of the field and we will make another shearing pen there and try to push in another four or five. "I like that," said Alan. "Make those lazy shearers walk about some more, eh?" The grin erupted. I opened the shearing pen gate wide and after two false starts, we set up more herding panels to guide the sheep, making a funnel to herd them into and six sheep were corralled on the third attempt. I had a strong desire to high five my team or run around like a footballer, turning cartwheels and generally showing off, but curbed the desire. Richard whistled around his fingers and gesticulated at the shearers. They waved at the other sheep, indicating they would run away if they started work, but then saw we were building another pen and shrugging ambled across the field to begin work. We grew hot and thirsty, chasing those sheep, but we could use the two pens to advantage, herding them in the way they wanted to run, away from those baaing in fear as they were sheared. The last three, seeing their relations bare skinned but unhurt, walked into the pen as if surrendering peacefully and our herding job was done. We turned our attention to the piles of wool, stuffing it into sacks and loading them on the wagon. The shearers finished their cutting and we were close behind them. The lead shearer clapped us on the shoulders and shook our hands and a woman came out of the house and gave us tankards of cider and a hunk of bread and cheese each. The well dressed man reappeared and gave a purse of coins to Richard and another to the shearers, He looked at me carefully, studying my clothes. Perhaps I should have worn my Tudor clothes but it was too late now. He walked over, slowly. "You are Marco," he stated with certainty. I nodded. Without any request for permission, he reached out and felt the material of my shirt, studying the buttons and stepping back to look at my trousers. I thought it was as well that they had a tie waist and not a zip. Thank goodness I was not wearing my cagoule. "I will visit you later to discuss these fabrics," he announced. He had Sir Nicholas's confidence but didn't bother to hide it with diplomacy. He was arrogant and I had a strong desire to refuse, but it would do more harm than good. I nodded again, keen to close the subject before everyone else started asking questions, like where did they come from and could they get some, too. This must be Lord Sheldon of Beoley. The man who would specialise in tapestry weaving and develop the sheep for wool industry in this area. He turned away from me and spoke to Richard. "I thought your team too small for the job, but you have done well. We will work with you again, perhaps." He walked to the cart, waved to the shearers to climb onto the back and they rode away. It seemed we were walking home.

I did not mind, except that Alan and Richard were now also paying attention to my clothes and my bag. I felt, mostly, embarrassed but also worried that even tiny changes to when buttons became popular might send ripples into the future which would eventually become tidal waves. To change the focus of attention, I asked about Hugh and Gilbert. "How ill are they?" "Almost everyone who suffers thus, dies." Richard spoke woodenly, his brain blanking out the words he spoke even as he said them. I was silent a while, afraid of changing the future, but wanting to save lives, especially Hugh, not yet a grown man, a canvas with an outline of the person he would become but no detail as yet filled in. "The monks of Weybourne had a man of medicine, He gave me some training in the use of herbs. Should I see if I can help them?" Richard paused in his stride and turned to study me carefully. I hated this intense attention. It made me feel vulnerable, but I held his eye. "It's not witch-craft you intend to use?" he asked roughly. "No," I said emphatically. "No spells, no calling of spirits or demons. Just foods that help the body clean itself of sickness." He swung round almost fiercely. "You won't do any more harm than the doctor, I suppose," he said. "Come to see Hugh, first then." He led the way to a shack set back from the main track. The smell of human waste was overpowering, but Richard ignored it as he strode to the doorway and waved me in. I went cautiously, afraid of infection, careful to touch nothing and inhale as little as possible. Hugh lay, curled, clutching his stomach. There was excrement on the floor, flacks of red blood in the yellowy brown mess and on his body, too where he had been too exhausted or lacked materials to clean himself properly. He looked at us apathetically, not sweating but with flushed hollow cheeks. "Not plague, anyway," I thought with some relief but the brown goo could easily be carrying infection. Hugh ran a tongue round chapped lips and croaked, "Help me." I already thought I knew the problem was dysentery, or typhoid or cholera, all waterborne infections, but I wanted to see the others to make sure there were no other symptoms. "Hugh, I will come back and help you, but I must check the others first. Where do you get your water?" "The brook," he mouthed, unable to get the words passed his swollen tongue. I left the doorway and we moved on to Gilbert's home where things looked much the same. Then, three more homes, the first where gaunt shadows of 4 children lay whimpering on a bed of hay, their mother looked thin, drawn out and weak. "Have you also been ill?" I asked. She nodded gravely. An old man slept, his breathing deep and slow. Richard tried to wake him but he slept on, a pile of bones in filthy rags. In the last house, a woman wept, holding a tiny child who could no longer sense her loving arms. It was Alan who pushed forward, taking the child gently, laying it aside and enfolding the woman in his comforting embrace. He turned his head to us. "My sister," he said. There was nothing I could do. We left them sharing tears. Richard looked at me bleakly. "What's to be done?" he asked. "Was Will's home by the same brook?" I asked to be sure. Richard looked startled. "Aye, down by the mill." "And everyone on the other side of the square is healthy?" He frowned. "All but Agnes, who nursed Will." "Show me her home," I said urgently. Richard led the way and we found a young woman wiping the face of her mother, who lay on the floor close to a stench filled bucket. Holding my breath I checked and found the blood flecked excretions as expected. "Its dysentery." I said, now sure of myself. The brook is the source but the faeces are also carrying infection. Richard, is there a village leader who can tell everyone they mustn't use water from the brook. Does the pump use a different source?" "Aye," he said. "Everyone we've seen is suffering from dehydration due to diarrhoea," I explained. "There is a tiny parasite, a worm, which has crawled into their insides and their bodies are trying to wash it out but it is taking all the liquid out of their bodies, and also salt and sugar." My mouth couldn't keep up with the thoughts I needed to utter to save these lives and others. What were the most important things? Richard nodded. "I will tell Richard Hawkesbury and Margaret Sterne and Hugh Lacye." he paused. "Should I tell the doctor?" "Yes, of course," I said, but I was worried about me doing his job. How would he feel about my interference. I didn't want to waste time arguing with him. "What is he like?" I asked. Richard shrugged. "I think he tries, which is more than the one before him who only wanted to leech the money from all and if you had nowt, could not care what happened to you, but he is ignorant of so much...." he tailed away. I nodded. "Tell him first and ask that I might speak with him." Richard ran off while I tried to organise my thoughts. We needed to dig a hole somewhere safe from all the watercourses and bury all the infected excrement and we needed to teach everyone about boiling water and washing their hands and not using the brook as a toilet, or even land upstream that would wash into the brook. Then we needed to rehydrate everyone with boiled water and small amounts of salt and sugar, I paused in my thinking, No sugar cane, We could try honey, and then there were all those other nutritional supplements I could buy in a bottle in 2019 but in 1564 would have to get from plants. Richard came back with the doctor, a surprisingly young man, also called Richard. He was holding a costume that had a mask like a duck's head and sacking. "You're the keeper at Shurnock and trained by the monks?" he asked. I nodded. "Marco," I said, suppressing the urge to shake hands in case I had touched infected material. "You have seen this before?" he asked, almost hopefully, but trying to sound factual and professional. Actually, I thought, no I hadn't, but somewhere along the line I had read a lot about it. Couldn't remember why. I lied. "Yes," I said."Tell me what we should do." he said simply. I explained the basic facts of dysentery, ignoring references to antibiotics and hoping we wouldn't need them. I had no idea how to identify the exact cause of the illness, or which antibiotic we would need and anyway they wouldn't be discovered for centuries yet. It was a relief that this doctor was prepared to learn. He had none of the pride I had expected. "We kill the worm by boiling the water?" he checked. "That's right," I confirmed. "But people don't have to drink boiling water?" "Er, no, We just give them already boiled water and then they can flush it through. Our bodies mostly can do that if they have clean water and salt and sugars." The doctor turned to the other Richard. "Start with Richard Hawkesbury and Mrs Sterne. Ask if they can authorise wood collection and then set a team of the oldest fit children to wood gathering. We'll have fires in all the homes that have a fireplace and organise water from the pump and Brandon Brook for the villagers to drink. We'll need to gather all the barrels we can for that. We'll need all the cauldrons and pans we can find as well, I think." My fellow field worker dashed off across the square and returned with another man exuding authority, but with sobriety and great experience. He had no need of bluster, assessing facts as he listened. He had been disbelieving as he approached but when we showed that all the original infections were along the Bow Brook, as Richard called it, he took charge of the logistics, calling out several villagers to lead teams and getting the carts harnessed for water transport. I was impressed by his ability and the villagers'obedience. No rabble rousing, no argument, they worked as teams with little friction. Richard Hawkesbury sent his son off on a horse to get permission from the magistrate – a Throckmorton, living elsewhere for the wood gathering, but sent the youngsters out without waiting for the lad's return. In the meantime, Mrs Sterne had also been alerted and gave herself the job of instructing the women of the village, with me listening in, on hygiene. "You say the waste is full of these worms?" she asked me. I wished I could make use of her intelligence to explain about bacteria and parasites but worms were more understandable and even a monk trained boy would not know about microscopes, so worms it would have to be. "They are so small, we can barely see them," I said, "But the sickness shows they are there. We need to bury it all and then wash in very hot water to ensure we don't have any on our skin. We can burn the dirty rags." I was glad I didn't have to gather the rags or clean the mess. My stomach churned and my throat closed at the thought. It was the women's work and silently and obediently, they made cloths from leaves and grasses and the fibres of hemp and flax, wrapped hemp sacking around their mouths and noses and set to work. "We need to move the sick people to a place with a big hole they can use as a privy away from the watercourses used for drinking," I told the doctor. Shovels were issued and the lad returning from the magistrate, was sent off to a farm with a barn to explain what was needed. The farmer returned, alarmed and shouting about not wanting his family or his animals infected, but Margeret Sterne proved to be the top authority with a blistering tongue pointing out that if he wanted labourers to help with his farm-work, he needed them alive. The farmer physically backed off from her tirade and turned the colour of beetroot. I was sent with the shovel brigade to sort the barn and ensure the hole was dug to the right depth. We were luckily at the bottom of a hill, the land stretching away on a flat plain. I dug with them, opening the blisters on my hands again, but not wanting to let the team down. They were mostly lads of about twelve and thirteen and dug with determination to outdo each other. I had done the best I could, not really knowing the facts, Water was arriving in barrels and cauldrons and carts carried wood to build a fire near the barn to burn soiled clothes and rags, as well as heat more water as it was needed. I wished we had soap. The best disinfectant I could think of was rosemary, but was it good enough? The doctor arrived and we discussed the amounts people should drink and how much salt and how much honey. I longed for the internet that would answer all these questions, or even a good medical dictionary or a set of encyclopedias. Common sense and a basic knowledge of germs was all I could offer. Some of the village women had come to offer the patients drinks and food when they could manage it, I was struck by the level of acceptance and the lack of questions. I felt a frightening responsibility for the lives of Gilbert and Hugh and the tiny children, and Agnes who was ill because she cared for others. "If anyone else gets sick, they must come here too and not use a privy in the village," I said. There was another man with authority on the scene now. He seemed more concerned with not wasting supplies, governing rations of food to be supplied, and the amount of wood to be burned. I recognised him as the magistrate from the court. He was arguing with Margaret Sterne and Richard Hawkesbury and another man called Hugh had joined the discussion. These were the powerhouses of the area and I tried to keep my head down, out of sight. I was afraid of their awareness of the outside world beyond this village that would pick me out in the searchlight of knowledge and nail me to the wall as an alien, a maker of magic, an intruder, a threat to their world. Margaret's firm voice rose. "We have already had six deaths. How many more should we lose before you think it important?" she asked. I could not hear the angry reply. "Every life is important," she proclaimed. I would have liked to listen further but carts were arriving with people on board. Hugh was helped from the first cart, and I saw him bedded down and helped to drink. The drink did not stay down, but I insisted he try again, and again in tiny sips and gradually his skin became less like brittle paper and became more supple. "You will get better," I promised him, "But you must drink, and keep yourself clean." An older woman stepped forward. There was a family resemblance. "I will keep him to it." she said with her jaw set resolutely. "Good," I said. It was dark, the villagers were not used to being awake beyond dusk and looked weary. There was little more to be done. Others could add prayers if they wanted, I would go back to Shurnock and sleep and return briefly to the barn before returning to Coughton tomorrow. My body ached with anticipated fatigue. I was asking too much of it. I groaned inwardly, remembering I still had to return everything from the forest and find the hens before I could eat and sleep. My luxury breakfast seemed planets away. I saw the doctor and told him I was going. He nodded, absorbed in his work, and I felt lonely leaving the community I had worked with that day and stepping into the night with its faraway stars but no one by my side.

The hens, thank goodness were pecking about in the barn, looking for the tiniest fragments of the grain I had thrown that morning. I gathered the things in the wood and dumped them in an untidy heap by the fireplace, almost deciding to not wash in hot water before bed and then remembering the agonies of stomach cramps and the dead child, I had witnessed. I set the fire and gathered rosemary, scrubbing my hands with it before again bringing tears to my eyes with the sting of near boiling water on blistered hands. I was too tired to eat and fell asleep instantly on falling onto the bed, not even bothering with the goatskin.

Chapter 10

I overslept the next day. Grabbing bread and cheese and
nuts, with cider to drink, I threw open the barn door and
chucked grain around for the hens to peck then half
jogged, half walked to the farmers barn. I could smell the
smoke of the fires before I could see it and found a woman
with hollowed shadowy eyes filling cups from a cauldron,
her face blackened by the smoke and ashes. I looked
through the door and found Hugh sitting up and sipping
from his cup. He gave me a shaky smile. Others were
sleeping. The woman with small children knelt, her face
tear-streaked besides her young, but one child was
missing. I looked away, blanking out my sorrow. I would
think of her tonight. There was no room for emotion now.
The doctor was asleep, propped in a corner. There was
nothing I could improve. I left for Coughton, my head a
jumble of thoughts. Would Hugh and Gilbert survive? Had
I done enough to stop more villagers becoming ill? Would
the farmer's barn be infected, and for how long? How
could I get to Himbleton to see the wise woman? Would
Sir Nicholas have reached London yet? Had he told Ralph
Sheldon about me or had he just known about me from his
wife, who was Robert's sister? Should I warn Lady Jane
that Sir Nicholas knew about me? I was almost on the
ridge before I remembered my attack, only three days ago.
So much had happened, since then, that it was almost
erased from my mind. I had seen no one. There was no
noise of axes, no smell of charcoal making. I marched up
and over the ridge and then, aware of my lateness, went
running down the steep sided ridge to make up time. My
tools bumped too much against my back to run across the

plain but I walked as quickly as I could, arriving breathless, and sweating, only about fifteen minutes late. With no wristwatches, it was possible no one would notice, and, I reflected, no one had actually set a clocking in time, I had mentally set that for myself. I walked in, laughing at myself. The stable area was empty. William had worked wonders. They would soon not be needing me. The beds were weed free and covered in black loamy compost. The raspberries were developing tiny green fruitlets. My herb cuttings needed some water but that was my fault. I hadn't mentioned them to William. I found him finishing the rose bed. "Is it done right?" he asked. "It is," I said with a smile. "Can you ride a horse?" I asked. He blinked at me in surprise. "I don't know," he said. "I never tried." I was thinking of my trip to Charlecote Manor. "I think you should come with me to Charlecote to see what their gardens look like and meet their gardener," I explained. He looked bewildered. "But why?" he asked. "One day," I said, "Perhaps quite soon, I will have to leave Coughton and I want you to be in charge, but you still have a lot to learn. It may be that the gardener at Charlecote can teach you what I miss." He was shaking his head furiously."But I don't want you to go," he cried. "I like working for you." "I like working with you, too, William, but life moves on and we have to learn to adapt with the changes fate forces on us." William's face showed I had delved too deeply into philosophy. "For now," I said, "You can start scything the grass along the path edges and take the grass to the compost heap. I am going to find out when and how we are going to Charlecote, and I have to see the Smith about new tools," I added remembering my agreement with Sir Nicholas. William ran off eagerly to fetch the scythe. I looked at my hands and was glad William was there to do the heavy work. There was a puffiness and redness about one of those blisters that was a little worrying. I should have bought salt in Droitwich. I arrived in the stable yard and tapped on the door to the house. No reply. How should I find someone to ask how to get to Charlecote? I called out. "Hello-o? Is anyone there?" I walked along the passage, quiet except for the echo of my feet on the flagstones. There was no one in the dining room. How far should I invade the house.? It was enormous. I didn't even know whose permission I needed to go. I had had instructions from so many different family members. Sir Nicholas was not there. Really, I needed Lady Elizabeth, although Lady Jane or Lady Anne would do. I could hear the thud of feet on a staircase and the high voices of children and then I saw four of them dash across the vast hallway my passage led into. I heard a strict voice admonishing them, telling them to be more decorous and a lady in layers of skirts with a plain bodice and a very straight back came into view. Without doubt, this was their governess. She saw me and drew herself up, straight as a pencil. "Yes?" she enquired. "I am looking for Lady Elizabeth," I said. "Indeed," she said, with disapproval. "To ask about a horse or other transport to Charlecote," I explained. "Wait there," she instructed. "I will find her." She gave me another haughty stare, instructed the children to take their hoops into the garden and returned to the upstairs regions of the house. It was Lady Jane who appeared, and descended the stairs in a rapid glide. "I said I would organise your horse," she said, "and give you instructions on the route to take. Come with me." We returned to the yard. She took me into the stable and indicated the saddle and bridle I should use. "I want William to ride with me. Is that all right?" I asked. She hesitated only very briefly and said. "Yes, of course. If you think that the right thing to do, He can ride behind you.

You are both lightweight. The horse won't mind. But walk only, yes?" "Yes," I agreed. Dropping her voice, she said,"What did you say to Nicholas? He came home at a gallop and called for our coach to take him to meet the mail coach to London, packed the fewest essentials and was gone. He looked excited. Bursting with it." I kept my voice low, too. "I had to tell him about the time slip." She gasped and looked worried. "He said he saw me come through that other time, when he was about nine. He was hiding in one of the trees. All this time he has known and was testing me to see what he could find out. He doesn't know that I have told you, but I thought you should know that he knows, too. He wants me to tell him all about my time but I daren't." The underlying, buried fears came to the surface as I spoke. "I'm afraid he will force me to go to London. If I won't tell him,,,,,, Lady Jane, Will they torture me?" Her worried eyes looked like deep pools, wide and scared. "I'm not sure," she said. "I.-I think that he will want to keep your secrets for his ears only. The torturer would report to others of the queen's advisors but he might take you by force to produce you to the queen and she might consider torture." My breathing became unsteady. "What can I do?" I asked. "Have you been to Himbleton yet?" she asked. I shook my head. I don't know how to get there and I haven't had time. So much is happening." I tailed off. There wasn't time now to explain. Her breath hissed with frustration. Just follow your brook downstream and you will find Himbleton. You must do it soon. It will take Nicholas just three days to get to London, a day perhaps to seek audience with the queen and two days back. You have just four more days, Marco." She was exasperated by my delay. There was a sound of feet echoing across the courtyard and the stable lad appeared at the saddle-room door. "Can I help you madam?" he asked.

"I'm just saddling a horse for Marco to take to Charlecote. He will also want his horse to take him back to Shurnock tonight." She turned to me. "The journey is too long for one horse," she explained. "Yes ma'am," the lad said and took the saddle out for us, saddling up efficiently in a quarter of the time it would take me. Lady Jane took me out and drew in the dust. "Charlecote is easy," she said. "Follow the back route from here. Any crossings, go East or South. It takes you to Stratford. Then follow the river to the East of the town and the grand building you will see there is Charlecote." "How long should the journey take?" I asked. "Two to three hours," she said. I couldn't help a glance at my wrist. "Why do you look at your bracelet?" she asked curiously. "Its a watch," I said incautiously. She looked enquiring. "It tells me the time," I said reluctantly. She gasped. "You are sure you are not a magician?" Creases of worry had appeared between her eyebrows and she drew back from me, slightly, as if giving herself space to run. "Truly, I'm not," I said. "In less than one hundred years, your inventors will work out how to make a clock that can be used to cross the sea safely and my watch is an adaptation of that." I thought of Sir Nicholas pulling facts from my head. Was I already part of this century. Just a piece of the jigsaw. Were the mechanics of clocks discovered because Sir Nicholas had seen my watch and knew what could be invented. My brain did its familiar jiggle, refusing to think too deeply about such frightening and incomprehensible considerations. Lady Jane made a gesture of erasure, rubbing out the conversation from her mind. "Just go," she said. The stable lad was loitering. It was impossible to discus anything more. "I'll go and fetch William," I said. She nodded, her mouth working as if she wanted to say more, but could not put it into words, and turned away, walking swiftly back to the house, straightening her back and pulling her shoulders up, blocking all emotion.

William was both excited and nervous but as with everything, he listened carefully and did what he was told and we left the stable yard with him hanging on to my waist, sitting behind me in the saddle, and bumping up and down with the horse. "I've never gone so fast," he shouted. "This horse could go a lot faster than this but we won't try today. Keep on holding tight. I don't want to lose you." I felt his arms wriggle round me more and his hands clasped each other tight. I could feel his chin bump my back as he turned his head, watching the scenery and after a while, I heard a sigh of happiness. It occurred to me that he would never have had a day without hard work from dawn to dusk since he was about eight. "Is this good?" I asked. "Yes," he replied and said no more. The horse walked on, also apparently enjoying the scenery and in no rush to get anywhere. Only I had a sense of growing urgency. I had another day's work at Coughton tomorrow, but if I left very early on Saturday, I should be able to get to Himbleton before most people were really out and about, even allowing for the Tudor habit of working from dawn to dusk. Then I could listen to the wise woman's advice and still get back in time to buy food at the market. I remembered Richard still had my pay from the sheep shearing. Well, he should be at the market, too so that was OK. We were riding alongside the river on a well used track, and came soon to the back edge of Alcester, not actually going in to the town but round its northern side. The smaller river became a bigger river, and we then found ourselves walking the north bank of the Avon , into Stratford and out the other side and there was Charlecote, towering above the trees. We trotted up the elongated drive, making William gasp at the splendour on show. "It is beautiful," he said. I agreed. Our hoof-beats echoed as we neared the buildings and a stable lad came out to meet us and led the horse to the mounting block. William slipped off neatly and I climbed more stiffly from the saddle. I resisted an urge to look at my watch and tell the stable lad we would be back in an hour or two. "Can you tell me where to find the gardener?" I asked. The stable lad looked uncomprehending. William laughed in his throat and interpreted for me. I could now understand most of what was said and converse with the aristocracy but local dialect, I still had not grasped. A stray thought of admiration wafted across my mind that Richard could speak with me and the locals with ease, almost bi-lingual. It was a skill modern day foremen did not require, except perhaps in terms of grammar. William was developing the same skill. The lad pointed around the house and gave William directions. It seemed odd to me that no one would have rung or even sent a note to make an appointment. No one knew we were coming but our appearance would not cause a flurry of panic. This was just the way it was. The gardener was forking manure around marrows. William gazed around in fascination at the vast organised garden with fruit beds, a knot garden, vegetables and the decorative rose garden, newly created. I tried to explain to the gardener why we were there and then William, again did the translating. The gardener was wrinkled from lots of sun. Well muscled but bent from too much spadework and carrying heavy loads. His hands were gnarled and calloused. I respected his competence and knowledge, passed from gardener to gardener, but now with the addition of new experimentation as plants began arriving from China and the aristocracy tried to emulate the queen's gardens. He took us round the garden and pointed at various shrubs and the roses, checking which I would like cuttings of. I named some of them for William and the gardener looked impressed by my knowledge, nodding as I explained their likely size with gestures and the best sites and soil type. At the end, the gardener had memorised a good sized list of plants and took us to a hot bed. Of course, no green houses yet, but here, hot air was forced from a fire under beds of seedlings and cuttings. He walked along the row, putting a mark against the plants I had asked for and told us he would inform his employer and they would organise payment from my employer and transport. Willliam translated. We shook hands, and smiling the gardener also shook William's hand and caused him to flush red with some nugget of praise and encouragement. I was just grateful I had had William to tell me what the gardener said and he hugged the gardener's special words to himself as a treasured secret. On the way back to Coughton, he talked excitedly about what we could do at Coughton if the master and mistress would let us and said he had never been so far from home before. I reckoned we had gone about eight miles and marvelled at how the world was to shrink as transport grew bigger and faster. I liked this slow old world where a trip to Stratford was an excitement to remember. The day was gone when we reached Coughton. William slid out of the saddle, his face shining with its happy smile. "Did you finish the grass scything?" I asked him, clambering down and walking the horse into the stable, to swap him for Midnight. He shook his head, worried he was in trouble. "Good," I said, "You can begin with that tomorrow. I will see you, then." Feeling as if I had already done far too much riding, I mounted Midnight and we set off for Shurnock. I felt safer on the horse as we passed the ridge and was grateful to the horse for carrying my load of tools.

I found myself whistling, enjoying these moments of peace in between the terrors of sickness, thievery, religious fervour and treachery. In two more days, I might know how to return to my true home, but supposing even the wise woman did not know? I tried to obliterate the thought, block it out. Ignore it. I must find a way. If I was taken to London, or in some other way imprisoned by Sir Nicholas until he had bled me dry of knowledge, I would never get back to the safe world of 2019 with only the dangers of car accident, electrical fires or electric shock or other such trivialities. Midnight turned into Shurnock without coaxing and the hens ran around clucking excitedly demanding more grain. "When are you going to lay me some eggs?" I demanded of them and then realised I had never actually looked for any. I needed to get those hens into a routine so that I knew where they went and where I might find eggs laid. I sorted horse and hens and went in realising we had had no lunch. There was a pile of coins on the table. Richard must have come and left them. My earnings from the shearing, forgotten in the efforts of the night. I made a fire, cooked bacon and toasted bread, realising I had forgotten to show my tools to the smith. Following the discussion with Lady Jane, my mind had been on what we said and not what I had promised Sir Nicholas. I needed to sort my hands. I boiled water, added rosemary and let it cool enough to put my hands in, whimpering quietly to myself as the burst blisters stung and burned. I studied them carefully. Most were just red, the odd flap of skin was white, but one was angrily purple beneath the damaged skin with an edge of white, dead skin surrounding the purple. I prodded it and felt a stab of pain. It looked infected. Somehow dirt had got through the blister and been imprisoned by new skin growing over the top. If I left it, the infection would spread and that tiny insignificant purple dot would turn to sepsis and kill me. I needed a needle, or scissors or anything else with a clean sharp point to puncture the skin before the infection spread. I wanted antiseptic cream or a good splash of TCP. I would have settled for an aloe vera plant, or soap to act as a drawing cream. Salt would help. I should have bought some in Droitwich. I should have bought needles from the tailor. I would have to use my teeth, but I had best clean them first. My teeth were furry. I used rosemary to scrub and sloshed hot water around my mouth. I put my hand to my mouth and tried to take the skin in my teeth but it kept sliding away. I was being too gentle, afraid of hurting myself. "Wimp, wimp, wimp," I chastised myself but I was sweating at what I had to do. I tried again, opening my mouth wider to take a bigger lump of skin and slide in. My teeth gripped and I edged them in, using my tongue to feel for the infected area, I bit harder and felt the nerve endings protest as I put pressure on the compressed swollen patch. I felt nauseous but knew I had to keep biting because once I let go it would be harder to begin all over again. Just get it over with, I chided. I managed to break the skin and held on, pulling now, fighting the part of me that wanted to let go, or at least freeze. The skin tore and came away in my teeth. I looked at what I had achieved. Some of the white ridge was gone but the swelling was still intact. I sniffed and blew air out threw my teeth. I would have to have another go. The palm of my hand was throbbing. I tried squeezing. The infection slid away from my thumb and finger. I could make the skin softer by soaking it more. I stuck my hand back in the hot water. Adrenalin flowed, making anger surge through me. I was not going to be beaten by a blister. I thought about using my secateurs but they were too awkward to hold, the blade too large. The pruning knife? Too jagged, the teeth too far apart and no sharp point to puncture with. Back to the teeth. Such a wimp. I was crying as I tried to grab the skin, causing stabs of pain when I nudged the infected lump. Finally, I got a grip around the sides again, caught hold of the dead lip of skin and bit harder, ignoring the insistent message of damage being done. I pulled my hand away from my mouth and another chunk of skin came away, no pain in the removal. That skin was completely dead. I felt a pop of released pressure and studied the damage. Clear liquid bubbled up, followed by yellow pus, but no blood. The throb had eased but there was more to do. I needed to get to the live flesh, to squeeze the dirt out and see cleansing blood flow. I felt relief, squeezing the pus out, putting my hand back in the water to cleanse and squeezing some more. A black blob of dirt popped out and was followed by an eruption of grass seed. Blood flowed. I had done it. I wiped the sweat from my face. That could have been bad but I had caught it in time. To be sure, I boiled more water and soaked my hands some more, both hands in case another infection was thinking of beginning. I sat back on my heels and rocked myself, creating a sense of comfort. I was OK. I mixed honey with more water and drank gratefully. It was so good to have different foods to eat. I could almost feel the nutrients I had been missing being absorbed and improving my well-being. I went out of the door to gaze at the stars before bed, a sort of meditation to give me peace before I slept. No cat tonight. I kept the door open a little longer in case his hunting had delayed him, but he did not come. I lay awake for a while, missing the feel of his body against my legs. Missing Bubble. Gradually my tiredness took control and I slept.

FRIDAY
The days were getting shorter. We were passed the longest

day. I felt as if I had lived here for ever. Life was gaining a routine despite the traumas I had encountered. I fed the hens in the barn and hunted around in the long grass I had given them to nest in. I found my first eggs and felt like I had discovered gold. Better than gold. You couldn't eat gold. I carried two into the house, leaving one in the nest to encourage more laying. No cat. Where was he? I walked round the time slips, hopefully but achieved nothing. Tomorrow, I promised myself. Tomorrow, I would talk to the wise woman and use her knowledge to make a plan. Today, I ate breakfast, and saddled Midnight, added my tools and set out to Coughton. On the way home, I would visit the barn and see how the dysentery patients were doing. The journey passed uneventfully, Midnight needing no guidance, confident in himself of the journey. We were in accord as to when to canter and when to walk. I enjoyed our simple relationship, and wished humans were as easy to deal with. Food, shelter, warmth and companionship. It should be enough for happiness. No one met me at the stable. I unsaddled Midnight and left him tied to a rail for the stable lad to brush down. William and I would be digging today mostly, and collecting the ripened fruit and fully grown vegetables so I didn't need my tools. I wanted to make sure I took them back tonight in case I could timeslip home before my next visit to Coughton on Monday. It was a shame I couldn't leave them for William, but then the smith might be able to make him some once he had seen mine. I found William, still scything. There was an awful lot of grass. We could do with some sheep, I thought. He waved when he saw me. I waved back and called, "I'll be with you presently." I returned towards the stable yard, swinging around the house to find the smith's cottage and work area, which we had passed on the way to Charlecote. He was pumping up the bellows, but stopped when he saw me. "Ah, I was expecting you," he greeted me. I unslung my rucksack and took out my tools, laying them on his workbench. He picked them up, one at a time, running his hands over the smooth, straight metal shafts, the plastic handles, trying the sharpness of the blade and working the handles, surprised at the lack of friction and the closeness of the blades. He took them out into the daylight and looked carefully at the screws, bolts, nuts and rivets, shaking his head in admiration at the workmanship. "How is it done?" he asked. "I don't know exactly," I said. Pointing at the screws and bolts I added, "but these undo so these parts are made separately and then joined together." He shuffled through his metal working tools and found a sharp edge that would unscrew the screws, and used his tongs to undo the bolts, laying out the flat blades. He picked up the saw and examined the teeth. He took up a piece of charcoal and drew diagrams on a piece of timber, then reassembled the tools and handed them to me. "The only things I can tell you, are that iron is sometimes mixed with other metals to change its softness and flexibility and that moulds can be made to pour molten metal into, and different amounts of heat and different times before cooling all make a difference to the end qualities of the metal." "Aye," he said thoughtfully. Tools made tougher can make drills to make holes, files to smooth, and threading tools make bolts, screws and nuts." "Aye," he said again. I left him pumping his bellows, and wondered how much I had changed the history of invention. With a start I realised this area led the world in needles, bolts and metal smelting. Was I already part of the picture? Perhaps I couldn't change history because what I did was already a part of the whole. It was all too complicated. I couldn't wait to get back to William and the simplicities of gardening. I spent the day neatening the edges of the beds and harvesting. With Sir Nicholas away, I wasn't invited to lunch, the cook brought me a dish of broth and a hunk of bread and I settled near the river to eat, immersing myself in the song of birds, the hum of bees and the whirring of grasshoppers. The background splash of a weir was soothing. I put the bowl aside and pulled my knees up to my chin watching leaves floating downstream. William had disappeared for his break but reappeared in good time. I took him along the riverbank, pointing out the dead reeds and excess brambles to be removed, showing him the irises and patches of marsh orchids and marsh marigolds which could be borrowed by a gardener for their beauty but would only grow in the damp ground. Then I showed him how to collect and plant cuttings and water them enough for them to thrive. "I will talk to Lady Elizabeth before I go. She can give you instructions about when the plants will arrive from Charlecote. Just make sure our new beds stay weed free." He had shrunk back at the thought of the lady of the house talking direct to him. "William," I said. "You work well. You have learned huge amounts with me. You will be a great head gardener one day. All you need is confidence in yourself." He gulped and flushed. "All being well, I will see you on Monday." My day was done, apart from reporting to Lady Elizabeth. I gathered my tools and saw William watching. "The smith is thinking how to make you tools," I told him. He drew his breath in and made a half leap of joy. "See you." I said and realised I would miss him if I left this time. I walked to the house and round to the front door, hauling on the bell pull. It hadn't felt right prowling around the house the day before. An invasion of their privacy. A man in smart uniform opened the door, eyed my working clothes with a sneer of one-upmanship but went to see if Lady Elizabeth would talk to me. She appeared with a parasol and a silk shawl and we walked back around the house so that I could discuss the layout of plants and explain the number I had requested. She seemed pleased. " I will send the hayman over with his wagon," she said and ride over myself to discuss payment. All thoughts of waiting until Autumn were gone. I said I would be back the next week. As I left on Midnight, I wondered if I would be on my way to London, or back in my own time by then.

 I left Midnight at Shurnock and walked to the farmer's barn. Gilbert was scooping water from the cauldron. He pushed lank strands of hair away from his face and gave me a gap toothed grin. He was stick thin, but the cleanest I had seen him. "I'm better," he said. "Going home." I grinned back. "Always boil your water, or use the pump." I said. "Yes," he confirmed. "Is Hugh better, too?" I asked. "Already home," Gilbert said. I was pleased. The vicar appeared from the barn. "Good evening," he greeted me. "You have saved me a few funerals, but not all." I had not expected the old man to survive, and knew we had lost two children. "How many?" I asked. "Four," he said bleakly. "The doctor still thinks you are a miracle worker." He nodded towards the village. "He was going to check on the thatcher's leg, but he has worked hard these two nights." I nodded and said. "He does his best, but it is hard without full knowledge," The vicar gave me a piercing look and I tried to button my run away mouth. "He might welcome some more of your knowledge to help with the thatcher," he said and headed off towards the village. I hesitated. I had almost forgotten the thatcher and his broken leg. My first aid knowledge said we needed to straighten the leg, being careful not to slice any blood vessels and splint it as straight as we could but my knowledge wasn't enough. I might make it worse. I might be already too late, but the thatcher couldn't lie there forever. Reluctantly, I followed the vicar. Striding ahead, the vicar never looked back, never saw me, so I didn't have to worry about holding a long conversation with him. He disappeared into the vicarage. I walked unwillingly across the square and stopped outside the thatcher's home. Peering in, I saw the doctor standing irresolutely in the middle of the room. The thatcher was sweating and shivering and the room stank of rotting flesh. I stepped away, gagging. Gangrene, I thought. I felt hot, furious with myself for not acting sooner. I wanted to run from my guilt and the consequences of my inaction, to blame the doctor for his unprofessionalism, the thatcher himself for being careless and falling in the first place but, although they could share the blame, I had to accept my share and do my best to make amends. No. That was impossible. No one could save that leg. Now the question was, could we save the thatcher? I pulled myself straight and stuck my head back through the door, calling to the doctor. He turned his head to me, and then came slowly out. He shook his head. "I should have acted sooner," he said. "The demons in his leg have invaded his body." "We might be able to save him," I said. The doctor shook his head despairingly. "We have to cut the leg off," I said and felt sick at the thought of sawing through flesh and bone. "If the leg is gone, so is the source of infection and we may be able to clean the wound and cure the fever with herbs. If we do nothing, he will soon fall into a coma and die. Removing his leg will hurt him for a long time but with a wooden leg, he might survive and have a good enough life." Sweat broke out on the doctor's forehead and he paled. "I tried once before with someone. There was blood everywhere, and he died when the blood stopped pumping." I wished I could at least ring my surgeon friend and ask for advice. I knew it was possible to amputate a leg. Men had survived the first world war with a stump for a leg. It must be necessary to put a tourniquet around the top of the leg. Did we have to cauterise the ends of the blood vessels to stop them bleeding when we removed the tourniquet? Could we tie the ends of the biggest vessels off with wool or any other kind of thread? So much I didn't know. "Are there any other doctors who can help?" I asked hopefully. "The barber doctored before me but he mostly just bled people to cure them, or kill them," Richard replied without humour. "Is there an animal slaughterer here?" I said thoughtfully. "There is Roger le Boucher," Richard replied. "Let's ask him if he can sever the leg with his knife, or axe or whatever he uses," I said, "But we must tie the leg tight above his cut first. Very tight." I looked in again at the thatcher. He was, thankfully, barely conscious. He might not even know what we were doing. "I think willow bark helps ease the pain." You get Roger and I'll get some bark." Richard hurried off to the western edge of the village. I realised I had no tools with me and called to the lady whose strip I had weeded asking if she had a knife. "What for?" she asked. She had such a firm toughness about her that I explained the whole thing to her. Surprisingly she said, "I have done this before. I will help. We need more boiling water, yes?" "Yes," I said as she handed me a knife. I hurried to the nearest group of trees and skinned off some bark. There was no time to create aspirin, but a sliver of bark between his teeth would save him biting his tongue and generate a tiny amount of painkilling drug for him to help him in his delirium. Roger and the doctor reappeared and I told them we had extra help. The doctor carried a strip of leather and a strong wooden stake. Roger carried a blade which was a cross between a knife and a saw with a strong sharp blade. The four of us squeezed into the fetid room. The decision made, we all wanted the thing done. Wasting no time, Richard wrapped the leather cord around the leg above the knee. The bottom half of the leg was a mess, the colour of my blister swelling but exaggerated, purples, reds, blacks and blues stained with yellow oozing pus. Roger seemed undisturbed, assessing angles and bone structure. "Wait," said the voice of experience. "You will need to burn the ends of the bleeding. You must heat three knives in the fire to keep them burning hot." She was throwing wood on a fire outside the hut and had brought another knife, taking the one I had borrowed and finding another in the rubbish of the thatcher's hut. With the fire burning hot, she nodded. "Tight with that cord," she said. Richard put the stake in a loop of the cord and twisted it as tight as he could. "Tighter," she said. "Marco, twist it more." I took the doctor's place and managed another turn of the cord. "Enough?" I asked. She nodded. I looked at the thatcher's face, not able to watch Roger wield the knife. There was no awareness of what we were doing. I thought we were probably too late. "Hold the leg still," Roger instructed Richard. I saw his arm rise and looked away, shutting my eyes involuntarily. I heard Richard gag and pushed harder on the stake determined to stop any bleeding. I found myself counting, my first aid knowledge said ten minutes maximum for a tourniquet. I would count and ignore all else. There was a sizzling hiss and a smell of burning flesh. Richard was sobbing as he worked, too young for the responsibility he was shouldering alone. "Get a grip, man," The lady's voice was firm and strident. It worked, shocking Richard into a professional frame of mind. He worked on, burning and burning and then I could see the shadow of his arm, moving up and down. He was sewing the flaps of the leg together. I had reached nine minutes in my counting. "I must ease the tourniquet very soon," I warned, "Just one minute more, man," Richard said. Roger had left the room, taking the leg with him, a trail of pus and just a little blood showing the extent of the dead cells in the leg. "I am done," Richard said. "Gently though, when you ease the pressure." I held my breath as I gradually untwisted the leather thong. The flesh beyond the cord changed rapidly from white to red and some blood spurted from the flaps of skin. I put pressure back on and Richard held a rag tight to the wound, binding it in as best he could. "Try again," he said. I eased the thong again, more slowly and there was just a dribble of watery red fluid that gradually eased and ceased. I unwound the thong more and more and the stitching held, the smallest blood vessels scabbing over. The bed was pus and blood soaked. The thatcher was unconscious. I had expected him to be screaming. It was a relief to have not had that to deal with. When, if he awoke, that was still to come. What herbs could we use to relieve the pain and the fever? Richard was ahead of me, talking to the lady and producing herbs from a bag. She already knew. I wanted to ask her if her last experience had worked but it seemed insensitive. We walked out shakily. "Come and have a drink," Richard said to me and Roger. Roger shook his head. He still had work to do, he said. I felt overstrung, shaky and a drink seemed a good idea. I followed Richard to his small house. He had a curtained off area with a bed bench as a surgery, a table and two chairs, fireplace with cauldron and a wooden bed in the corner. There was a set of shelves with china and glass bottles and actual books sharing a shelf with mugs, plates and dishes. He knelt and lit the fire and boiled a saucepan of water, taking soap and washing his hands and arms carefully, insisting I did the same. The soap smelt strongly of disinfectant. I looked in amazement at my clean skin. I had got used to being grubby. I would have liked to use that soap all over. Only then did he take one of the bottles and two mugs and slosh liquid into them. He threw his mug back in one go and refilled the mug, hurling himself into the chair. I sipped carefully, heat spreading with the descending alcohol to my stomach. Not used to the powerful spirit, I felt tension easing, my brain throwing off the horrors I had witnessed. Richard placed his mug on the table and rubbed a hand over his face and raised hollow eyes to my face. "I'm useless," he said. "I might have killed him, but I have at least, ruined his life with my tardiness. I was afraid to set his leg. Afraid of hearing him scream as I worked." I put my hand on his forearm. "No," I said. "The main fault was his for using a ladder with rotted wood. You have done your best. Only learn from what has happened so that you may do better another time." He took another swig from the mug and refilled it, topping my mug up too. "Drink," he encouraged me. I knew I was less affected because I had looked away from the grisly amputation. I had not had to sew through flesh or cauterise the vessels. Could I have done that? No. I would have been sick all over the floor. "You are a brave man," I said. "You have faced your demons and conquered them. It will be hard to get through the thatcher's anger and his pain and his despair but you and he will come out stronger." He studied my face carefully. "You are a strange man, Marco," he said. "Sometimes, I feel you are not of our time." I stared at his face in turn, trying to read how he judged me but the emotions were too complicated and the alcohol was having an affect on both of us. I shrugged, not knowing what to say. He giggled. "I am drinking with a man from the future. How about that?" He leaned towards me desperately. "Help me," he pleaded. "Teach me what I must know." I stood up, unsteadily and walked around the room, avoiding his penetrating stare. What could I say? I sat down again. "There is too much to learn," I said. "Too many diseases, too many things to go wrong." I drank again, feeling fire light my mind. "The most important things you already do. Boil and heat to kill germs. Use disinfectant. When the plague comes, kill all the rats. It is spread by fleas on the rats and don't let people mix for the fleas will jump from one man to another. Talk one doctor to another to learn from each other, learn all the herbs and what they do. Other plants will come from other countries with many useful powers. Only one other thing, if you find a man called Edward Jenner*, believe in his findings for he will help destroy many diseases." I looked at the man opposite, who still watched me intently and had stopped swigging alcohol. "To save your mind, concentrate on those you save." I was afraid of telling too much, marking myself as a demon, changing the future. I stood again, balancing against the table as my head swam. "I must go." I wavered to the door and stumbled through it. The sky was black, no moon tonight. I giggled as I fell over ruts in the ground and found myself running to keep my balance, steadying myself against a house wall and then trying to walk solemnly down the middle of the street, the houses blacker shadows against the trees and the sky. It took hours to get home, falling into the roadside ditches and laughing at myself as I climbed out. The laughter became tears as images of the last two days crossed my mind uncontrollably, but the tears washed away the horrors and by the time I reached Shurnock I was able to throw myself on the bed and sleep. The dreams were turbulent. People cutting each others' limbs off, horses demanding to know where I was planting the roses and threatening torture if I did not tell. A world folding in on itself because I had

*   In fact Edward Jenner was not born until 1749 and died in 1823

given away The Secret of the Future and had to get it back. It* made no sense.

---

*

Chapter 11

SATURDAY

I woke with relief, but found myself going back over the dream, sorting bits out and trying to correct my actions as I thirstily drank rainwater from the barrel. I wasn't hungry. I would take bread and cheese to eat later. It was still dark, but the rimlight of dawn could be seen through the tops of the trees. I sloshed water over my head to clear the dreams and the hangover. What did I need to take? I wore my long trousers and old torn shirt as evidence of my story and shoved my cagoule in my bag along with the food, my full cup and the secateurs. I carried my shears in case the brambles were thick along parts of the stream. Still no cat. I was missing him, missing Bubbe. I threw grain for the hens, seeing there were eggs but not collecting them yet. Midnight, I took to share the grass with the sheep, using the saddle and bridle straps to create a long tethering rope from high up in one of the apple trees. I stroked his nose and emotionally thanked him for looking after me. I was too tired, not able to think sensibly. I had to go or I would not be back in time for the market and I could not manage another trip to and from Droitwich with all the food I needed. I walked to the brook and headed west. It was another warm day and I splashed into the water, the easiest way to avoid the bankside brambles and nettles. I felt like a child, remembering carefree holidays in Devon and Cumbria, playing in the wide rivers, hopping from stone to stone and looking for fish in the fast flowing clear water. Another stream joined mine from the North and, realising this was the stream from Feckenham, carrying death in its unseen microbes, I climbed out and walked on the bank, my feet sloshing in my soggy shoes. I emptied the water out and wrung out my socks. They would dry as I walked. Thank goodness for the Summer. The ground was marshy here. I hopped from tussock to tussock, or clambered on exposed willow tree roots, occasionally sinking into mud to my knees. This must be completely under water in Winter, I thought. There were reed beds, partly harvested, difficult to navigate in the early dawn light. More streams joined mine but I came to a fording place where many stones had been laid and track users had worked to raise the height of the track and from then on, the going was easier. I must have reached the track linking Bradley Green to Himbleton. I began to wonder what I was going to say. What would she be like? I was imagining her as a witch in one of Shakespeare's plays, cackling, toothless and speaking in rhyme, Was it safe to be honest with her? I could think of no other way to get help. I found myself walking slower, afraid of this momentous meeting. If she could not help, I would be in despair. How would I cope with knowing I had to deal with Sir Nicholas's thirst for knowledge and Richard Crispin's pleas for help. How long could I struggle on with this tough way of living, alone and isolated? And how long before the clergymen of Worcester discovered me and threw me out? Ahead of me, was a shack, and standing, looking at me with eyes shaded from the dawn sun, was a heavily shawled woman. She was not dirty and ragged but she was wrinkled and gap toothed. It was hard to judge age as I had learned that although the aristocracy were fit at fifty, most folk would die before they reached forty and their hard lives and poorer nutrition bent their backs and wrinkled their skin before they reached thirty. She looked ancient but her skin was pink and her hair brushed. "I have been waiting for you," she greeted me. I blinked. None of my planned opening lines fitted this situation. "Oh," I said stupidly. She waved me towards her. "Come and sit," she said. She was still agile, sitting on a low stool outside the shack in the slanting sunlight she said simply, "Tell me what you wish for," The words catapulted straight from my heart. "I want to go home." She nodded. "For some people, that is not so," she said. I felt the stupid tears brimming again. "I miss my cat," I said and it sounded daft, but she was, I suppose a microcosm of my whole existence, safety, warmth, food, security and love. The most important things in life. The woman looked at me sideways. "You came from the future because you also existed in the past. At Shurnock, time is twisted by the turbulent events there, many family treacheries, people fleeing, soldiers fighting, even the house itself is changed and changed and changed by each family that lives there and the building and rebuilding has turned time into an earth tremor. It is like a river eddy turned into a whirlpool by the repositioning of the bedrock." "Yes," I interrupted, "but how do I get back?" "You need to understand the workings, Marco, Margot, to get your head right and then you need a meeting of time. Every changing of time is caused by a meeting of two bodies in the same spot from two different times." I thought back and realised that at every blur of the centuries there had been another person on the spot – the gardener, the kitchen maid, Lady Jane and the clergymen. "But how do I know when they are there?" I cried in exasperation. "That is fate," the lady said. I had another disturbing thought. "And how do I know if it is the right time?" "That is also fate, but I know that you cannot return to a time between your birth and your leaving for in the universe you exist in, that is an impossibility." I sat silent. Too many half questions forming to know where to start. "How do you know these things?" I asked. She laughed and her voice was young. "I slipped back from a time beyond yours, when man has made such a mess of the planet that everything is ending. The land is a desert. People live only underground to avoid the burning heat of the sun and only pockets of fertile land on tiny islands survive. Shurnock was the edge of a vast sea, dykes holding the water back. The land inside built higher. I was running from people desperate for the last land to survive on. The last source of food. Mankind had gone full circle and was back to living life like this," She swept an arm to embrace Tudor England, " but with few of the skills for survival the Tudors have. We were trying to repel invaders from the sea just as we did with the Vikings and the Danes and the Saxons centuries before but the weapons more advanced, more lethal.. As I ran, the earth tremored and I was here. I tried to return to a time before my time, to warn people of what was to come. I tried to return to when I was a child to change the way we were living but I think that is impossible. I managed, once, a time before I was born but was scared of what I might make worse by speaking out and encountered you when you return from here." I drew in breath to interrupt but she hushed me. " I will not speak of that. You may have echoes of a memory when we meet in your time and that will be enough. I do not know to the exact day when you will return, but hold on to the fact, Marco. You WILL RETURN and find your cat, safe and well." The stupid tears welled again. I wiped them away angrily, overwhelmed by feelings of homesickness. "What must I do?" I asked. "Just look after yourself. Live your life here by the principles you set yourself and walk your gardens at Shurnock often. Do not will it to happen. It will occur when the time is right, and probably when you do not expect it." I looked at her, feeling my emotions naked in front of her vast knowledge and perception. "Why did you stay?" I asked. She shrugged lightly. "The world was ending. I had nothing to return to. I do not know if warning you of the future can change it, but I will try. Tell, people, Marco. They must return to the land and value it above all else or the end will come sooner than they think." She had taken my hands in her urgency and shook them, gripping tight, making desperate contact eye to eye. "I already know," I said, "But I feel a droplet in an ocean of non-believers. I will try, though." She nodded. "Perhaps it is impossible to change." she said. I suddenly remembered the cat. "The cat at Shurnock," I said , "Changes times. I saw him go. How does he do it?" She laughed again. "Cats have knowledge beyond all other creatures. They have immense powers of observation and can twist human beings to their will. I suspect your cat has created human routines that he uses to meet them between centuries and so cross at the moment of contact. Does your cat not always know the times to meet you coming home?" I smiled. "Yes, she does," I agreed. "How do you live here safely?" I asked. She shrugged. " I am a good grower, a good herbalist and give knowledge when asked but otherwise keep my nose out of everyone else's business. They think me a little strange but do not fear me and so I live safely. I have helped many of them and so they now look after me." I nodded. There seemed nothing else to say. I stood. It had been good to talk honestly with someone who understood. Part of me wanted to say, "Let me stay here with you, I feel safe here," but she had built her new life here alone and I wouldn't encroach, "Thank you for your help," I said. I half laughed. "Its been nice knowing you," I sounded modern and American. She laughed too. "Have a nice da-ay." The accent was definitely American. I waved and turned to go back along the stream and into a more hopeful future. Adrenalin hummed and buzzed ready to return to my time, but bits of our conversation floated through my head and I reckoned I had a few days at least to get through. She had made no promise that the time would be soon. The thought was sobering. The bright day was not living up to its promise. Puff ball clouds were blowing in. changing the light from dazzling to grey and back again. I hesitated at the ford. Should I visit Bradley Green? But no, time was short. I had food to buy at that one day a week market. I walked as fast as I could and branched left to follow the Feckenham stream, finding my way through the trees, recognising the big tree I had climbed in my first days here but this time walking boldly up the track, passed the farm and onwards to the village square. I was greeted with smiles, only the odd person reacting with fear, backing away and making the sign of the cross. There was nothing I could do to convince them I was no demon. It was hard enough just communicating on a day to day level. I bought the food I needed in a sort of daze brought on by general fatigue and information overload. Hugh sat weakly in a doorway, leaning on the wall for support. I still had money to spare from the sheep shearing. I bought another two bread rolls and took them to him, "You must eat now," I said, "But only small amounts at a time," He went to push the food away, but I was insistent. He took them and tore a small piece off. He ate it slowly, chewing carefully but after swallowing, his body awoke and called for more, knowing this was what it needed. He ate another piece, chewing faster. "Slowly," I reminded him. With difficulty, he put the bread down and gave me a lopsided smile. I thought of Gilbert, also unable to work and wondering if there was any charity in this hard world, then I remembered the court room and the request for aid for the thatcher with his broken leg. It came not automatically, but on request. I used my last penny to buy Gilbert food and took it to him. He was lying, exhausted. I was furious that no one was helping him. No one bringing water or helping him with a fire. Then I reassessed. They had cleaned his house. There was only so much time to spend after their day to day chores were done. I took a bucket back to the pump and filled it, slopping water as it bumped against my leg on the way back to his home. He watched me blankly as I filled his cup and insisted he drank and then tore off a nibble of bread and ordered him to eat. It wasn't enough but I couldn't go barging around demanding the setting up of a welfare state. I would talk quietly to the vicar and the doctor and maybe Sir Nicholas, if I saw him again.

I returned to Shurnock and walked hopefully around the grounds but I knew my frame of mind was wrong, willing it to happen, instead of allowing it to happen. Still no cat. I ate and sat in the herb garden, letting the patchy sun warm my clothes and the sound of happy bees fill my mind. Gradually, I fell sideways and slept. I slept until teatime, my mind and body using this quiet time to heal themselves. The hens woke me, pecking for grubs near my ear. They set off down the path, gurgling and chuckling as they found a tasty morsel, their feet kicking sideways as they ran and the path blurred ahead of them and the cat stepped into view. He trotted cheerfully up the path and rubbed against my leg before heading indoors, tail raised, anticipating bacon. I couldn't help running to the spot. If I could only meet the cat and step the other way as he came through. I thought. He was watching me smugly and with amusement from the doorway and then circled slowly inviting me to fetch some food to share. He was frustrating but loveable. We shared eggs and bacon and I thought wistfully of the not yet discovered potato.

Church tomorrow and then a day of rest. Would Lady Jane come on her way home from church? Where was Sir Nicholas in his journeyings to and from London? I hoped the queen was refusing to believe his tales of a person from the future. Surely they would think him mad. For all his zealous patriotism and threats to have me imprisoned, I didn't want him locked up for madness. I just wanted him delayed.

SUNDAY

It was good to have the cat to sleep with. His deep purr was soothing and I had no dreams. We rose in the dawn light again. We had passed the longest day now and the mornings were getting darker. We ate, I fed my menagerie of animals and went to Church in my new shirt and Tudor breeches and jacket, feeling smart. I even washed my face. As the villagers filed into the church, I was greeted by a few. These were people I had dug alongside and instructed in herbs and cleanliness. I counted heads as the vicar's sermon rolled over me. More than 200 in this tiny church. Lady Jane was not there. Her cousin sat with several children around her, fidgeting on the pews, the youngest swinging her legs energetically until an older sibling gave her a smack. The farmer's barn stood empty now, all the villagers that had survived were being looked after in the village. I was still tired. I collected herbs for seasoning, walking all round the grounds swinging from hopeful to exasperated and back. Superstitiously, I did not carry my tools, thinking this was trying then to force fate into letting me through. I was coming to love this house with its baaing sheep, ducks, coots and moorhen, the hens and the cat. Despite its turbulent history, it was becoming an oasis of calm for me. I slept again until supper time and ate bacon and pea soup with bread and drank honey dissolved in water and slept again.

MONDAY

I woke yawning, traversed the grounds, pulling out weeds, checking on my growing seedlings and cuttings and fetched Midnight. As we travelled, I wondered if the plants would have come from Charlecote. I had advised waiting until Autumn but as with most of my customers, the eagerness to create a garden would override common sense. We would just have to water more. At least this Tudor sun had less heat, less burning power than that of the 21st century. I wished I had paper and pen to write for William what he must do each month of the year and then realised this was useless because he could not read, As we planted, I would tell him. Would he know what month it was? No. I would have to describe the seasons in terms of the leaves on the trees, the amount of rain and snow. He was waiting on the drive, running up to me excitedly and making Midnight skitter, "Steady," I said to both horse and boy. "The plants are here," he said, taking hold of the strap near the horse's nose and leading him to the block. I dismounted as the stable lad appeared to collect the horse and William took my hand and pulled me through the arch to where a whole stack of sack wrapped cuttings lay. William could barely keep still in his eagerness to plant. "Well. Fetch the barrow, then," I said and he ran off while I began to sort what we had. He returned also at a run, the barrow bumping noisily as it bounced on the uneven surface. When did gravel arrive, I wondered. We loaded the roses first. I was impressed with the Charlecote gardener's grafting. Where had he learned his skills? I sent William off to unload the roses while I sorted the other cuttings and the seedling trees for the avenue. July was not the ideal planting month but the plants had travelled in the cool hours before dawn. If we watered well we might get away with it. I sent William off to find empty barrels and a watering can and we set the barrels up to soak the roots of our poor thirsty plants close to where we wanted them planted. Thank goodness, I thought we were close to the river. We dug and planted until lunch, both of us forgetting the intended morning break. There was a great deal of bustle going on at the house. The cook sent a maid out with my lunch – ham, cheese, lettuce and bread and a flagon of cider. William smiled at her shyly and she tried to look scornful but I could see the lips curling into a return smile before she scurried back to the house. We could see coaches rolling along the impressive drive up to the house and wagons appeared from the Stratford track. "What is happening?" I asked William as we ate, me sharing the food I had been given. " 'T is the young son's birthday tomorrow. There is to be a big party." William said. "He is coming of age." There seemed to be more and more children running around on the grass at the side of the house. "Are you not invited?" asked William. "We are to have the afternoon off and eat at table in the kitchen," I shrugged . I had heard nothing of this, probably because I did not live within the grounds. "Well," I said, "We had better get this lot planted properly today, as tomorrow we may well be fully employed cutting flowers for decoration." I had no clue when table decoration became fashionable. William jumped to his feet and grabbed his spade. By the end of the day, we had planted all the roses and all the cuttings but the trees were still sitting in their barrels. "We'll just heel them in in a loose trench tonight," I said and tomorrow you can plant them properly in the places we've marked. Don't forget to stake them like I've showed you, I will be back on Thursday." I was headed back to the stable, when Lady Elizabeth called me.

"Marco, we have just realised you have not been invited to share our feast tomorrow. George is to be 21. We ladies would like to invite you to the main table but my husband thinks you are below stairs," She put a hand to her mouth as if gagging herself from further indiscretion. "Perhaps I should not come. To save argument," I suggested, "Oh. You must come. We think Sir Nicholas will return tonight and join us to fight our cause." I rather felt Lady Elizabeth enjoyed stirring up trouble and annoying her husband and wasn't keen to be the subject of debate, but refusing would put me more in the spotlight and annoying Lady Elizabeth might cause more trouble. I gave her a small bow and said I was grateful and would be pleased to attend. "At what time?" I asked. "Oh, from luncheon until nightfall, and probably beyond for the gentlemen and George," she said. I bowed again. "Thank you," I said. Midnight was unsaddled in his stable. The lad had assumed I was following last week's pattern. Rather than make a fuss, I would walk and make the most of enjoying this countryside. I might not see it many more times without its busy car filled main roads and modern houses and factories. I would miss the natural noises and clean air away from the smoky villages. I found myself still jumpy on the ridge and descending the Shurnock side. I had to hope Sir Nicholas's warning would over-ride any tendency towards retaliation for informing the Throckmortons of my attack. The hillside was silent. I felt watched but no one appeared. I let out a breath I had not realised I was holding and wriggled my involuntarily tensed shoulders. All was well.

The cat was still with me and we inspected the garden together, me watching carefully for the cat to open a door to the future. He blinked smiley eyes and rubbed around my legs but he opened no doors to the future. Instead, we ate together in silent harmony. "I'm going to a party, tomorrow," I told him. "I have no present to give. I hope that will not matter." There was an itch of worry over Sir Nicholas's return but surely his nephew's coming of age would be more important than his dealings with me. The cat was not particularly interested. Suggesting instead we look for eggs in the barn. There were three, I took two while the hens ate their grain. I cut more wood into logs and collected more kindling and dry grass and leaves and we slept again, no longer missing the radio or television contact with the outside world. America did not exist in the European mind and the affairs of China, Africa and the Middle East were irrelevant. The Europeans were in turmoil but I could do nothing about the greed of kings and princes and their hungry snatching of lands.

Chapter 12

TUESDAY

We had a morning free to weed and plant and water at
Shurnock. The weeds were sprouting again and took a fair
bit of hoeing but I was done in good time to walk back to
Coughton, stopping on the ridge to look over the Queen's
forest to the west and the more open land with its vast river
plain to the East. The River Arrow was much more
powerful than it appeared in 2019. I looked northwards.
Right up there, out of sight there would soon be mills
making paper, grinding needles as well as corn. This was
the real beginning of the industrial revolution. There were
real fields appearing. Sheep were becoming more popular.
Soon there would be the first factories weaving woollen
cloth. At what point should we have stopped
industrialising to keep the world safe and balanced? It was
hard to know. Perhaps on the first day some child
announced, "I'm bored," I walked on to Coughton,
pondering the problem. The answer did not matter because
I could not change history but the repercussions of the
discovery of oil, say were pretty terrifying. Were we
alright with coal? I had arrived at Coughton. There were
footmen greeting coaches, not in the full splendour of later
history, but well dressed and in uniform, showing off the
wealth of this powerful family. I was wearing my smartest
clothes but still felt untidy compared to the peacock
fashion of the time. The footmen ignored me and I walked
in with a group of five children and their parents. Lady
Elizabeth was there in the grand entrance hall with her son,
who looked fed up with the meeting and greeting, stiff in
his smart clothes. I avoided the formal greeting but caught

Lady Elizabeth's eye asking in gestures if I should attend the grand party. She waved her hand shooing me towards the noise filled living room. I entered, feeling shy. So many people talking loudly in groups. All knowing one another. I was surprised to hear someone calling my name. I turned, searching for the speaker and found it was Lord Sheldon. He beckoned to me and I wriggled through the crowd, finding it odd to be one of the tallest in the room. I was used to being hidden by other people's height. Lord Sheldon put a hand on my shoulder. "My dear," he said. "This is Marco of Shurnock. The monk I told you of. Marco, this is my wife, Anne, who is one of Robert's sisters" I bowed. "How do you do?" I asked. "I am well,thank you," she replied. "But your clothes are not unusual, except your shirt is of wool," I was finding this a difficult conversation. "Yes, ma'am. Your husband is talking of the clothes I work in. They give me more movement for chasing sheep." Lord Sheldon laughed. "I was impressed with your speed and technique. Had you done this elsewhere?" No Sir," I said "But I have seen it done before," I stopped myself in time from mentioning sheepdogs. "We are interested in fabrics," Lord Sheldon said. "We have seen tapestries in France and plan to make them here, at Beoley. This is why we have the sheep and collect the wool." He paused and sipped from a goblet. "Would you like to visit us and see the work we are doing?" I was fascinated. To watch the first English tapestries woven would be an incredible experience. I couldn't see any harm in it. "Yes, I would," I replied. "Would you bring your other clothes for my wife to see?" I supposed it was alright. They couldn't weave cotton until it was discovered in America. I wouldn't take the T-shirt, though with its screen-print picture. Anne clapped her hands and turned to her husband. "Perhaps we could collect Marco tomorrow when we return to Beoley?" she suggested. "And the carpenter could bring him back as far as Astwood Court in the afternoon on his cart." Lord Sheldon approved and I could think of no objections. "It will not be an early start. There is much celebrating to do yet today," Lord Sheldon warned. Another couple appeared at his shoulder. "My brother-in-law, Clement and his wife, Katherine," he introduced them. Clement looked remarkably like Robert, the head held high, confidence in the set of the eyes and mouth. "This is Marco, garden designer to Robert," Clement ran his eyes over me in assessment and I visibly saw him dismiss me as of no account, almost shouldering me out of the conversation. I felt an instinctive dislike of him and was glad to leave the group. There was a table filled with goblets filled with a golden liquid. I thought it might be mead. I took a goblet and stood watching the intermingling groups. There were groups of teenagers chatting together, the lads trying to impress and outboast each other, the girls characters exaggerated by the occasion. Some supercilious, some shy, some confident in themselves and not slow to offer an opinion, others quietly listening, observing, learning how to behave as one of the group. The clothes and mannerisms were different to my time but the development into adulthood from child seemed identical. I found Lady Elizabeth at my side. "You are watching my daughters," she informed me, "Muriel, Anne and Elizabeth. Already they are interested in the young men. Indeed, Muriel is betrothed to the tall young man, Thomas Trensham." I knew that name, I thought but couldn't remember why. Anne is only fourteen but Robert intends that she marries her uncle Brian to keep his late sister's money in the family. She would prefer that young boy standing next to her, William Catesby. Hot headed but of a good family. I was looking at the mother and father of Robert Catesby who would die as a result of the failed Gunpowder plot. Who else in this room would become famous in time? Almost as if she read my thoughts she said, "Let me introduce you to some people." The family, it seemed was extensive. I gave up sorting the brothers, uncles and cousins so many with the same names. She introduced me as her garden designer which gave me status and sounded pompous, She was showing off. Her son, George had attached himself to the younger group and they went outside to sprawl on the grass and swap stories, more than twenty of them, the family features striking. They were undoubtedly almost all related. I thought Elizabeth was slightly drunk, giving away family secrets better kept as we toured the room. We finally arrived at Sir Nicholas's wife. A small boy in his best clothes was whispering in her ear, while an even smaller child played with pebbles a her feet. She laughed at what he said and gave him a hug, but her face was strained and her eyes sad. She let the boy go and said,"Arthur, take Nicholas to your nanny and then you can go and play with Frances and Ursula and the Georges and Edward, No fighting. Arthur picked up his small brother awkwardly and there was a squawk of protest. "Hold his hand and he will walk," Anne instructed. Arthur allowed the squirming bundle to slide to the floor and then pulled him upright by his arm. He marched out of the room, the baby was half carried and half walked beside him. Anne smiled, "Lucky babies are tough," she commented. "And that little one is stubborn, like his father." Elizabeth had gone to greet some other guests. "Shall we walk?" Anne suggested, "I dislike the noise of all these people." I agreed. We walked away from the house, passing a group of aproned women minding a gaggle of infants. "The next generation of

Throckmortons," Anne observed. She patted her stomach. "And there's another one here," She sighed. "I wish Nicholas had not dashed off to London again. Do you know why he went in such a hurry?" she asked. "I understand he had something important to discuss with the queen. An important invention of some sort," I replied. She sighed again. "He can never stay in one place for more than three months without feeling the need to move on and the queen has him bewitched." "Lady Jane was sure he would return today for George's birthday," I offered. She smiled a shade wistfully. "Yes. Robert has sent the coach to Warwick to meet the mail coach. I expect it is late." As she spoke, the Throckmorton coach came into view. "And there he is," she said a mixture of relief and annoyance in her voice. Just like a parent who has been worried sick by a late returning child and I realised that an advisor to a Tudor monarch strode a dangerous path. Imprisonment and execution the punishment for a false step. She hurried to meet him leaving me behind and they embraced as he descended. I had expected him to be impatient with her but in fact, his care for her was evident, love on both sides. He spoke to her for a short time and she pointed at me. To my surprise, another man was climbing from the carriage, young, lithe and dressed like a peacock. I saw Sir Nicholas introduce him to his wife. The man gave her an exaggerated bow and then they all went into the house, Anne following the two men. I decided I had had enough of the gentry and their arrogance and politics. I would go and eat with William. The party in the kitchen was in full swing. A long table with people squeezed on benches and the cook doing her best to keep order. Smiles and laughter filled the air and William squeezed up further to make space for me. There was a huge sliced ham and raisins and the vegetables we had harvested and rough cider to drink. I relaxed and felt happy in this simple crowd where no one had to watch to avoid a knife in the back. They had all lined up earlier to wish their master's son a happy birthday and been given a penny each as a gift. William was holding his tight in his fist, looking at it every now and again and giving it a rub. I had no idea where he could spend it.

Eventually, I left to walk home, feeling lonelier than I had ever felt before. I walked the herb garden and the orchard and over the moat to the wood and slumped by the front door, unwilling to go into the empty house. I felt the brush of fur and reached out automatically to stroke the cat. I wasn't completely alone, but how I ached for Bubble. I had no room for food, just offering a nibble of cheese to my black and white companion. I felt restless and couldn't sleep, walking instead under the stars, watching their reflections glint off the surface of the moat water and startling the ducks from their slumber. Mum would be watching the light from these same stars and watch the same sun and moon as the earth turned beneath them. I would send a message of love to her by moon and starlight. I clambered to my feet and went to bed at last finding sleep.

WEDNESDAY
The rattle of a coach awoke me. It was very late. The cat sprang to the floor and I stumbled out to see Lord Sheldon peering out of the window of his coach. "I am coming," I called and hurried to get ready. Hens, drink, bread and cheese, clothes for inspection in bag. I hurried to the coach. "Ride on top," Lord Sheldon instructed, and I climbed up beside the coachman. What a way to view the world, I thought, once you got used to the eternal dust, and

holding on to avoid being thrown off as the coach traversed the deep rutted surface and swerved around branches. I felt severely shaken and bruised by the time we reached Beoley but what an experience. On top of the world. Beoley was growing fast as the word about paid work spread. There was a shanty town developing just like the one at Droitwich, except that these people held their heads higher. They believed they had an important skill to offer. Snatches of conversation carried an accent like French. The coach pulled into a yard area and we all climbed to the ground. "Come to see the weavers," Lord Sheldon invited. The room we entered held three looms making the room noisy as the shuttle was thrown backwards and forwards and there was the clack of footpedals as the threads were pushed up and down. I could see bobbins of coloured thread spinning in turn. The weavers were focussed on their task, obviously experienced. I could see the finished cloth lying clear of the loom. It shone with the bright golds, red, bronzes and blues. I could have watched the work all day. It was amazing. "He likes it, Ralph," Anne Sheldon squeezed her husband's arm. "Its incredible," I murmured. A boy ran in with more threads on bobbins and added them to a wooden box. "Did you bring your clothes?" Ralph asked. "I did," I confirmed and pulled them out of my bag. There was one man watching the others work. He started forward and shouted at one of the weavers, pointing at the colour on the shuttle and shaking his finger. The weaver looked sheepish, and changed to a different colour shuttle. Ralph called him over. "Look at this," he said, handing the man my trousers and shirt. The man rubbed the cloth against his fingers, put it to his lips and smelt it. "Yuk," I thought. They must stink of body odour and moat water intermixed with manure and goodness knows what else. He took them to the door and out into the daylight and shook his head in awe. "What is this?" he asked. "Cotton," I replied. "Where from?" I could hear the Flemish accent, strong but his English was good. I shrugged. "I am not sure, but I think, America, or India." He made a grunted exclamation, exasperated. "What is cotton? What animal?" I shrugged again. "I think it is a plant." He turned almost angrily to look at the loom with its unevenly spun wool. "So fine, so smooth." He looked at Lord Sheldon almost avariciously. "You buy me this and I will work miracles," Lord Sheldon looked at me. "So. How do we get it?" I shook my head. "I do not know," I said honestly, and then had to resort to deceit. "The cotton must come on ships from America. Perhaps it was bought from the Dutch or the Portuguese, but I was not involved in making these garments. I was just given them." The overseer let out a frustrated tirade of Flemish, almost kicking the loom and startling the weavers. Lord Sheldon watched impassively. "I will make enquiries," he said practically. He took my arm, "Come and see my spinners." We moved to a dark room where women and children were combing and twisting the wool by hand. I was surprised. "Do you have no combs, and spinning wheels?" He patted my arm excitedly. "I knew you would improve things." What had Sir Nicholas told him? He took me to a desk where there were blank scrolls, ink and a quill pen. "Show me." he stated, "I'd rather draw in the dirt," I suggested. His eyebrows rose. "I thought all monks could write and draw." I shook my head, "Never any good at it," I apologised. He dragged me back outside and handed me a stick. I frowned trying to remember how exactly a spinning wheel worked. "Well, the comb is simple," I said, drawing one pretty much to scale. "You'll need an engineer to check over the spinning wheel design but its a bit like this."

I did my best to draw the wheel with its crease for the wool, weights to change the wool tension, how to get the wool twisted and the same thickness but I had never studied it carefully. It would need improvement. I tried to explain this to Lord Sheldon, then added. " I believe the system works best if workers have their own homes with the wheel in a shared room with good light and the spinners work best if you provide their food so that they are not tired from also tending their crops." Lord Sheldon was staring at me with his mouth open. He shut it with a crack and snap of his jaw. "You could build across the road so that they have little distance to bring the wool and you could easily keep an eye on how they work. You could even train apprentices in weaving if they lived there." I had not realised Anne was still listening but she came forward and took her husband's hands. "It sounds a marvellous idea," she said. "Should I fetch the carpenter to look at these drawings before they are washed away?" He nodded and when she had gone, he turned to me and asked, "What is an engineer?" How could I explain? I tried. "A scientist. Someone who knows how the world works and can use what he knows to make things that do what you want doing. I cannot do that. The man who drew your looms might be an engineer." I saw he understood. Anne brought a man smelling of wood and linseed oil into the room. He carried a mallet and chisel, absent mindedly. He scratched his beard with the chisel as he looked at my drawings. "This is to size?" he asked. I pondered. "Fairly close," I said but it depends on the height of the spinner to get the pedalling efficient. He considered. We need William le Wright to make the wheels, I think. I can make the other parts." He walked around the drawings using his arm and hand to make measurements. It was odd to see a chippy without a pencil behind his ear and a measuring tape and rule in his pocket. The Tudor memory for detail was impressive. I could see him making sense of what he saw and storing the information in his mind. "Can you do it today?" Lord Sheldon asked. "I can begin today," the carpenter replied, but I have not the right sized timber. My apprentices will have to prepare it. I was watching the history of manufacturing, I thought, right in front of my eyes. Lord Sheldon sounded exactly like a modern go ahead factory boss. I knew in my head what the spinners and weavers homes would look like. They were still standing in 2019. I started wondering if I could time slip here. Beoley was another island of dramatic history. Not so much war and political strife, but the success of tapestry weaving in Tudor times leading to lots of building and then a decline as tapestries became less popular and cotton production in Manchester and Liverpool took over, but as a small village, it survived and remained unchanged, an island of stillness in history. I had stopped listening to the discussion swirling around me, and suddenly realised someone had asked me another question. "Sorry?" I apologised. "What did you ask?" The carpenter repeated, "Have you any thoughts on the looms?" I shook my head. "They are fine, only perhaps you can use the power of water one day to turn the mechanisms, but you will need a team of artisans to make it work. All different skills." Lord Sheldon and the carpenter looked at each other, calculating. "We need to go to Bordesley," Lord Sheldon said quietly, hopefully. The carpenter nodded, his face blank as his mind raced, but he was plainly excited. "We should go now, while the water is low and then I will go for more wood and take Marco home. Yes?" Lord Sheldon agreed. "Marco, I do not know if you are an angel or a demon. Your knowledge is.......frightening." I didn't know what to say, so I stayed silent as the carpenter led the way to his cart. He gestured to the plank seat and I climbed up next to him. We were being led by a mule. The journey home would be a long plod, especially stopping off at Bordesley first. I resisted an impulse to check my watch. I was aware of Lord Sheldon calling for a horse. We set off and I was fascinated to recognise the contours of the land as we travelled. We were, I thought, crossing the golf course, travelling along the river until we came to a bridge strong enough for the cart to cross, and then back along the other side until the jagged stumps of the abbey came into view. "I can't take the cart closer," the carpenter said. "It would bog down in the marsh." We dismounted. He studied the ground as we walked along the river edge, and, paused at the site of a mill. He looked around carefully. I felt disorientated. Surely this was not where the mill I knew in my time stood. I looked more closely at the broken, rotting sluice gate and the ruins of the mill, and thought, this is not the same place. The mill wheel was smaller and the remaining foundations a different shape. My mill was further up stream. Lord Sheldon arrived, leaving his horse attached to the cart. He too assessed the river flow and they discussed extending the mill pool, where the water could be diverted from and controlled and all sorts of other things which I did not understand. I found it hard to believe they had such a breadth of knowledge, but then the populations were smaller. Communities had to pull together to get things done so I supposed they all got hands on experience of all sorts of work. The only strange thing was that the history of this mill that I knew said it was used for needle making, not wool spinning. I stood and listened and said nothing wondering if their grand plans were going to fail. Eventually they ran out of things to say and agreed to talk with more experts. "Come on, then, Marco," the carpenter said. "Let us go home ." We headed back to the cart and were soon rattling up past the new church site and then on up the ridge. The clopping of the mule was almost drowned by the rattle of the cart wheels and the carpenter was deep in thought so I enjoyed watching the scenery go by without conversation. It was good to have had a day without manual work and without even the exercise of walking or horse riding. I felt as if I was on holiday. The carpenter dropped me at Astwood Court, where he apparently lived and I walked carefully back through the trees, this time choosing the correct path and coming out onto The Saltway right opposite Shurnock Court. I felt ridiculously proud of myself for not getting lost. I ran over in my mind the things I had said to Lord Sheldon. Was it wrong of me to encourage an employer to look after his workforce by providing a good roof over their heads and food to eat? I had reckoned they would reward him with better work, as much in gratitude as because they were fitter and better able to concentrate after a good night's sleep in proper shelter. He might have thought of those things himself or the Flemish weavers might even have insisted on it, so perhaps I had again only fitted in with the history that was already happening. What about the mill? Would I return to find Redditch famous for wool products and not needles and motorbikes? I ran a hand over my hair and face. I must learn to stay silent or at least offer the simplest answer to questions I was asked. I wandered hopefully around the gardens, under the apple tree and beyond the barn to the moat. Birds sang, the hens ran about chuckling and the cat rubbed around my feet, but Shurnock remained undisturbed. There was no shimmering or blurring of the centuries and a small part of me felt relief. I liked this natural world I was now part of and found myself caring about the futures of the villagers and

William. I wanted to be around to talk to Lady Jane and find out why she was at Coughton Court and what she thought about the world around her, but, on the other hand, I did not want to endanger her by getting her associated with me if I fell foul of Sir Nicholas as a result of withholding information, or if my knowledge gave me a reputation as a demon who had to be killed or driven away. I pushed the thoughts away and went to cook, thinking it best to finish the bacon before it went off and wishing for pasta or rice or potatoes as a change from bread. I fed the hens while my saucepan cooked my food and the kettle created rosemary tea and sat lazily watching them peck away. I had eggs to spare and boiled one in the bacon pan. The food tasted gorgeous. The cat thought so, too. In the last of the evening light, I cut more logs and collected more kindling. There was the smell of the weather breaking. I took as much as I could inside, shooed the hens into the barn for the night and satisfied and tired out, the cat and I slept.

Chapter 13

I woke not knowing what day it was, missing the radio and my diary which kept me on track. I worked things out again, Monday-Coughton. Tuesday, George's birthday, Wednesday-Beoley so today was Thursday, walk to Coughton. I looked at my trainers. They were wearing out, the heels almost worn through and the thread breaking along the toes. Had I got to go all the way to Droitwich for new shoes? The pair I had been given by Sir Nicholas were way too uncomfortable for day to day use. Could I afford a new pair? Was Alcester nearer? It might be from Coughton. I put the trainers on gently. Nothing I could do about them today, anyway. The routine tasks were a soothing pattern and I left for Coughton in good time, my mind centred on gardening. Today William and I could get the avenue trees planted so I carried only my secateurs and trowel. The route was so familiar now that I was aware more now of the wildlife than of the road I walked. There were deer amongst the trees, and a vixen with half grown cubs. There were swifts and swallows swooping across the sky, their shrill cries excited as they chased the midges and flies. The hum of bees was loud above the chirrup of finches and tits. It still felt odd not to have to keep out of the way of cars and lorries. Not even a tractor in this rural scene. William proudly showed me the work he had done and puffed his chest out as he told me Lady Elizabeth and Lady Anne had admired our work. "Are we planting the trees today?" he asked. "I got the barrels of water ready." I patted his arm with approval."We are," I said, "Dig them up and let them have a drink while we pace out the spacings and make the holes." We worked companionably and by lunch time had just four trees to do. We looked back along the avenue at our staked in trees and exchanged a look of pride. I didn't tell William that I knew what they would look like in 500 years time. It added to my sense of pride to think of their eventual height and splendour.

Sir Nicholas had a way of appearing silently and unexpectedly. I turned from admiring the avenue, and there he was. "You are invited to lunch, today," he told me. "We have another visitor you might like to meet." He turned and gestured for me to accompany him. I turned first to William, "Just water in the ones we've planted and them have lunch, William," I said. He nodded. He knew. Sir Nicholas had paused to wait for me. I hurried to catch him up. He looked tired, his face thin and shadowed, the skin taut over his cheekbones. Rattling around in a coach, I had learned did not allow for any sleep, and he had been travelling for five days. Did he sleep in inns between coach trips? I did not know. I was already wearing my Tudor costume, my other clothes were getting too ragged to wear regularly. I needed needle and thread to hold them together. We walked into the dining room together and I bowed to the ladies. The young man from the coach was there. He came forward and gave his sweeping bow. "Francis Drake at your service," he said with a mocking smile. I stared, couldn't help it. He was younger than all the pictures I had seen of him, but of course he was. It was twenty four years before his battle with the Armada, about thirteen before he sailed around the world. My thoughts stopped right there. He had come to see my map of the world. I had not drawn it yet because I had received no paper or ink or quill pen. He held out his hand and for the first time I shook hands, feeling the callouses of a sailor's hand. The ladies were fascinated by the sailor at their table and no one asked me anything. I ate quietly and listened. He held no rank as yet but had such confidence and a great deal of charm. George appeared bored but I thought it was a front. He was still listening. Sir Robert was also silent, hiding ignorance of the subject under discussion. Sir Nicholas had a small smile in place, amused by the ladies' interest. Sir Robert might have been slightly jealous of the attention Elizabeth was lavishing on the visitor. Sir Nicholas was more confident of his wife's affection. Lady Jane had given me a look of alarm, remembering perhaps that I had asked her from the future about this man but still, his charm and stories had her addicted, wanting to know more. His mind was quick. He was very intelligent. I would draw the map, I thought and mention the importance of wind and tide in naval battle. It would take thirteen years for him to raise the capital, build the ships, gather stores and sailors and then sail the world. I wasn't changing history, I was part of it. Discussion after the ladies left was short, Nicholas excusing us and explaining that Francis had a coach to meet to return to his ship, presently docked in London. I was heading back to the garden but Sir Nicholas put his hand on my arm and guided me firmly into a room, which I supposed was a study. There was a table, scrolls of paper and quills and ink. "Francis has come to see how you would draw the world." He gazed into my eyes, half command, half entreaty. I thought there was no harm and ducked my head in assent, stepping over to the table. I unrolled the curled paper and stuck the ink bottle on one corner and a paperweight on another, holding the base with my hand. The quill needed dipping often. I was always useless with an ink pen. The map was pretty basic. No sea serpents nor whales. There were a lot of islands missing but it gave an idea of Africa and America and how China could be reached either way. Francis was looking eagerly over my shoulder as I drew. When I had done my best, he tapped the map with a finger. "How many days sailing is this ocean?" I shrugged. "I do not know. It depends on the type of ship and the winds, but I know it is difficult to get through the doldrums, which are about here, and there are good winds that make it easier at other latitudes. Oh, and also the weather is dangerous in about October with rough seas and hurricanes. Another thing is, it is a shorter distance across away from the equator because the earth is like a squashed ball, so it depends where you cross." He smiled a devilish grin. "It is complicated, yes?" He looked again at the map, a look of longing, almost avariciousness in his eyes. "The distance from America to China is the same?" I shrugged again and pointed to the Chinese coast and how it wriggled away from America further south. "It depends where you aim to land." His finger moved to the top of the map. "What is to stop me going over the top?" "Ice," I said. "Thick enough to stop a ship and then break it." I pointed at Cape Horn. "The winds are difficult and there is some ice but this is the only way round. Like all things to do with the sea, it is important to get the tides and winds in your favour. It is best to be there in December when there is less ice." He raised his eyebrows. "But that is Winter!" he said. I shook my head. "No," and sighed. How did I explain the whole universe to people who believed the earth was the centre of the universe. "Wait," I said and went to fetch some pebbles, the roundest I could find. I gave one to Sir Nicholas and put him in the centre of the room. "You are the sun," I said. I gave Francis the earth and positioned their arms to hold them up. "I am the moon," I said. "The moon goes around the earth every twenty eight days, and causes tides," I explained walking around Francis. I took Francis' spare arm and led him round Sir Nicholas. "The earth goes round the sun every 365 days but it also changes it angle", I twisted Francis's wrist as we traversed the room to show how the seasons worked."So in June, we have Summer but the southern half has Winter." The two men looked me in astonishment. "How do you know these things?"|Sir Nicholas said and there was fear in his hoarse voice. I felt suddenly afraid. We were back in the realms of witchcraft. I had to bring the conversation back on to safe subjects. "Explorers draw their maps, and as they travel, they notice what happens to the moon and the sun and the stars and they wrote this, too. The people who taught me, read what the explorers wrote, so I learned." Francis's eyes were shining with excitement and he could hardly keep still. He snatched the map from the table, rolled it up and tucked it into his doublet. "Nicholas, I must leave at once," he said, "and return to the queen. Will you sort me a horse, or a carriage? I will ride to catch up the mail coach." He strode briskly to the door, looking back to see if Sir Nicholas was following. I dithered, unsure if they were finished with me or would have more questions. Sir Nicholas hurried to the door and as he did so, he produced a key. In a smooth movement, he exited the room, pulling the door shut and inserting the key in the lock as he did so. With alarm, I realised he was going to lock me in. I dived for the narrowing gap, crying out, wordlessly, getting my fingers onto the heavy oak surface but with not enough power to stop the swing of the door so that my fingers were trapped agonisingly between door and door jamb. I drew in a gasp of pain. My trapped fingers prevented the door from latching and Sir Nicholas swung the door back at me, banging it against my head and body, loosening my grip and sending me reeling into the room. "You don't have to lock me in," I shouted as I struggled to my feet. "I'll tell you anything you want to know." Sir Nicholas said nothing, pulling the door towards him again. I ran forwards as the door shut and pulled at the thumb latch, hearing the key turning in the lock, but I had managed to open the door enough for the latch to miss its target, and I pulled harder. Nicholas gave a hiss of anger and yanked at the door again so that my bruised fingers slid from their hold, and the door shut, but there were voices in the passageway. First a lady's voice and then the high pitched voice of a child. The key had not turned. With trembling hands, I fumbled with the latch, pulling the door open and found Lady Anne holding Arthur's hand. "Arthur was desperate to meet you, Francis, before you left," Lady Anne was explaining. "He wanted to ask you questions that I could not answer." Francis was enjoying the adulation and crouched down by Arthur, holding his shoulders. "Ask away," he said. I edged out of the room, feeling hot, light headed and shaky. It seemed Sir Nicholas was not prepared to imprison me in front of his wife and son. "How big is your ship?" Arthur was asking. Francis replied. "The ship I mostly sail in has thirty men to sail her and can hold stores for thirty days." "And, are you the captain?" the eager voice asked. "Not yet," said Francis, "But one day soon, and I plan, one day to be not just a captain, but an admiral." "Gosh," said Arthur as I sidled down the corridor and found my way out into the sun. I broke into a run, headed towards the stable yard, no plan in my mind but to get away. I had no idea if Sir Nicholas would try to recapture me, whether he had intended taking me to London or meant to keep me at Coughton. If he was playing a lone game, I had a chance because he could not get more men to capture me. If he was acting for the queen, I could expect a group of henchmen to be on my tail. My luck was in. Midnight stood, saddled and bridled, ready to go. Adrenalin was pumping through my blood making the impossible easy. I undid the tethering rope and leapt into the saddle, shocking Midnight into movement as I struggled to find my stirrup. He spurted into a gallop that nearly unseated me and I clutched at the reins, working my fingers forward to get more control and better leverage to keep my balance over the powerful shoulders. I just hung on, letting the immense muscles flow beneath me. I could not steer my frantic horse, but just waited for the fear to ebb.

Gradually, Midnight realised he was not in danger and slowed to a canter and then a walk, his sides heaving from his exertions. Holding the reins in one hand, I reached forward to pat his neck. Our panic was subsiding as if we were mentally linked. He had chosen to flee along our normal route home. I nudged him back into a canter, more controlled, but still frighteningly fast for a novice rider. I concentrated only on staying on and increasing the distance between me and Sir Nicholas. If he chose to chase me, I had only the time it would take him to extricate himself from his family encounter and saddle up. He was a far better rider than me and might easily catch me. Midnight slowed to climb the ridge and I let him choose his own pace to keep us both safe. His flanks still heaved with the effort of his speed. On the ridge, I hesitated. If I went to Shurnock, Nicholas would easily guess my route and might overtake me. If I turned either way along the ridge, I would be harder to find but also could easily lose my way, and I was back to the same old questions. Where could I go? How could I earn money? How would I shelter or eat? Tramps were whipped until they returned to their homes, but I had no home. Sir Nicholas had not wanted to be seen imprisoning me so if I went to Feckenham, I might be safe. I looked back towards Coughton. No sign of pursuit. I nudged Midnight down the ridge, and once on level ground, we cantered. I was not sure of Midnight's stamina, how far he could gallop and anyway, I was not fit enough to sustain a gallop. At the entrance to Shurnock, I hesitated. I could pack up all my stuff in case I needed to leave. My mind blurred with panic. I had left my tools at Coughton. I needed them for survival. I berated myself for my stupidity, but looking back, I had not had time to detour to the garden. It would have just given Sir Nicholas time to hatch an excuse to detain me. He was a skilled diplomat, his brain trained in fast thinking. I would have been no match for him. I turned in to Shurnock. I would pack up the food and drink and all my clothes, even the goatskin and be ready to leave if I had to. If Sir Nicholas came to find me, he might even think I had gone already. As I packed, I saw my loppers and saw by the fireplace and managed a wobbly smile. I remembered now that I had thought we would only dig today. Only my secateurs gone. I hadn't taken any other tools. I used the goatskin as an extra bag for the food and fastened everything onto Midnight. We had no food for him. The stable lad had not expected us to be leaving so early. I threw grain for the hens and felt sad to be leaving them. I looked around at Shurnock, as empty now as when I had come, but with vegetables and trees now planted, the beds weedless and tidy. "Bye house," I whispered. "I don't know if I'll see you again." It had looked after me well. I led Midnight over the moat and out on the Feckenham track. Midnight nuzzled my neck, glad of my company, glad to not be carrying my weight on his back with all the supplies. I had my rucksack on my back, stuffed as full as possible in case I had to abandon the horse to get away along a ditch or into the trees., I set off along the track but I had gone only a few paces when someone came running along the road from Feckenham. I paused. Surely Sir Nicholas had not already got news of me to Feckenham. I could make no sense of the runner. I realised it was Hugh. I walked forwards, undecided. Hugh shouted and waved at me. Midnight was startled by his actions and froze, his ears flicking questioningly. He backed off a couple of steps, taking me with him as I held his bridle. I turned to reassure him, stroking his nose. He snorted at me and rolled his eyes, suggesting we might flee. Hugh could hardly stand as he reached us, bending over to support his knees and then standing to suck air into his lungs." Marco," he gasped. "The clergymen," he paused again to gather breath. "Hugh," I said, sit down. "You aren't fit enough to be running yet," He folded up on the track side and looked up at me, urgently pulling in air. He tried again. "The churchmen have been talking to the vicar," he pulled in another breath. "They know you should not be here. They're coming here. To whip you out. They were collecting ropes,,,,,when I left. Marco, you saved my life....You have to get away." I understood, but which way could I go? Not back to the ridge, not towards Feckenham. I would have to go back to the moat and then go through the forest on foot. I clambered onto Midnight's back to go back along the track to Shurnock. "Thanks, Hugh," I said. "Now hide lest they link you to me. You have saved my life, too," I kicked Midnight into a canter for the short distance and then hauled him to a stop by the moat. I unstrapped the goat skin and my bag, slapped Midnight's rump to send him back into Shurnock where I hoped Sir Nicholas would find him and slipped into the trees, half running, half stumbling on the rough ground, watching my feet and the ground just in front of me, feeling bramble briars and branches whipping at my face, I had no hands free to ward them off. The load was too heavy. If I had to run, I would have to lose the goatskin. Suddenly, there was a shout from ahead of me and I saw running men. They had anticipated my escape this way. I swung round and headed more south but there were more running feet. I would have to head back to Shurnock and then back towards Coughton. Maybe I could slip down the stream I had fled down those many weeks before if I met Sir Nicholas on the road. I dropped the goatskin. I needed speed now but didn't dare stop to drop my rucksack. It bumped heavily against my back, knocking me off balance. I was back at the bridge over the moat. More shouts from down the track. The cart with the clergymen was trundling towards me and the whips stood out against the background, harsh and threatening. I sprinted over the bridge and round the side of the house to the front drive to leave by the other bridge, but a mounted horseman was coming over the bridge, Sir Nicholas. I skidded to a halt. No where to go. I turned back to the house and ran in through the porch. No where to hide. If they came to the doors, I was trapped. I ran straight across the great hall, like a frightened rabbit with a fox on its tail and tugged open the back door. Everyone was around the front, I had one chance to get away, swimming the moat, or hiding in the reeds until they gave up the chase. I catapulted out of the door, kicking it shut behind me and started to run through the herb garden but Sir Nicholas was coming around the house still on his horse, a whip in his hand. A man appeared from the barn end of the house. I would have to jump into the moat. I shrugged the tools off my back, dropping them in the middle of the garden and running on. The door burst open behind me and I sensed a man right behind me, felt the shift of air as he raised an arm to hit me. I pivoted, my arm raised to ward off the blow, A stout piece of wood hit my arm and I fell backwards, twisting to break my fall, my ears full of the cries of pursuit, and shouts of triumph and suddenly the shouts died to nothing and my shoulder hit gravel. I kept rolling, trying to escape the next blow,hearing the crunch of small stones beneath my body, curling my legs up and ducking my head down knowing I had reached the end and hoping whatever they did would not hurt too much. My arm was numb and would not work properly, I put my other arm over my head and closed my eyes and a voice said, " Bloimey, Whire didyoo cum from?" The invective was Black Country. I slowly opened my eyes. A man in white overalls and carrying a paint brush was looking down at me with wide surprised eyes. I uncurled slowly, and found I was tucked up against a wall, my bag still attached to my arm. Looking around, as I struggled to a sitting position, I found the herb garden had gone. There was just a patio area of paving slabs and, turning, I saw the moat was now a closed off lake with a tennis court beyond the small lawn. "Eh, Jack," the man gave a sharp whistle through his lips, "Coom an' give us an 'and." He crouched down, putting his brush on top of a tin of paint and reached in his pocket, taking out a blue mask and putting it on his face, I looked around again, more carefully. The house was fully built and had scaffolding up. Another man appeared. "Wha's oop?" he asked. The first man pushed his chin out at me. "Dunno whire she cumfrom. Joost appeared." The other man looked down at me. I struggled to my feet, feeling uncomfortable under their stare. "Are you awlright?" Jack asked. I nodded. I felt awful, disorientated, my arm throbbing now, making me feel sick but I needed to be alone while my head caught up with what had happened. Carole had not mentioned renovation work, so who were these men, and what was the mask for? Perhaps the paint fumes were toxic in some way. I was back, I should be feeling relief but the fear was lingering like the aftermath of a nightmare. I looked around again, not quite believing that I was looking at gravel drives, paint in metal pots, men in polyester overalls. I swallowed, finding my voice, "Yes. Thank you. I banged my arm when I fell, but I'm OK." I stepped around the men. My tools were gone, the patio empty of everything but scaffolding and paint. I pulled myself upright and walked towards the mews cottage with the brambless bed. My bicycle was gone. I turned slowly and feeling unstrung and shy walked around the house and grounds, looking in the stables and even the cottage but there was no bike anywhere. I returned to the men and asked if they had seen my bike. They shook their heads, looking concerned. "It's not in the house," Jack said. Nothing for it, but to walk home, then, I thought. On the way out, I checked the old barn where the tools were kept. It was empty. Nothing. No wheelbarrows, no forks or spades. Had Carole found a buyer and moved out? I'd only been gone well, how long? three weeks? I felt numb. No emotions. This must be shock. Even my arm had returned to numb. I looked at the lump where the bone had deflected the blow to my head and prodded it. Was that a broken bone? My hand refused to react to my commands. There were pins and needles developing from elbow to fingertips. I looked down at my woollen shirt, dusty breeches and tights. The incongruous trainers on my feet. No wonder the men had stared. I still had my bag. I leaned against a tree and pulled the bag open. Trousers and ragged shirt. Struggling with the useless arm, I removed the tights and breeches and pulled on my trousers. That felt better. I was back. I still felt numb, unable to process the thought. I would go home and eat and drink. Three weeks. I would still have tinned food in my cupboards and pasta and yes, coffee. I just had to get home. Six miles. I could do that. I put my hand in my pocket and unbelievably pulled out both modern and ancient coins. Two pound coins and one ten pence. No buses from Feckenham but I felt so ill. I would maybe catch a bus from Astwood Bank. I walked across the fields, enjoying the sun on my face and the open fields with sheep skittering away and baaing as I passed. No forest. There were hedges and barbed wire fences and stiles to climb over with metal footpath signs. Yellow painted arrows. I felt dislocated. It was as if I floated in a bubble, though my feet were on the ground. Unreality shimmered around me. Twenty minutes on, I arrived on a tarmac road and there was Astwood Court, its partial moat linking the times but the old buildings swept away. I was thirsty. No other feelings, just a dryness of the throat and cramp in my toes, kidneys protesting at the lack of lubrication. Just hold on, I thought. Either I would get a bus, or I would buy a drink in Crabbs Cross at the Co-op. I toiled up the long hill, looking steadily at the ground, and jumping almost into the hedge in fright at the noise of a van belting up the hill from behind me. Traffic. So loud and smelly. I had forgotten the extent of the noise. I reached Astwood Bank. So much traffic. The added noise of an aircraft overhead and someone using a hedge trimmer. I wanted to put my hands over my ears to block out the startling volume surrounding me. The main road was worse. I found it difficult not to shy away each time a van or lorry passed. It was hard to believe I had only been away for three weeks, such was my disorientation. I felt as one does when returning from a fortnight's holiday where cars drive on the opposite side of the road, but multiplied one thousand per cent. My arm was throbbing again. I leaned on a lamp post while a wave of giddiness passed.

My arm was swelling below the break. It should be in a sling, I thought. I remembered the tights and with difficulty made a sling and inserted my broken arm into it, trying to spread the material to support the arm each side of the break. If I could find a straight stick, I would try to splint it. I walked unsteadily on. The shops seemed to have receded, the road lengthening like stretched elastic. I told myself to just keep putting one foot in front of the other. No use sitting and weeping. That would get me nowhere. I reached the shop, at last, and found there was a queue right out of the door. More people were wearing those odd blue masks and everyone stood on a yellow circle on the pavement. Something was odd. Was I dreaming or had that blow actually reached my head. Maybe I was unconscious. I hoped I wasn't going to come to while I was being beaten. Feeling woolly headed I joined the queue. The lady in front of me kept flicking angry glances at me. I didn't know what I was doing wrong. Someone came out of the shop and we all moved forward one circle. I rubbed a hand over my face. I felt awake but I couldn't be. I was so thirsty that I thought I would faint. I leaned on the shop window. The world was beginning to flash in and out of focus. The queue moved forward. The lady in front turned to me."Are you alright? If you're ill you should be isolating." I blinked stupidly at her. "I'm not ill," I said, "I'm just very thirsty." She looked at me with a worried frown. "Have you hurt your arm?" I looked at it blankly. "Yes," I said but couldn't think of an explanation. "I suppose you are too frightened to go to the hospital." she said sympathetically. "It looks bad. I think you should go." I didn't understand why I should be frightened. What an odd conversation. "I'll go later," I promised her. It was her turn to go into the shop. It didn't look that crowded but a shop assistant on the door told me I must wait for someone to come out. "Where's your mask?" she asked me. "Pardon?" I said. "You can't come in without a mask," she said. I was definitely dreaming, or......had I changed history so that this was how the world now worked in 2019. I thought back but couldn't think why anything I had said or done would lead to the need for a mask. Had I anything I could use for a mask? To the bemusement of the shop keeper I emptied my bag onto the floor, buttoned my ragged shirt and pulled it over my head. I stuffed the other stuff into the bag using my knee because my arm seemed to have become totally useless. I stood and almost fell as the world swam again. Low blood pressure due to dehydration and shock, I thought. A man came out. "Two metres," the assistant said, letting me in. What was she talking about. I stumbled to the fridge which buzzed alarmingly and selected a drink, two drinks. I was very thirsty. I reeled over to the counter. The lady who had been in front of me was just paying. She backed away from me hurriedly. "Two metres!" the man behind the counter said. What were they talking about? The lady said,"She doesn't understand. I think maybe she is not all there." She was sympathetic. I had to agree. I seemed to have left part of my brain in 1564. I held out my pound coins. "Don't you have a card?" the man demanded. "Er, no," I said. Why was he so aggressive? I thought he must mean a Co-Op loyalty card. "I don't shop in a Co-Op very often," I apologised. The world was sliding into yellows and grey shadows. If I didn't drink soon I knew I was going to faint. He shook his head disgustedly, picked up a bottle and sprayed his hands, then snatched the coins from me, rang up the sale and gave me my change, carefully avoiding contact with me. I must look filthy, I thought but what disease was I likely to give him? I took my drinks and left the shop, noticing yellow arrows on the floor but not understanding what they were for. As soon as

I was outside, I looked for a place to sit. The floor at the side of the shop would do, I slithered to the floor, back supported by the wall and opened a drink using my teeth, my hand would do nothing. Gurgling the fizzy water down to half way, I then sipped more slowly. What had happened to the world in the last three weeks. I felt uneasy, slightly guilty that I had changed something important. The grey and yellow shadows faded away. I put the second bottle in my bag and put my shirt mask in there, too. I finished the bottle and stood up carefully. Thankfully the world remained stable, no giddiness. I pushed off the wall, threw the empty bottle in the bin and set off steadily for home, It seemed unreal to be walking on pavement, to be hemmed in with houses. As I reached Headless Cross on the top of the hill, I saw there was still an inn where I had drunk my soup. The village green had only tiny trees and was invaded by a car park but the sense of familiarity was steadying. I felt ill, wanted to lie down on the grass and sleep, but more than that I wanted to be home with Bubble. Please let her be alright, I thought. Come on Margot, only the downhill to do. You can do this. The blisters on my feet were hot, expanding and sore. Just one foot after the other. It must be teatime, I thought. No people in the streets. Even the bus had only one passenger as it whooshed past me. I reached the town centre and still there were no people, not even outside the pub. It felt spooky. Just half a mile to go. I stopped by a seat and opened my second bottle, sipping slowly, enjoying the moisture on my tongue and throat and the sight of the police station, the college and shops. I was back. It still felt unreal. Standing up again was difficult, painful. I was stiffening up. I stubbornly raised my head and straightened my back. Last half mile, just ten minutes more. It was good to look down Easemore Road and see the familiar row of Victorian houses with the base of the hill outlined with hills, trees and the square church tower. Nothing had changed here. All downhill. I could do this, easy. I walked on, promising myself I would be home in just 800 strides and counting them off in my head. At last, I reached my road, and there was my house. I stopped in front of it. The porch door was fine but someone had smashed the glass of the inside door and then boarded it up. I would have sighed if I had had the energy. I'd have to get a new panel sorted. It would have to wait until I felt better. It suddenly occurred to me that I didn't know where my door key was. When did I last see it? I felt in my trousers, knowing it wasn't there. Had it been in my bicycle? Please don't let it have been in my bicycle. I never put it in my rucksack. I had emptied the bag hundreds of times and not seen it. Did I leave them in the hall or bedroom at Shurnock? I didn't remember seeing them. I crouched on the ground and emptied my bag again, stupidly feeling around the corners of the bag, numbness invading my brain refusing to accept defeat. I shook everything out and then I heard a jingling from my cagoule pocket. I took a half breath in and held it. All the time I'd been away I had only worn my cagoule in the house when my other clothes were wet. I'd taken it out in the bag and brought it back unused. I felt the pocket and yes, there were keys. Couldn't get the zip undone with my broken arm. Why was everything so difficult? I took a deep breath to push down the futile anger and wedged the cagoule with my knee, pulling the zip with my one good hand and wriggling my finger into the gap to get the keys. I held them up in triumph and smiled exultantly at them. Struggled to turn the knob on the porch door, but finally managed, Key in the lock, Heard the familiar homecoming noise of the latch opening. Almost fell into the hall. It smelt of old damp newspaper. "Bubble," I called. "Bubble

I'm home." But no little brown cat came running down the stairs to greet me. No face peeping cheekily round the door. I searched the house but she wasn't here. I slumped in the hall and let the tears fall until there were no more left to cry. Rested my head on my drawn up knees and wrapped my one good arm around my head. Felt totally spent. Slowly, I fell sideways, nursing my broken arm and slept. I woke, cramped and cold. It was dark. I hadn't even shut the door. I shuffled to it on my knees and pushed it shut. Stood up and found the light switch didn't work. Too dark to check the fuse box. It didn't matter. I was used to natural light and there was even a street light shining through the windows. I climbed the stairs and fell into bed, too tired and hurt to undress. Tomorrow I would deal with things. I slept again and woke stiff and confused. Where was I? Gradually I pulled together the details of warm, soft bed and curtains at the windows. There was daylight filtering in through glass windows. No need to undo shutters. I was in my bed. Had I dreamt everything? I tried to move my arm and the nerves screamed at me to stop. I looked down at my woollen shirt. No dream. I needed a coffee. The water was turned off. I fetched water from the water butt. The kettle would not work. I tried a light. No electricity. I checked the fuse box. It looked fine. Power cut? Better check the neighbours. It was still early. I had a wood-burner, I was good at lighting fires. I could make a coffee on that. I swore at my broken arm, striking a match awkwardly, trying to hold the box in numb fingers. It was ironic that I was still having to use a wood fire to cook. I could hear movement next door. I looked down at my clothes and decided I had best wash and change first. I looked longingly at the shower. Here I was in the 21st century still using cold water from the water butt to wash in. It was good to use soap. I really stank. It was odd how I had hardly noticed when everyone smelt the same. I washed and scrubbed as much of me as I could reach one-handed and felt fresh. I dressed in clean soft clothes and put on dry shoes. How odd to look in a mirror. I brushed my hair and used a toothbrush. My gums bled but how great to have clean teeth and the taste of toothpaste. My tongue kept exploring the glossiness of clean enamel. I hobbled out of the front door, wedging it open with the pile of junk mail on the mat. I knocked on my neighbours door. I needed to know what had happened to Bubble. When my neighbour opened the door, she looked blank and then surprised and then almost angry. "Margot," she said. "Where have you been? Why didn't you say you were going away? We've had the police and everything asking questions. Your mum's been coming round every week to see if you've come back and she's been so worried." There were too many questions. I waved them away with my hand. "Do you know where Bubble is?" I asked. "She's with your Mum, I think," my neighbour replied. She noticed the empty sleeve of my shirt where I had left my arm inside. "Have you been in an accident?" I could see her trying to piece together a story that fitted. I hadn't really thought about explanations. I couldn't say "No, I went back in time and got bashed by a mob," "Sort of," I said. "I'd better go and ring Mum. Er Is your electricity on?" "Well. Yes," she said. "Oh," I said. Mine isn't." "Well, no," she replied. "Your Mum had it switched off after the first month you were away." I thought I had misheard or she had meant to say week, not month. But surely Mum wouldn't have acted that quickly. "You do look ill," my neighbour commented. I felt ill, still drifting in time. " Is your phone still working? I thought they might have switched that off too?" Why had everything been switched off so quickly? "I don't know. I'll try it, " I said.

She stayed on her doorstep as I returned home and picked up the phone. No dialling tone. It was plugged in. I rubbed my sleeve across my face for comfort. Everything was impossible. I poked my head back out of the door. "You're right, Its not working." My neighbour rubbed her nose. "Shall I ring your mum for you?" she asked. "Yes please," I said. "I've got the number," she said. "Your mum gave it to me when she moved." She disappeared into the house and came back with a mobile, pressing buttons and listening to it ring. Moved? I thought. How could she have moved. I thought the guy had died and everything was delayed. No way had she got everything packed and moved in three weeks. I could hear the ringing end and my mum's voice said hello. "Margot's home," my neighbour said. My mum asked her to repeat what she'd said. "She's standing in front of me," my neighbour said, paused, listened, then said to me, "She's coming down." "Down?" I said. "From her house." "Down?" I repeated, feeling stupid. "Oh," my neighbour said. "Perhaps you don't know she has moved to Redditch, about six months ago." I felt as if I was sinking into the ground, hollow inside. Was this me changing history or was this not 2019. I felt panicky, my breath came short and fast and my mouth dried up. "What's the date?" I asked. There was a pause while the question was absorbed and the date calculated. "6th July" she said. I tried to control my breathing. How stupid to ask what year it was. I glanced around for clues and my eyes focussed on a car registration plate. The car was shiny and the registration plate showed the year. 2020. My mind reeled. I had lost a year. My neighbour was still talking but for a moment I couldn't focus. ".....tea?" she was saying. I nodded. "Sit down," she said. My legs obediently folded under me. A mug of tea appeared it seemed in seconds. Time was still wobbling around me. Rushing forward and receding like the tide. "Here," my neighbour said. "I daren't ask you in," she said. "Will you be alright? You're so pale. …..You haven't got it, have you?" She held out the mug at arms length so that I too had to stretch to reach it. "Got what?" I asked. "The virus," she said. Was she talking about dysentery? How would she know I had been in contact with people all those centuries ago that had it? "No," I said. "You can leave the mug under the tree," she said. Things were too odd. I nodded vaguely and sipped the too hot sugar filled tea. She retreated into the house. "Shout if you need me," she said as she shut the door. I did as I was told, leaving the mug under the tree and going back indoors. Where should I start? I needed the phone to ring the electricity company and couldn't contact the phone company without a phone. The tea had given me energy but what could I do with it? The police arrived before my Mum. It seemed both Mum and my neighbour had obeyed instructions to ring them if I reappeared. They pulled out the little blue masks and put them on before knocking on the open door and inviting themselves in. They introduced themselves politely and one produced a notebook. "Can you wear your mask?" the older of the pair asked. "I haven't got one,|" I said. They exchanged glances and one returned to the car and came back with a mask in a bag, his hands in gloves. He tossed it gently to me and I struggled one handedly to hook the elastic behind my ears. I must be still dreaming, I thought. Maybe a tree fell on me and I'm in a coma. I felt concussed. "Can you tell us where you've been?" said the older man. "Can you explain what happened?" I was silent. How could I explain? I found my voice. "I-I -I don't remember." I rubbed my arm across my face again. It felt real. Would it feel real in a dream? "I seem to have lost a year." They looked at each other, seeking each others thoughts in a kind of telepathy. "What do you last remember before today?" I answered simply with the truth. "Someone broke my arm with a big stick and then I walked home from Feckenham, and I bought a drink in the co-op and everything was strange." The policemen exchanged another look. They studied me carefully. "And before that?" My nerve failed me. "I was gardening at Shurnock Court, and then nothing until yesterday. Did I have an accident? Did I bang my head?" I was asking them to tell me it had all been a dream, a coma induced nightmare but the bruised fingers from the door, the bramble slashes, the broken arm, and my clothes were evidence hard to deny, and if I had been in hospital, how did I leave without remembering? "We don't know," said the policeman. "We traced your movements to Feckenham on 13th June 2019 and found your bicycle, which you can reclaim from the police station, but no one admits to seeing you after that. Who were the last person you remember from before you lost your memory and who do you remember seeing yesterday?" There was a commotion at the door, a car engine coming to a halt and a car door slamming and my mum appeared carrying a cat basket. A furry face was pressed against the bars. I leapt forward, tears springing weakly to my eyes. "Bubble," I cried. Mum had put the basket on the floor and was unzipping the door. I knelt by the basket and put out my hand . "Bubble," I said lovingly, my throat closing with emotion. Bubble scrutinised me, considering and studied the policemen's legs. It had been a toss up whether she would scratch me and bite me in fury for abandoning her for so long or rub me and love me. The big policemen might be a danger. I was not. She rubbed against my hand and then gave in to her rush of emotion, rubbing against my legs, my torso, my arms and hand and purring, climbing onto my legs and rubbing my face with her forehead. I stroked the wriggling body, wiping away the tears with my sleeve. Then she sat back, looked into my face and swiped my arm with her paw, claws only half sheathed. "I'm sorry," I said. My mum laughed. "I feel like that, too," she said. "I've been so angry with you for not telling me you were alright. Why didn't you?" There was such a mixture of emotions on her face I couldn't read them all. "I couldn't," I said. "I would have done if I could and I didn't know I'd been away so long." Mum's anger softened and she reached out a hand to comfort me. "We'll talk about it later," she said. "Let me get you a meal. You're much too thin." "No electricity," I said. "Oh, I forgot," she said. "Everything is switched off. It seemed safest." She looked at the policemen. "I expect you have more questions. I will go and buy some food and be back in half an hour?" The policemen nodded. She looked at me. "I have a mobile phone you can use to get the telephone and electricity reconnected," she said and handed me a pink phone. Wow, I thought. Fancy Mum having a mobile. I was glad my mum wasn't the suffocating sort, pushing for answers, smothering me in hugs and answering for me to the police. She left matter-of-factly to get things done. I felt better with Bubble rubbing and rubbing as if to mark me as her property only. She tried to climb on my lap and curl into a ball. I twisted so that my legs made a wider space and she settled, my hand tickling her ears. The policeman repeated his question. "Before," I said, "There was no one at Shurnock. I didn't even see anyone on the way, because it was so early." "What time?" the note taker asked. "I left about 6.30, but I can't remember exactly, only that it was a beautiful day and no one around," He scribbled in his book. I said slowly, "I don't know who the man was who hit my arm." If I wasn't careful, the painters at Shurnock would get the blame. I was running and he was behind me and maybe I blacked out because the next thing I remember is being at Shurnock again and there was a man with a paintbrush asking where I'd come from, but I'm sure it wasn't him who broke my arm, and not his friend either." The policeman was looking frustrated more than anything. "Why are you so sure?" "Their clothes and the shape of their bodies and he was so surprised to see me and they were nice, too." The policeman thought and then said, "Describe the man who hit you, What was he wearing?" I thought back. It wasn't one of the clergymen in their black cloaks, but a man of muscle in breeches and a loose fitting wool shirt, his beard long and dark, his hair also long with lose curls. I describe him hoping that no one now in Feckenham matched the description. "And can you remember your surroundings?" My mouth answered without the intervention of my brain. "I was in a herb garden." The phrase took me back to the moment and I felt the acceptance of capture, the moment of pain and the terrible fear as if I was back there and almost fell apart again but Bubble pushed against my hand, purring and reminding me I was safe They tried for more details but I couldn't tell them any more. "I'm sorry," I said. "Everything else is just a jumble. Like a bad dream. Like being back in time. It doesn't make any sense." The policeman checked his watch, made a note of the time. "I think we had better take you to the hospital to get your arm set, and we will also need you to talk to a police psychologist. He will ring you...." He paused, remembering the cut off phone. "He will ring your mother to make an appointment." He scratched his head and looked at his partner. "Are we allowed to take her to the hospital?" The other man shrugged. "Dunno." he said. "I'll radio." He left the room "Bloody virus," the policeman muttered unguardedly. My mum was back, carrying fruit juice and sandwiches, chocolate, cake and oranges. She looked at the policeman, frowning. "Can I offer you cake?" she said. The policeman smiled. "You can offer but I have to refuse," he said. "Thanks, anyway." She handed me the food and drink and had some herself. It felt odd drinking juice out of a straw, eating sandwiches and cake at the table, The other policeman returned and said, "We're doing it unofficially," "Ah, Right," his companion said. "In our lunch break, eh?" I was ushered into the car. The passenger seat man turned and said, "Have you got your card?" "What card?" I asked, remembering the co-op man. "Your bank card. No cash these days, In case of the virus." My mum appeared at the window. "Use mine," she said. "You only have to swipe it." I was still not in the real world. I took the card, wondering where the dream would take me next. It was the hospital. More masks. A swab test, yellow circles and footprints. Crosses on seats. Time blurred. I watched television in a nearly empty waiting room, and gradually pieced together the news of a serious pandemic with thousands dying while I sat and waited for my arm to be fixed. The doctors and radiologists looked strained and tired but were still kind. Apparently, I was lucky. One bone snapped in my forearm but the other holding it almost in place. I felt the doctor pull it straight and then it was plastered. They looked into my eyes and checked all the other things doctors like to know about and I was free to leave. I could see the bus driver thought I was an imbecile not knowing how to use mum's bank card but it seemed a broken arm gave me an excuse for a stupid head and he never suspected the card wasn't mine. It was turning out to be a long day. Mum gave me emotional support as I tried to get my phone back working and my electricity back on. So many automated voices saying "Due to covid virus, Only in an emergency....." and then the people explaining that due to the virus no one could fix things for a week or two. Mum took me to her house, along with Bubble and I enjoyed a long hot shower, washing my hair with shampoo and my body with soap and I slept in pyjamas. "What happened, my love?" she asked. "Do you remember Lady Jane?" I asked. "Yes," she said. " I went back in time...." I said. She looked into my eyes, searching for I knew not what. "I'm not insane," I said. "I have proof."

Chapter` 14

Only Mum knows the real story. I haven't been able to retrieve the note I wrote in 1564 and hid behind the skirting board, but I showed her my clothes and she carefully examined my breeches and tights and the woollen shirt and could find no explanation for them other than the truth. I hope the note has been eaten by a mouse. The police psychologist was puzzled by the unlikely memories and the police grilled the poor workmen until they nearly confessed to a crime they didn't commit. It must be still in the records as unsolved. I'm nearly back to normal now but I no longer garden at Shurnock and I know that one day, I will meet a lady who still lives in that long ago time but in fact is a lady from the future.

Notes
Translation of the French when talking to the vicar:

Good day, I am working in Shurnock, for the church and I would like to visit your church for god, "
"Welcome," he replied. "When you're done, come to the vicarage, over there." He waved in the general direction of his house. "We can talk more comfortably there,"

"Thank you,"

What city are you from? " she asked. "Guildford," I lied thinking of the nearest big town to Weybourne Abbey. "I learned from the monks at Weybourne and then I worked in Evesham and Worcester in the gardens. I am a gardener and now I work in Shurnock until a tenant is found. Also the clergy say I must work in the village for all the people for the meats. "

"Well," the vicar's wife said to me. "Maybe you work here today and we give you lunch, yes?" "Oh, yes please," I said, the relief strong in my voice. They had understood. She looked at my back pack and then waved at me. "Come here,"

Other Books by Margot Bish

For Adults and teenagers
A Difficult Age   short story in paperback and e-book
'Tis The Irish Way   e-book

For children
The Long Day Out   for three to five year olds e-books
How could I Forget?
The Perfect Home

Through The Storm for 9 to 12 year olds paperback
hardback and e-book

About the author

My career choices at the age of six were: writer, teacher, postman or something outside. I have, at the age of something over fifty, achieved them all – I teach sailing, act as volunteer warden on a nature reserve, work as a professional gardener for all the Summer daylight hours and some of the Winter ones, too, and had a paperround for about ten years which is simpler than a postman but just as ejoyable. I also tried several years working in offices and factories but much prefer the solitude of writing and the company of birds as I garden. Human beings are much too complicated.

When I am not working, I love to sail dinghies and spend time with my cat who co-authored this book and is in charge of time management in case I forget to eat and sleep.

My thanks to my mum who suggested the route of self publishing so that you can enjoy reading my books.(I really hope you do) and I can enjoy writing them.

Printed in Great Britain
by Amazon